ANGEL

OF THE

CRYPT

C.J. Laurence

ANGEL OF THE CRYPT

DEDICATION

For my new, old friend, Katie C. Your constant support and help is invaluable to me. Thank you.

CHAPTER ONE

Makeysha

The day it happened was extraordinarily beautiful. I remember it like it was yesterday. For two thousand years I have walked this earth, damned to eternal loneliness, cursed to forever wander the lands, helping souls crossover into the next world.

I have seen many things in my time on Earth. Wars have ravaged the exquisite nature blessed upon this world, forever scarring it and reshaping its future. Humans are cruel, narrow minded creatures, and I see now why this was the worst fate God could have subjected me to. I long to go home, to converse with someone of my own kind once more, to stretch my wings and fly in the beauty of Heaven.

But I cannot. My damnation allows me only to fly from graveyard to graveyard, assisting lost souls in the seven-day period it takes for them to split from their fragile human shells. It's tiring, drifting to all the different places but it keeps me busy and the comfort I get from helping souls is enough to keep my spirits up; just.

What saddens me the most is the surprise on their faces when they realise I'm an angel and that the supernatural and an afterlife does indeed exist. "I knew it!" the believers say, or "I can't believe I didn't think this was real," from the sceptics, but the instant they cross over, they are 'washed' through the Cave of Hypnos, rinsing their memory of this human life, blanching them ready for their next.

It means none of them remember me. But I remember them. Some have already achieved Nirvana and gone on to greater, higher levels, such as Heaven, but others still have lessons to learn. Those are the ones I see time and time again, each meeting an exact replica of the last. One soul has met me thirty-three times, but he remembers none of it. I wish I could influence them otherwise, but I can't. Not unless I want to upset God again.

I'm already on thin ice, if he even knows what I'm doing. I had enough of helping souls years ago. Call me selfish but two millennia doing the same job, never resting, never having anywhere to call home, I decided a few years ago that I'd had enough. It was my time for a break, for a vacation if you like. It just so happened that I kind of never went back to my job. I tried, I really did, but it hurt too much, reliving those same conversations over and over, so I stayed put, in the place I now call home—Odd Fellows Cemetery, New

Orleans, Louisiana.

The humans condemned this peaceful graveyard years ago. Initially they were going to refurbish it, but they never bothered. Instead, they left it to ruin and permanently closed it. This proved perfect for me, so I took advantage of it.

Is it sad that I've lived there for years and no one knows? Humans can't see me, except for a special kind—supernatural hunters. Supernatural creatures can see me, unfortunately, but I haven't ran into too many, thankfully.

I've been away for a couple of months, travelling and sight-seeing. After resting for years and just letting the days blur into one another, I decided it was time to go and see all the attractions that I have always adored—the pyramids, Stonehenge, the Mayan temples, the colosseum, and loads more. Admittedly, I did help out some lost souls along my journeys.

Now though, I'm back and looking forward to settling back down in my cosy crypt in the city I feel the most at home in. As I fly through the aurora borealis, looking for my home, my mind wanders back to that fateful day that changed my life forever…

Heaven—Two Thousand Years Ago

I woke in my chambers, bright yellow rays of sunshine blazing through my window. My wall length window gave the perfect view into Heaven, never failing to amaze me with its splendour. Fluffy white clouds as far as the eye could see, all basking in the shining sun.

The particular castle my chambers were in was a magnificent gothic style building. White bricks, black slate roofs, turrets, and ornate decorations with gargoyles and other nightly creatures, I felt truly privileged to live in such a stunning place.

Six other castles, similar to mine but with colour changes and different architecture, were also in Heaven, each one named after God's archangels. My castle was Gabriel, and in my opinion, was the best castle to be in. However, I'm sure all my fellow angels felt the same about their own castles, too.

The archangels were in charge of the angels who stayed in their castles. Gabriel was a fantastic boss. He was firm but fair. A couple of the others, Barachiel and Uriel, were nothing short of drill sergeants. I was glad I wasn't in their 'clan' as we called it.

Today was Selaphiel—or Thursday to humans. That meant the angels in her clan could rest today whilst the remaining six castles carried on with the many tasks needed to keep Heaven running smoothly.

We all shared tasks so we could develop our skills as a whole, rather than just one area. Today, I would be cleaning The Great Hall—a magnificent temple like building where God held daily meetings with his archangels and closest confidantes.

I threw back my covers, stretching and yawning before making my way over to my wardrobe. Angel dress code wasn't very exciting. Female angels always wear brilliant white maxi dresses, complete with gold sandals that are rarely visible because of the long dress. Male angels wear a brilliant white suit, complete with gold shoes.

Quickly changing out of my plain white pyjamas, I slipped a dress on over my head, slid my feet into a pair of sandals and made my way into the bathroom. The colour theme in here was the exact same for the rest of my chambers and the rest of the angel world—bright white. I had wondered on more than one occasion if humans chose white for their hospitals in order to feel closer to angels.

I scrutinised my appearance in the mirror. My long blonde curls were all fluffy and unkempt, the absolute definition of bed hair. I ran my slender fingers through it, teasing the knots out and shaking it free. I brushed my teeth, flicked my hair over my shoulders, and nodded to myself.

"Today will be a good day," I said to my reflection.

She didn't reply.

Humming to myself as I walked back through my chambers, I opened my door and checked the corridor was empty before stepping out. Coming out of such clinical whiteness and into the halls of such ancient beauty never failed to amaze me. Aside from our modern decorated chambers, everything else in the castles was as it should be.

I had heard whispers that actually, what we 'saw' in our chambers was merely a layer of painting of some sort, all the original bricks and ornate decorations were underneath the mask of whiteness. I hadn't dared experiment with my powers to prove the rumours right or wrong. My track record of being a model angel wasn't brilliant at best.

As I looked at the sun becoming brighter and stronger, I realised I was late. Again. I sighed. Breaking into a jog, my sandals slapped against the old brick floor as I raced through the narrow halls to join the rest of my clan outside.

Angels don't eat as such. We survive on energy drawn from the sun. This was a daily ritual called sun gazing that we did together, in our clans, barefoot on the clouds. The divine energy from the sun's rays soaked into our bodies, giving us more than enough energy to work from sunrise to sunset without needing a drop of physical food. It was an invigorating experience that I loved.

I finally made it to the top of the grand staircase, and despite having been yelled at many times, I hopped onto the smooth wooden railing that lined the wide set of stairs. I knew this had just been polished yesterday which meant my descent to the bottom of the hundred steps would be slightly faster than usual.

As the end of the railing came closer, I prepared myself to jump off. This is where it usually went wrong. Inches away from hitting the huge wooden ball sat on top of the end post, I pushed myself off. Perfectly timed, I missed the bottom two steps and landed on the grey stone floor on both feet.

"Yes," I whispered to myself, grinning from ear to ear.

"MAKEYSHA!"

Hearing Gabriel's voice bellow my name sent a shiver right through my soul. I rushed out of the huge open doorway, pleased I didn't have to wrestle with the two monstrous sized oak front doors. The sunshine blinded me momentarily. When my vision came back into focus, there stood my clan, all in rows, looking at me and waiting.

Gabriel stood to my right. Twelve stone steps lead down to the clouds and my patient fellow angels.

"I'm sorry," I said. "I thought I was early."

"You thought wrong," Gabriel said, his golden eyes burning with ire. "And stop sliding on my railings."

My cheeks burned with heat as I scurried down the stone steps to find my place amongst my clan. Apnastin, the newest male angel to join our clan, motioned for me to take the spot next to him.

"Thanks," I whispered, trying to ignore the burning stares from the others.

"You're welcome," he said, flashing me a smile.

"My Angels," said Gabriel. "Please remove your footwear and stand upon the clouds with the bare essence of your being. Look into the sun and invite its energy to fill you up. Imagine your body overflowing with hot, yellow energy. Harness the divine energy you are blessed to bask in and allow it to fuel your day."

The same speech, every day, without fail. Gabriel had a little bit of OCD. I think he was secretly afraid that if something happened slightly out of routine, then the rest of his day would be cursed as a result. I hadn't ever shared my opinion though. That might just cross a line I couldn't get back from.

I blanked my mind and indulged in the familiar feeling of sun gazing. Looking into the sun wasn't dangerous for angels. When you took into consideration that our eyes are the windows to our souls, closing our eyes wasn't really an option when we needed soul food.

My body started to hum with the addictive warm buzz that happened as the sun recharged my body. Heat trickled through my veins, inching its way to every last cell inside me. My soul started to lift, feeling weightless and happy, full of joy. I felt good. I felt full of life.

The sun crested over the horizon, blasting us all with its full power. I revelled in the strength of its energy, wanting to soak up more and more of its divine offerings.

"And that will do, Angels," Gabriel said, clapping his hands together once.

We all tore our gaze away from the powerful solar energy and slipped our feet back into our shoes.

"Have a good day, Angels. Any problems speak to me directly. See you at sunset. Sharp."

I cringed as he said 'sharp.' I knew that was aimed at me. We met at sunset every day to discuss the day's events and partake in 'clan building exercises' which usually consisted of fun games like charades and Pictionary. Magic not allowed, of course. All the castles, once inside, were magic free spaces. I found this ironic considering the rumours surrounding our chambers.

"What are your duties today?" Apnastin asked.

"Cleaning The Great Hall. You?"

"Ditto."

I smiled at him, noticing his striking features for the first time. High cheeks bones, plump pink lips, a gentle curving nose, and trademark golden hair, I'd seen less attractive angels.

"Fancy flying with me?" I said.

"Sure." He stretched out his magnificent white feathered wings, flapping them a few times to iron out the kinks.

I held my arms out as I stretched my own wings. For some reason, it seemed to enhance the stretch, making it feel ten times better. I had experimented, it wasn't just in my head. Releasing our wings inside the castle was forbidden which always made this even better after keeping them cramped up all night.

Pushing up on my feet, I soared into the air, my wings flapping to give me lift. Apnastin joined me, shooting upwards in a manic spiral display.

"Someone's full of energy," I said, surging upwards to catch him.

He grinned. "I'm a morning person. Come see me at two o clock and I'll be dead on my feet."

I laughed at him as we flew higher and higher, seeking out the thermal current that would take us to The Great Hall. In Heaven, each thermal current had its own direction, kind of like humans with their tarmac roads. The current for The Great Hall sat at the top of Heaven, metres above any other updraft.

Powering through other currents disrupted their energy and flow but flying straight up was the quickest way to get to our thermal, even though many angels frowned upon it. Apnastin blasted through a current, inches away from two angels heading towards the laundrette. The ripples from his sudden invasion threw the two angels from Raphael's castle backwards.

"Hey!" one of them shouted, flapping his wings to right himself. "Take the long route like everyone else!"

"No can do, sunshine," I replied, laughing as I followed Apnastin up.

I kept my focus on Apnastin and our thermal, ignoring the burning stares from the two angels we'd just upset. They'd get over it.

Without any more upsets or near collisions, we found our thermal and relaxed, allowing its current to float us along to our destination with little energy needed from our wings.

"I hear you're quite the trouble maker," Apnastin said, flashing me a cheeky grin.

I looked across at him, as we were now side by side, and smirked. "Oh really? And who told you that?"

"Just whispers I've heard around the castle, that's all. It seems you're the topic of conversation almost every day."

"I'm not sure I like the sound of that," I said, raising an eyebrow.

He laughed. "It's nothing bad. It's more the angels not understanding how you don't care about being told off all the time."

I grinned. "I'm used to it. Every human life I had I was in trouble for one thing or another. I guess it's just a part of who I am. I don't conform to rules and authority very well."

"How many lives did you have?"

I giggled. "Twenty-seven."

"Wow," he said. "That's quite some going. Over how many years?"

"Somewhere around three thousand years. How about you?"

"Thirteen over five hundred."

I balked. "Oh my goodness. That's bordering on archangel territory."

He grinned. "I know. Gabriel has already spoken to me about the next level. He wants to see how I perform for a few decades as an angel first though."

"That's amazing. Congratulations."

"Thanks."

I mulled over the soul flying next to me. The general basis was the less lives a soul lived, the better, as it took less lessons for you to achieve Nirvana. The same went for the amount of years it took you to live those lives. Generally, the shorter the time period it took you to live your lessons, the better. My record of twenty-seven over three thousand was horrendous. It basically meant I'd been a stubborn ass who needed long breaks in between lives in the hopes I might learn something.

They'd hoped wrong.

Apnastin, however, had only had thirteen lessons in five hundred years. He was obviously a quick learner who conformed to what God wanted. The total opposite of me.

For archangel territory, the number of lives had to be below fourteen, and the number of years below six hundred. All of the current archangels were below ten lives and four hundred years. I'd never wanted to be an archangel anyway. All the responsibility and pressures weren't something I wanted to be bothered to deal with. Not even for my own castle, clan, and enhanced powers.

We flew on in comfortable companionship. After several minutes, The Great Hall finally came into view in front of us. Resembling an ancient Greek temple, the huge building was a sight to behold.

The entire thing was made from sparkling white marble. It shone back at us, the gold flecks within the marble highlighted like gems under the sun's rays. The ornate columns, all twelve of them, were huge masses of intricately decorated marble. Decades of work had gone into this magnificent building.

"Wow," Apnastin breathed. "That's incredible."

"Have you never been here before?"

"Yes," he replied. "But it still never fails to take my breath away."

"It is quite something, isn't it?"

He nodded and slowed down, putting himself upright and using his wings as an air brake. I followed suit. We both landed on the bottom step, marvelling at the creation in front of us.

"Let's make it shine then," I said, running up the steep steps. "Do you know where the equipment is kept?"

"Yes, the cupboard at the back of the hall. Behind God's seat."

I nodded, my heart hammering inside my chest. I hated going in there, disturbing their meetings, and having to open the squeaky door behind God's seat. Silence always fell as soon as they realised they weren't alone, making me feel like a trespasser and that I had to get out of there ASAP.

Apnastin opened the giant double doors that led into the hall. The only thing that gave away they were doors were the two huge gold lion head door knockers. I held my breath as we walked through, expecting to be hit with the immediate silence that usually fell around the cleaners when they walked in.

But that didn't happen today.

My mouth dropped wide open at the chaos unfolding before me. Apnastin looked at me, wide eyed, and mouthing, "What the…?"

I shook my head and shrugged my shoulders.

The glass table that seated God and all of his confidantes lay smashed into pieces, millions of shards of glass spread all over the floor, glinting under the sunlight. God and Lucifer were in each other's faces, bright red, pointing, and shouting over one another. The rest of the confidantes had seemingly split into two sides, each group pointing fingers and yelling at the others.

"I told you to leave them alone!" God yelled, stabbing a finger into Lucifer's chest. "And you ignored me."

"Because I didn't agree with your decision, and

neither did half of this table."

"The vote has to be a majority before you can action anything."

"I know," replied Lucifer. "But not doing anything was also technically actioning something."

"Are you seriously trying to get out of this on a technicality?"

"It's not a technicality. It's a cold hard fact. You wanted to do nothing. I wanted to do something. Either way would result in one of us getting what we wanted."

"And you insured that it was your way that won, not mine."

Lucifer shrugged his shoulders. "Yes. You snooze, you lose, my old friend. Not my fault I have more initiative than you."

God narrowed his eyes at Lucifer—his closest confidante. His golden coloured pupils turned black. His long sunshine yellow hair also coloured itself darker, making him instantly unrecognisable. The air around him started to crackle and sizzle with energy and power.

"You will leave this realm immediately," he said, his voice booming around The Great Hall.

The two groups of archangels and confidantes ceased their bickering in an instant. Seconds ticked by. The atmosphere grew fraught with tension.

I looked at Apnastin and whispered, "Should we leave?"

"You go nowhere!" God yelled.

I looked at God, jumping back in shock when I saw his dark features staring straight at me.

"Call Heaven to order," he said, pointing to The Golden Horn in the corner of the hall. "Things are going to change here today."

My mouth dropped open. The antique Golden Horn, which was a huge feature decoration in The Great Hall, hadn't been blown for thousands of years. When it was sounded, it called all the angels in Heaven to The Great Hall to be addressed by God for something serious and life changing.

"What?" I said. "Seriously?"

"Just do it!" he bellowed, before turning his attention back to Lucifer.

Apnastin sprinted over to the Horn and within seconds, was blowing a deep breath into its mouthpiece. A rumbling trumpeting sound echoed around us, calling all of Heaven to order. The world around me shook and vibrated as the Horn blew on and on, demanding attention immediately.

Barely a minute passed before angels started appearing, all shocked at the scene before them. Some of the female angels started crying, saying this was the apocalypse, our time had come. We were going to die.

"Get a grip," I said, rolling my eyes at one angel in particular. "It's just a stupid row."

"Don't you see it?" she said, her golden eyes full of fear. "This is what he talked about. He knew it was going to happen!"

"Who?"

"Joshua. God's son. He said there would be a great turmoil that would rip Heaven in half, forcing us to choose between two great powers. I can't believe this is happening."

She broke down in tears, sobbing her little heart out.

I shook my head and sighed. What a drama queen. Rumours of God having a son had banded about for years. Some people believed it, others didn't. Earth didn't seem any more peaceful than normal, which if God did have a son down there, something would have changed drastically.

Then there was the matter of *how* he'd had a son. As far as we all knew, creatures in Heaven could not reproduce with each other; including God. If he had fathered a child, then he would have had to have done so with a human. Which was forbidden. That brought about its own trials and tribulations. Of course, those who believed, said it was a necessary break of the rules to save Heaven and Earth.

I thought it was all a load of poppycock. I'd believe in what I could see, touch, and feel. If I met the dude, then fine, but that would make me question God's integrity, too.

God turned towards us, his change of appearance frightening some people. "My people, my Angels, I am sorry to take you from your duties, but this is a necessity I cannot avoid. A great betrayal has happened in Heaven and I must call upon you all to cast a vote."

The whispers, cries, and fidgeting stopped as everyone stood and listened to God.

"There are souls, down on Earth, who have the ability to communicate with us. They have the power to pass our message on to their fellow humans, spreading love and joy all around."

"Isn't that what Joshua is supposed to do?" someone called out.

A collective gasp sounded around The Great Hall. I scanned my eyes over the hundreds of golden-haired heads, trying to locate the owner of the voice.

God glared at a central point in the crowd of angels. "That is not the discussion here."

Silence.

"However," God continued. "As we have all witnessed, the humans are a primitive species at best, still taken with war, jealousy, and rage. We, in The Great Hall, cast a vote just last week, on whether to speak to these humans or leave them be. It resulted in a fifty-fifty split. Some of us felt they needed to be left longer to mature before being given the knowledge of their powers. Others felt the knowledge of this power could be their turn to the right path."

Whispers and murmurs started flying around, each angel already taking sides with what they felt was the right thing to do.

"Lucifer, upon realising that by doing nothing meant I would be winning, decided to visit these humans and inform them of their powers."

Some angels shook their heads, frowning. Others started to clap and cheer.

"What I want to know is, my dear Angels, what is your opinion?"

A sea of blank, unsure faces stared back at our powerful leader.

"Please," God said, opening his arms wide. He smiled, returning some golden colour to his eyes and hair. "Take your sides. Let's have a Heaven wide vote. Those who agree with me, please stand to the left. Those who agree with Lucifer, please stand to the right."

The Great Hall filled with grumbles, heated discussions, and scuffling feet. Over the next several minutes, Heaven's angels were split fifty-fifty.

Except for me.

I stood, rooted to the spot, not knowing which way to turn. Neither of them were right. How could I be expected to pick a side when I thought they were both wrong?

"Makeysha," Gabriel whispered, leaning towards me from my left. "What are you doing? Make your decision. Now."

I turned to my boss and shook my head. "But I don't have one."

"What do you mean? Don't be so ridiculous. Get over here. Now."

"But I don't agree that they should be kept in the dark."

Gabriel widened his eyes, their golden colour brightening as his rage flared. "So you agree with Lucifer?"

"No…" I said, shaking my head. "I don't think they should have been told either."

He frowned at me. "But they are the only options, Makeysha. Pick one."

"No. They could have had their powers revoked. Why do they need them in the first place? Or tell them they can have them, but only when they've done X, Y, Z first."

Gabriel faltered. He opened his mouth, but nothing came out.

"That is not the debate here," God bellowed, making me jump. "Now choose a side, before I choose it for you."

"You shall not!" Lucifer said, shoving God in the shoulder. "You shall not choose for her, giving your side more points. If she has no choice, then let her be choiceless."

I started to tremble as the two great powers in front of me stared at each other like a pair of warring bulls. I couldn't choose. My opinion on the matter was not an option they wanted to hear. I would not pick a side and they couldn't force me to.

"Are you disagreeing with my decision?" God said, turning back to me.

All the eyes of Heaven fell upon me. I felt like I was on trial for some great crime. "Yes, I disagree with your decision."

God flicked his hand through the air, flinging me to the right-hand side of the room. I fell down, startled. My heart beat inside my chest, hammering ten to the dozen as I found myself with Lucifer's followers.

"Wait," Lucifer said, holding his hand out. "You said you disagreed with my decision also?"

I started to quiver uncontrollably all over, but I couldn't be untrue to myself. "Yes," I said, my voice a weak whisper.

"Then I don't want you either," he yelled. Motioning his hand through the air, he tossed me away from his believers, putting me back into the middle of the room.

"Makeysha," Gabriel hissed. "What are you doing?"

The panic in his voice started to make me realise I was in a dire situation. Heaven was split in two halves, with no room for grey areas and loopholes.

"I'm sorry," I said, my eyes filling with tears. "But I don't believe in either choice."

"Then be choiceless," God said.

Choiceless? What did he mean by that? Fear climbed through me like jungle vines. "I don't understand…"

God opened his hand, his palm facing towards me. An invisible force grabbed a hold of my limbs, lifting me into the air. A startled cry left my throat as I looked at the marble floor metres beneath me.

"Makeysha, you took many lives over many years to learn your lessons to be here. It seems even they have not been enough to calm your nature. There is no room in Heaven for people who refuse to follow me loyally."

A loud rumble resonated around me. The skies darkened and the air seemed to be charged with power. I looked over at my fellow angels, only to see them all looking down, shocked expressions on their faces.

Looking over my shoulder, I saw the sparkling marble floor of The Great Hall had disappeared, an ominous black void left in its place. I could see the dark energy swirling around, lining the edges of the black hole.

I turned back to God, panic rising in me like a tidal wave. "Please, no…"

"I forbid you to be in my realm, Angel Makeysha. I hereby cast you from Heaven, never to set foot here again."

He moved his hand down, lowering me into the dark energy mass. Then, with his free hand, he took hold of Lucifer and his followers.

"And you are all traitors. Disloyal to me and my message to the people of Earth. You shall also be forever forbidden from setting foot in Heaven again."

The invisible force that had a grip on me suddenly released, dropping me into the black hole. I found myself falling backwards, able to see the crowd of angels, and Lucifer, also falling through the void with me.

Screams and shouts of surprise and anger banded around. Some angels tried to release their wings, only for them to be burned up or broken up from the rate of our fall. The darkness around us started to lighten into blue skies. I dared to look behind me to see what we were falling towards.

My answer was Earth. A huge crater sized entrance, the colour of burning flames, stared directly back at us from the centre of Earth's mass.

"That is our new home," Lucifer shouted. "All angels head for the opening."

I found myself thinking about the colour orange. Could orange really be the new white? As I wondered what our new home would be like, I felt my body being pushed to the right, out of the way of the stream of falling angels.

Panicking I would miss the doorway, I looked behind me again. I choked on terror as I realised I was miles off course to land where I needed to. As the earth's landscape came rushing up to meet me, I closed my eyes and braced for impact.

My back hit the solid ground, knocking every bit of breath from my body. I lay stunned for several minutes, watching the flow of angels descending into their new orange abyss, miles away from me. I willed my body to move so I could hurry to them, get into the entrance before it closed.

"Except you."

Lucifer hovered above me, his magnificent wings outstretched and gently flapping in the wind.

"You didn't believe in me either, Makeysha. I don't want you in my domain. You can stay here, on Earth, forever cursed to wander the lands by yourself. God has left your powers intact and I will grant you the same comfort. From here you shall assist souls in parting from their shells. You belong to nothing and no one."

I opened my mouth to speak but he was gone. In the blink of an eye, he'd soared into the sky, heading towards the last of his faithful followers plunging into their new realm. I don't know how long I laid there, broken, empty, and utterly alone.

Finally sitting up, I turned my head left and right at such a rate of knots as I looked around me, my hair flew back and forth with the quick movement. That's when I noticed it; my hair. My gentle golden curls had vanished, jet black waves staring back at me instead.

I couldn't help it then. I sat and wailed like a banshee.

ANGEL OF THE CRYPT

CHAPTER TWO

Ronin

There's no smoke without fire. That's what my mom and dad had always told me. I wasn't religious, not in the traditional sense anyway. My family, and a number of others like mine, looked at the Bible as a fantastic story. A brilliant creation from a mind that existed thousands of years ago.

In our world, all of these magical beings existed—and still did. Angels, demons, dragons, witches; any monster you could think of, it lived, it breathed, and it did so right here on Earth.

Our family, and the others, hunted these creatures, damning them back to the pits of Hell. We all agreed on the viewpoint that Lucifer's fall from grace had turned him bitter, fuelling his dark actions and thoughts into vengeance on God.

God, unable to bear seeing his beloved humans being tortured by Lucifer's demons, had turned his back on us, picking ignorance for the sake of his sanity. We could handle the fallout though. The angels had underestimated the power of human determination.

Ever since I had been old enough to understand stories, I had been taught about the tale of one angel. There apparently was one who refused to pick a side and her punishment was to walk the earth alone. Some said the feathers from her wings could turn water into gold. Others said the sound of her voice could coax diseases into leaving bodies. I believed she was nothing but sad and lonely. If she truly did exist.

My parents, and most of the other families, believed she could be our fighting force against an age-old war between angels. Centuries ago, God had sent his angels down to Earth to help battle the demons back into Hell. Those angels blessed certain humans with special powers, enabling them to help in the fight. But, as time wore on, the visits from his angels became less and less, until eventually they stopped.

However, the powers in the humans remained, and they passed on to their offspring. Hence, me, here today. A supernatural hunter with inhuman strength, speed, and intelligence. We have limited magical powers in that we can 'influence' the environment around us. For example, if I step outside in the morning and inhale a breath of fresh, damp air, I may think to myself, "It smells like rain." At that instant, it will start to rain, because my thoughts influenced it to do so.

We lived in the De Soto National Forest, right on

the border for Mississippi, Alabama, and Louisiana. We inhabited around one thousand acres, of which, no one knew we existed, of course. Our families had settled here way back with the aid of the angels, their powers marking our territory and gently deflecting unwanted humans away from our borders.

"Ronin!"

I sighed as I heard my mom yell. All I wanted this morning was to clean my bow in peace. Was that really too much to ask?

"Ronin, where are you?"

"Down by the creek," I shouted back.

The foliage behind me rustled as Mom blundered through the forest, not caring how much noise she made. Dad always taught us, regardless of our surroundings, we must always be quiet.

"If you start being noisy at home, it won't be long before you slip up out on the field, son," he said to us, over and over.

"Ronin," Mom said, pushing her way through a thicket of twigs and branches. "I've just had a call from Wanda. She's ready for you to go see her."

I rolled my eyes. "Mom, I don't want to marry Leyani. How many times?"

"Ronin," she said, standing to my left. Out of the corner of my eye, I could see her feet were shoulder width apart, which meant she was most probably giving me her 'attitude' pose with her hands on her hips. "We've discussed this. You can't marry any old human. It has to be someone from within the hunter community. The Shipton's are the only family we've never tied ourselves to. It would be a fantastic coupling and your children would gain a whole new level of skills never yet introduced to our family."

I ran a cloth over my bow strings, sighed, and then looked up at my mom. Yep—there it was. The 'attitude' pose. Her brown shoulder length hair sat inches above her shoulders, swaying back and forth as she shook her head at me.

"Mom, I'm not attracted to Leyani. She's far too young for starters and I just don't want to sleep with her. End of. Why not let Brandon have her? He's been obsessed with her since he knew what females were."

"Because Leyani wants you, Ronin, not Brandon." She gave me a sympathetic smile, her bronzed cheeks creasing. "And she's not that young. She's twenty-four."

"Ten years is a big age gap, Mom."

"And you're not getting any younger, either. The rate you're going, you're going to be forty before I get any grandchildren."

I chuckled and stood up. Placing my hands on Mom's shoulders, I grinned. "The rate Brandon is going, you'll have plenty of grandchildren before I'm forty."

"Ronin…"

Talking about my little brother always exasperated her. Six years younger than me, Brandon had a lot to learn in terms of self-control and his sex drive. My parents hated it as they'd done nothing but try their best to teach us to be respectable men who kept their urges under control. After all, we couldn't afford to be distracted by a beautiful woman. Chances were she would be some sort of creature we'd have to kill anyway, or if not, she would certainly lead to us dropping our guard and being killed.

"Will you just go and talk to Wanda anyway? Please?"

Seeing the pleading in my mom's big brown eyes, I sighed and gave in. "Fine. I'll go see the old witch about tying together two bloodlines, and then tell her it isn't going to happen, and I wasted her time."

"Maybe some time away will do you some good. It'll give you time to think about things. Maybe by the time you get to Wanda, you'll feel differently. Hey." She clapped her hands together, her eyes lighting up with joy. "Here's an idea."

Oh no.

"Take Leyani with you. Get to know her a little better."

"Err…no."

"What harm could it do?"

I stepped back and bent down to pick my bow up. "Listening to her talk non-stop about crochet? A lot of harm. To my mental health."

"Crochet is a very handy skill for a young woman to learn. It will save you a fortune in clothes when your children are growing up."

"Oh yay."

"Ronin. Come on. Please. I'm trying to help you here."

"No, Mom," I replied, giving her my best smile. "You're trying to help yourself."

"How do you figure that out?"

"Because for some insane reason, you want babies in your house. It's not going to happen. Not yet anyway."

"But I'm the only mother with a son over the age of thirty who isn't married!"

"In our community, yes, maybe, but not in the whole world, Mom. Chill out. No one is judging you."

"Ha," she said, snorting. "You haven't been

subjected to those judgemental sympathy ridden looks from Mary Whittaker. Then you'd understand."

"When's Dad back?" I said, figuring maybe getting away for a few days wouldn't be a bad idea seeing as she was on one again about my lack of marriage.

"This evening."

"Right," I said. "I'll pack a bag and leave when Dad's back."

Mom leapt forwards and gave me a hug. "Thank you. I promise you won't regret it."

"Don't make promises you can't keep, Mom."

"I'm not," she said, drawing back and winking at me.

She turned and skipped back to the cabin, humming away to herself. I followed, grumbling to myself about my inability to say no to my mom.

CHAPTER THREE

Makeysha

As I caught sight of the purple and blue hues emanating from my cemetery, I came back to reality, forgetting my emotional history. Swooping down to Odd Fellows, my heart filled with peace and a broad smile swept across my face. This was the only place on Earth that elicited such a reaction from me. That's how I knew it was home.

My existence on Earth up to now had been nothing but miserable and lonely, except for the joy I felt when I was within the walls of this cemetery. Sat on the corner of two busy roads, Canal Street and City Park Avenue, most would think it a noisy place to choose to be, but the crumbling white walls lining its boundaries were surprisingly efficient at blocking out the hustle and bustle of the city beyond.

Bundles of trees also helped block out the noise, and the pristine cemetery backing onto its southern boundary line provided an added element of serenity and tranquillity. It saddened me that two cemeteries could be kept in such different states; one completely forgotten and left to ruin but the other so clean and well cared for. Still, the souls still being laid to rest in the neighbouring cemetery would give me something to do if I so desired.

I straightened myself up and used my wings as an air brake as I came in to land on the overgrown grass circle in the centre of the small graveyard. The instant my feet touched the ground, I sighed with relief; I was home.

The cemetery sat a little outside of the main action of New Orleans, roughly three miles from the heart of this beautiful city: the French Quarter. Canal Street provided a direct vein to the thriving life happening in this small part of the city. I had always admired the liveliness going on down there but had never ventured downtown. Lots of creatures lived, worked, and passed through the city and as much as I hated being alone, I also didn't want to come across undesirable creatures either.

Perhaps though, it was time to change that. I couldn't stay here much longer without indulging in the beauty of the city that wrapped me up in its arms.

I ventured to the crypt I called my home. When I left to go on my travels, I returned it to its original state that I'd found it in. Whilst I was here, I could shield its pristine condition from the outside world, but being away from it, I couldn't do that.

The crypt was a large sandy coloured derelict structure. Its doorway had been broken open, the headstone laying in several pieces on the ground. 'Renee Howard' had been laid to rest here, but at some point, had been removed, leaving the crypt wide open and empty.

Black gothic style wrought iron railings lined the small plot that belonged to this family. Roughly around thirty square feet, it wasn't a huge space to claim as my 'chambers' but it was mine.

I stepped inside the empty tomb, sighing with sadness as the stained walls, creeping vines, and dead leaves slowly claimed its historic beauty.

I closed my eyes and held my hands out, calling my magic to the surface. I'd kept my magic usage to a minimum during my time on Earth, just in case Lucifer decided he didn't like me having my powers. For things like this though, I saw my magic as an aid. As the familiar buzz of warm energy trickled through every part of me, I couldn't help but smile.

In my minds eye, I envisioned the mould stained walls being painted over with fresh white paint. I pictured the leaves being swept out and carried away on the wind, and the vines retreating backwards, finding new places to creep through and slowly claim.

I opened my eyes to see the golden shine from my eyes reflecting back at me from the brand-new white walls, what I imagined becoming a reality within seconds. I stepped outside and focused on the cracked, broken bricks, shining my powers over them to plaster them back together. I gave the railings a new lease of life and then finally weeded out the pesky wildflowers that had taken a hold in the ground around me.

Compared to the rest of the graveyard, my home stood out like a sore thumb, but no one ever came in here anyway, except for the odd creature. A huge oak tree sat inches away from the west wall of my crypt, providing some cover. I looked up at its huge leafy branches and decided to shape them, so they hung lower to cloak more of my small home.

I sprouted some new leaves, just for good measure, to make it a little bushier as the branch draped across the roof of my crypt, its leaves partially blocking the entrance. It wasn't a perfect disguise, but the drooping branch definitely gave an initial impression of it being delipidated. Of course, if any curious creatures decided to investigate further, they would find me, but I would deal with that then.

I clapped my hands together and skipped back inside my home. My bed would be all I needed now to complete my arrival back home. I'd missed a comfortable bed on my travels. Picturing a giant cloud, and enormous fluffy pillows, I filled the space inside the crypt with my picture-perfect bed. I coloured the sheets and covers with a soft pink and lilac mix. Once it was complete, I stepped back and squealed in joy.

Finally satisfied, I lowered my hands, allowing my powers to subside beneath my layers once more. The longer I stared at the bed, the more I wanted to be in it. I jumped through the open doorway and allowed my soft new bed to envelope me in its warmth. Crawling beneath the duvet, I couldn't have had a bigger smile on my face.

CHAPTER FOUR

Ronin

I was finally on the road, away from my mom's nagging about marrying a woman I didn't want. Wanda was a powerful witch and one of the few good ones. When Lucifer first settled in Hell, he unleashed his demons on the earth to do all sorts of weird and evil stuff. Part of that happened to be having sex with humans. The result of those couplings were a stream of children born with magical powers—witches, wizards, and warlocks.

The difference? Warlocks were born of a female demon (née angel) and were much more powerful than a witch or wizard. They could do everything a witch and wizard could, and then some. Warlocks were not only rare, but extremely good at hiding in plain sight.

Witches, born of a female human, played with spells, herbs, rituals—the usual interpretation of a witch, and could be male or female.

Wizards, also born of a female human, had a distinct ability to control animals and the minds of those around them. They could also be male or female.

What Lucifer hadn't accounted for was nature versus nurture. Some of these created children were exactly what he hoped for; badass powerful people who wanted nothing more than to wreak havoc on their fellow humans. However, some were good. Some wanted to use their powers for the better, or even not at all.

Wanda happened to be one of the good ones. It was easy to spot a good witch from a bad one—you simply looked at their ring finger. If it was crooked, all bent up and wonky like a twisted tree branch, then they were bad. I'd never met Wanda, but I knew my mom had worked with her for years regarding marriages in our community.

Supernatural hunters only married other supernatural hunters. It wasn't just to ensure the purity of our bloodlines but also to guarantee the secrecy of our kind. Each family had its own strengths and weaknesses, all down to general genetics and how the angel's powers had affected our ancestor's DNA. It also made sure we all worked together as a team.

When marrying two families together, a witch had to be involved in order to transfer one family's strengths to the other. It wasn't fair that the children from the union were the only ones with the benefits.

The Shipton's were an excellent hunting family. All of them were small and petite in size, power and strength being their weaknesses, but what they lacked in size they made up for in cunning and strategic planning. It would be a valuable asset to our bloodline, sure, but we'd more than managed thus far. I didn't see it as a vital marriage in order to further ourselves.

Leyani was an attractive girl but she was exactly that; a girl. Her size and delicate features reminded me of my mom's fragile china tea set that we weren't ever allowed to touch. She was also a 'home girl' always baking, cooking, or making something with her mom. I didn't want to be married to a girl's mom as well. One female was more than enough for me to deal with, thank you very much.

Wanda lived in New Orleans, in the French Quarter. Apparently, the best place to find her would be at her workplace; The Historic Voodoo Museum. I mean, where else would a witch work?

The drive was only a couple of hours, so nothing too dreadful. As I neared my destination of 724 Dumaine Street, a sheen of sweat broke out all over my body. I didn't like dealing with witches, even the good ones. Their ability to conjure anything from anything seriously unnerved me. Vowing to never let my mom hear the end of this if it went bad, I pushed on, only ten minutes to go until I reached my destination.

Currently on the I-10W, I took exit 236C and dropped on to St Bernard Avenue. Houses littered the side of the interstate, all neatly cut gardens, and new looking garden fences. As I carried on, trees lined each side of the road, shadowing the path ahead. I crossed the intersection and headed underneath the overpass.

To my left, several closed down and derelict buildings stood on the side of the road, graffiti on nearly every wall. Abandoned cars with smashed windows were strewn around like trash. Unease started to climb inside me as I thought of what creatures could be lurking around.

On the opposite side of the road, houses lined the roadway, each a different colour, giving a mix of pastel blues, yellows, pinks, and reds. Considering the ugliness facing them, they were a pretty distraction. Given the time—just after nine p.m., there weren't many people about and I had to wonder if crime was rife in this part of town.

Coming to another intersection, I headed right onto North Rampart Street, the scenery becoming noticeably different the instant I crossed over. Gothic style lampposts lit the streets up from the neutral ground, the grass on which they sat neatly landscaped. The buildings were bigger, older, and well cared for, their architecture giving away the years they'd sat here already.

The streets were clean, the cars newer, and the houses well cared for. My worry for skulking creatures lessened somewhat. I turned left onto St Philip Street, the surrounding area changing once more. The road was bumpy, cracked, narrow, and empty of people. Parked cars lined the side of the street, outside well kept, immaculate houses.

All of the houses had wooden shutters on the outside. Whilst I appreciated the originality of the cottages, the Creole townhouses were my favourite by far with their fancy ornate iron railings and old age looks. No two buildings were the same and it gave the area a beautiful unique quality that paid diligence to the its rich history.

I turned right onto Royal Street, passing between two pink Creole townhouses, marvelling at their beauty. Several hotels appeared, all flying American flags and carrying various banners on their balcony railings. I briefly wondered whether I should stop and book myself into one now.

Looking at my sat nav, I realised I was literally around the corner from Wanda and decided to push on. I turned right onto Dumaine Street and kept my eyes peeled for a museum. Several trees lined the left-hand side of the road, blocking my view partially. Then, as a well-cared for pink townhouse appeared to my right, I noticed a drab grey coloured Creole house opposite it.

Had it not been for a wooden sign swinging loosely in the cool breeze, I would have sailed straight by. A side street ran down the side of the pink house so I swung my black SUV into it and hopped out, pleased to be stretching my legs. I locked it up before heading across the street to what looked to be a closed Voodoo Museum.

As I reached the dark green double wooden doors, they opened, and there stood who I presumed was Wanda. A petite white woman with short cropped dark hair, the yellow lights from the room behind her cast her physical appearance into shadows.

"And it is to the angels we must be eternally grateful…" she said, waiting for me to finish the rest.

"For without them, Earth would wither and diminish into the realms of Lucifer."

It was a saying, along with several others, that all hunters were brought up with. We used them as passwords, for situations like this. It was a fail-safe way of making sure that who we were meeting was on our side.

"Hi, Ronin," Wanda said, stepping aside.

I walked into the brightly lit room, surprised at

how much stuff someone could fit into one cramped space. She closed the doors behind us and brushed past me to sit on a wooden stool behind the small counter.

Now in the light, I could see her face properly. High cheekbones, a strong jawline, and soft brown eyes, Wanda must have been a sought-after lady in her younger years. Crows feet edged the corners of her eyes, and various lines and wrinkles added to the features on her face. I guessed she must be mid-fifties.

"I'm fifty-five," she said, her eyes twinkling with mischief. "Good guess."

I cringed as my mouth dropped wide open.

"Some of us are psychic," she said, grinning as she tapped the side of her head. "Might want to remember to keep your shields up."

Trying to ignore my burning cheeks, I nodded. "I'm sorry. I had no idea." I mentally cursed my mom for not telling me. "I'll make sure I keep my shields up. Thanks for the tip."

Mental shields were something all hunters learned to build. We could, after years of practice, flick them on and off at will. We didn't keep them up all the time because it was so mentally tiring. After a while, mental tiredness takes its toll on the body, too. Generally, we only needed shields when around creatures such as demons and vampires, and the odd werewolf if they happened to be an alpha or luna—an alpha's mate.

"Please, take a seat," she said, motioning to the small stool underneath a huge picture of hand drawn tribesmen.

I eyed up the sturdy object, debating if my bulky frame would squash it, despite its robust appearance. "Will it take my weight?"

A gentle laugh sounded around the room. "I've

had bigger men than you on that chair."

Gazing around the vast collection of weird and wonderful items around me, I said, "This is quite a collection. Is it all genuine?"

"Every last piece. Some of them were very hard to come by."

Intricately carved wooden figures, animal skulls, wooden crosses, flags, voodoo dolls, tribal masks—anything you could think of was in this room. I made a mental note to come back another day and learn more, but not tonight. This evening we had different business to tend to.

"Your mother tells me you're going to be marrying Leyani Shipton."

I tore my focus from what looked to be the leathery corpse of a cat on the far wall and smiled at Wanda. "Not quite correct, I'm afraid. My mother wants me to marry Leyani Shipton."

"But you don't want to?"

I shook my head. "No, I really don't."

"Then why are you here?"

I shrugged my shoulders. "Because my mom asked me to come and see you. She thought by the time I'd driven down here that I might have changed my mind."

"Have you ever felt like marrying her?"

"No."

"So it's definitely not cold feet then?"

I laughed. "No. I just don't want to marry her. She does nothing for me."

"I see," she said, pursing her lips. "Well, luckily for you, unless both parties are committed, the unification ceremony won't work. There is no benefit here for your mom to make you marry Leyani."

"That is the best news you could have given me, Wanda. Thank you. I'm sorry to have made you wait all this time after closing just to tell me that."

Wanda waved her hand through the air. "It's nothing. I practically live here anyway." She nodded her head towards the wall behind me. "That pink house across the street is mine."

"It's lovely," I said. "It was the first thing I noticed when I came down here."

"Thanks," she said. "Now, one more thing. Has anyone ever spoken to you about the colour of your eyes?"

I jerked my head backwards and frowned. "No. Why?"

A mysterious smile tugged at her pink lips. "Amber eyes are extremely rare among humans, let alone your kind."

"Ok…"

"The angels have golden coloured eyes." She narrowed her eyes and peered at me. "And yours, when the light reflects from them, have a similar colour."

"And what does that mean?"

"It means that you're closer to the angels. You have more power, more strength, more speed, and more intelligence, than your counterparts. It means that you're the closest human to being an angel and the closest angel to being a human. Does that make sense?"

"What are you telling me? That my dad isn't my dad?"

Wanda laughed. "No, he most certainly is. Think of it like a genetic anomaly. Every few hundred years, something in the gene pool happens and creates a throwback, but more often than not, those throwbacks are special in one way or another."

"So I'm a throwback?"

She nodded. "For whatever reason, you have more angel like powers than any of your kind. That is why your eyes are the colour they are. It's like a signal to other creatures of your heritage."

"So what about amber eyes in humans?"

"They're nothing like the colour of yours. Most often they're taken as being hazel, it's only the light reflecting from them and catching odd flecks of green and brown that give off the appearance of amber. Yours though, yours are quite something else."

"So why hasn't anyone ever mentioned it before?"

Wanda shrugged her shoulders. "Could be that they don't want to or they just don't know what it means. Or maybe they don't want to point out how you're different to others. Could be anything."

"If they did know, and didn't mention it, why would that be?"

"Because if you're more angel than they are, chances are if anyone is going to find the legendary lone angel, it's going to be you."

I barked with laughter. "She's a myth. No one has ever seen her, heard her, or even caught a sniff of what might be her."

"How do you know it's a her?"

I stalled and thought about her question. "I don't know…it just kind of came out."

Wanda smiled. "See? You're more in tune with your angel side than what you think."

I shook my head. "It was a slip of the tongue, a wild stab in the dark. I could have just as easily said 'he.'"

"But you didn't." Wanda took a breath to

continue, then stopped. She froze. Putting her index finger to her mouth in a shush motion, she pointed to the doors.

I frowned and mouthed, "What?"

She lifted her arms, showing me the hairs standing on end. Something was lurking outside. Just as I stood up, my heart did a backflip—a tell-tale sign I'd learned from my body over the years that a creature was nearby.

All of my weapons were in the car, except for a serrated hunting knife I kept clipped to my belt regardless of where I went. I carefully popped the button off and slid it free from its sheath. As I approached the door, the hairs on the back of my neck stood up.

Vampire.

Each creature had a different effect on a hunter's body, and this was the classic sign for my body to tell me a vampire was around. Tightening my grip on my knife, I slowly unlatched the door, half expecting to be rammed in the chest as they burst through it. My knife was more than capable of taking out a vampire. Wood didn't hurt them like all the old tales and legends tell; they slept in wooden coffins for goodness sake. What really hurt them was silver; which my blade was coated in.

The only way to extinguish one was to slit the throat and drain all the blood. Once their blood had been pumped out of their cold bodies, then you removed the head, took out the eyes, and the fangs, and burned it all—in separate piles. Taking the head off before the blood had been drained would result in a headless corpse running through the streets at warp speed. It was not a pretty sight and damn hard to catch.

I opened the door, peering out into the dark, empty street. Nothing moved. Nothing made a sound. The eerie silence unnerved me, tripping me into high alert.

Then I heard it. The slightest scrape of shoes on stone. My eyes darted to my car. There stood a tall, lithe figure, dressed in a long black coat, peering into the back of my Suburban.

Mothersucker.

I slipped out into the street, keeping my back pressed against the cool bricks of the museum. My plan was to sidle up the street by a hundred yards, cross over, then come back down the other side so I could creep up on him.

Vampires were fast, but not overly intelligent. More often than not when they were homed in on something, focused, they tuned out of everything around them. Hopefully, this dude would do the same.

Tiptoeing up the street, I dashed across the road, then slowly made my way down the other side of the street. The last house sat back from the sidewalk. Its front garden was lined with black wrought iron railings that enabled me to clearly see my SUV.

The vampire moved along the side of my car, edging around the back of it. He looked up and clocked me. His silver eyes glinted under the moonlight. We stood for several seconds, staring each other out. Then, he turned and fled.

I gave chase. Whilst my speed could not match his, he certainly wasn't disappearing from my sights. He headed north on Dumaine Street, then sprinted around the top corner, turning left. I pushed forwards, desperate not to lose sight of him.

The silvery glow his aura left behind lingered in

the air for several seconds, like a snail's trail, the only hint a vampire left of their presence. I followed his silver specked trail, my lungs burning for oxygen but my legs pushing me faster and faster. Running out onto the main street, I just caught sight of the end of his coat billowing behind him as he turned alongside a park.

Pushing myself more, I bolted across the street and down by the square. He'd gone, but the faintly vanishing silver specks gave me all I needed. After a couple of twists and turns, I finally caught sight of him again. He was running at top speed, about a quarter of a mile in front of me. The route he'd chosen was a direct straight line. I grinned, thanking the Universe for the vampire's stupidity.

It didn't dawn on me to begin with that the path he'd taken was all back alleys. It was only when I noticed figures hanging around in the shadows that I realised these parts of the city were less than desirable to be in at this time of night.

I hoped that regular humans knew to steer clear. I didn't have time for any rescue missions right now. We ran for what felt like an eternity. He looked back over his shoulder every few hundred yards, no doubt surprised to see me still there, keeping him in my sights.

As we neared the edge of the mid-city limits, my body started to scream at me for relief. We must have covered a good three miles or more in a matter of minutes. I would not let this bloodsucker walk free though. His head was mine. I gritted my teeth and ignored my body's cries of agony.

Come on. Do something stupid, give me a break.

The vampire darted left, taking an alley back towards the main street. I hoped he'd run out in front of a car, something to stop him even if just for a second. He burst out onto the main street, heading right. My footsteps echoed around me as I pounded down the empty tarmac. He took another right, just behind some kind of herb shop, and leapt over a black iron gate into a cemetery.

Now I've got you.

Cemeteries sucked all the powers out of vampires like a leech. They became nothing more than a regular human with a thirst for blood once inside hallowed grounds. I grinned as I hurdled over the gate. Figuring I had a few seconds to catch my breath, I stopped and sucked in some deep breaths of air. I never knew how good fresh air could taste when your body screamed for it.

Before my legs locked up on me, I started moving again, skirting around the edge of the graveyard, looking for any signs of movement. There was no way he'd manage to jump back over that gate without his supernatural abilities. He was trapped.

Idiot.

I crept along the rows of deserted and neglected crypts, doing my best to avoid tripping over the layers of vines inching across the broken pathways. Then I saw it; a brief flicker of something long and black.

Sprinting towards it, I ran full pelt into a sandy coloured crypt, hit something solid, and then fell face first onto the softest, fluffiest bed I'd ever come across.

What the…?

The tip of something hard and cool pressed into the back of my neck. I stayed motionless, wondering what the hell to do next.

"Is this one of your friends?" a female voice asked.

"Are you going to kill him if I say yes?" a male

voice replied, hissing.

Wait. She had the vampire and a knife pressed to the back of my head? Who the hell was she? Wonder Woman?

"Don't lie to me," she said, her voice icy and cool. "I don't take well to your kind, let alone when you invade my chambers."

"Go fu—"

His words turned into screams. From the corner of my right eye, I could just make out a blinding white light. It shone brighter and brighter before then enveloping us back into complete darkness.

"You," she said, pressing the tip of her blade into my head. "Up. Back it up nice and slowly."

I put my hands on the bed and gently pressed myself up. Very carefully, I crawled backwards onto my feet and slowly stood up. Still facing into the crypt, I could see I had in fact fallen onto a bed. A huge bed that filled the entire inside of this family tomb.

What the...?

"Turn around, wise guy," she said. "Nice and slowly."

I kept my hands up so she could see I wasn't going to try anything smart. As I turned around, I noticed a pile of ash at her feet—the remains of the vampire. How had she killed him? There was no fire and no blood.

When I looked at my captor, I nearly choked on my breath. Burning golden eyes, hair the colour of a raven, and two magnificent fully stretched white wings—she was the missing angel. The legend. The one everyone spoke of.

Our eyes locked. And that's when my world changed

Chapter Five

Makeysha

My bed was pure bliss. I never wanted to leave it ever again. I allowed myself to fall into a deep sleep, so deep, I had no dreams. My peaceful slumber was abruptly interrupted by a long, wet tongue sliding up my cheek.

"Hmmm, you're going to taste so good."

The raspy voice sent a chill down my spine. I opened my eyes to see a man above me, his sharp-nosed features inches from my face as he leered at me. The silver aura beaming off him, combined with the silver colour of his eyes told me all I needed to know about him; vampire.

What this stupid critter hadn't accounted for was me being an angel. Even at my base level of angel powers, I could take on most supernatural creatures in the blink of an eye and kill them. I'd never had to do it yet though. Most would see the colour of my eyes and run like the wind.

Since I'd been sleeping, this one I had to forgive for the small transgression. He couldn't hurt me though; his fangs would merely bounce off my neck, my flesh too strong for his teeth to penetrate. After all, Lucifer hadn't wanted to cause harm to angels directly; only indirectly through God's precious humans.

"I suggest you leave while you still can," I said, keeping my voice calm and matter of fact.

He grinned. "And not have a taste of angel blood? I don't think so."

"You can't drink from me without breaking your teeth."

"No…maybe not, but this little thing will surely help."

He lifted a hand to reveal an intricately carved dagger made from ivory, its sheath made of feathered white gold.

I gasped. "No…"

"Yes," he replied, his grin turning maniacal. "Now who has the upper hand?"

His weapon was one of seven I knew to be in existence. A dagger made from a unicorn's horn, its handle created from Pegasus wings. The only known thing that could not only draw an archangel's blood but kill one. It would easily take me down.

The heavy thud of footsteps alerted me to someone else's presence. Sensing this would be my only distraction, I jumped up, headbutting the vampire square in the nose. He jerked backwards, giving me enough room to speed through the doorway. I didn't know if he'd come with back up or not, so I grabbed a hold of him on my way out, prising the dagger from his bony fingers.

I kept one hand around his throat, squeezing just enough that my fingernails spilled a few drops of his blood onto my hand. He kept still. His blundering companion pelted into my crypt, faceplanting my gorgeous new bed.

Great. Not even one night and I need new sheets.

I called my powers back, loving the sizzling feeling crackling through my veins. I felt more powerful than I ever had done. Perhaps these daggers had more of an effect on angels than we all thought. Using my power, I magically pressed the dagger to the back of the man's neck, controlling it with my mind.

"Is this one of your friends?" I asked the vampire.

"Are you going to kill him if I say yes?" His words came out as a hiss, his voice strangled by my grip.

"Don't lie to me," I replied, glaring at him. "I don't take well to your kind, let alone when you invade my chambers."

"Go fu—"

I heard his thoughts before he spoke them. I didn't like swear words at the best of times. I fixed my stare on him and wished him dead. Pure energy and power shot from my eyes, its radiance becoming more blinding with each second.

The vampire screamed as the white power seared his flesh from his bones, then turned his skeleton into nothing but ash. Within seconds, he was nothing but a heap of dust at my feet.

Wow.

Night swallowed me once more. No evidence was left of the amazing power display I'd just unwittingly unleashed. Feeling on top of the world, I turned my attention back to the other man, still pinned to my bed by the unicorn dagger.

"You," I said, pressing the tip of the blade into the back of his head. "Up. Back it up nice and slowly."

He put his hands on the bed and pressed himself up onto all fours. Painstakingly slowly, he crawled backwards onto his feet and slowly stood up. Despite no silver coloured aura, he was obviously something to do with the vampire.

"Turn around, wise guy," I said. "Nice and slowly."

He kept his hands where I could see them and shuffled around to face me. His eyes went straight to the pile of what was a vampire. Then our eyes locked. I gasped. Those eyes. Shining amber eyes, an athletic muscular body, hair as dark as my own—he looked part angel. Power emanated off him in droves. His rugged, handsome features would rival any male I'd ever seen.

I dove into his aura with my mind and saw nothing. How could that be? "What are you?" I said, opening my hand for the dagger to return to it.

"A man," he said, his voice all but a breathless whisper.

"No, you're not. Your eyes...you're no ordinary man."

"You," he said, his voice still a whisper. "You're a myth, a legend. You can't be real."

I pursed my lips. "I can assure you, I'm very real. Now, answer my question. What are you?"

"A hunter...I'm a hunter. You're...you're an angel."

"You here to kill me, hunter?" I held the dagger up to his throat. "You want some of my blood, too?"

He frowned, then shook his head. "What? No. I was chasing the vampire."

"For what? This?" I held the dagger up in front of his face.

"No, to kill it. I wanted to kill it, but you got there first."

I narrowed my eyes at him. "So you'd never seen that vampire before tonight?"

He shook his head.

I let out a breath, easing some tension. I lowered my hand holding the dagger and smiled at him. "Sorry. I wasn't expecting to be nearly killed tonight so forgive me for being a little on edge."

"Killed? Angels can't be killed by a vampire."

Waving the dagger in front of his face, I said, "They can with one of these."

His eyes focused on the knife. "Can I have a look at it?"

"No!" I said, snatching it back and holding it to my side. "You think I'm stupid enough to hand it over to you after just telling you it can kill me?"

"I don't want to kill you," he said. "I've just never seen one of those before."

I studied his face for several seconds. He seemed genuine. If he had an aura, I'd have been able to read his truthfulness, but he didn't have one because he was a hunter. Unions between humans and angels were illegal, as was angels giving humans powers. As a result, he had no aura because the Universe didn't recognise he existed.

"You try anything, and I'll turn you into a pile of ash like your friend," I said, hesitantly holding the dagger out to him.

He nodded and lifted the weapon from the palm

of my hand. He took it so delicately, it surprised me seeing such care coming from such a big man. His hands were the size of shovels. Turning it over and over, he scrutinised every detail of it, then handed it back, smiling.

"That's incredible." He paused and cocked his head to one side. "You said 'one of these.' Is there more than one?"

I nodded. "One for each archangel."

"Can they only be used once or something?"

I nodded. "If you stabbed one archangel with it, then stabbed another, their powers would accumulate and transfer through the blood. Or so the whispers say."

He raised an eyebrow. "So theoretically, one archangel could kill all the other six with one of these, and then become the most powerful angel ever?"

"Yes…" I said, realisation dawning on me. "But the whispers say that no one body is capable of holding such power. That the archangel would explode from the sheer amount of energy and power contained within them."

"Where are these normally kept?"

"In our castles."

"Your castles?"

I sighed. "Yes. Each archangel has a castle and their own clan of angels, like me, that live in the castle. Each castle hides one of these daggers within its walls. I mean, what better protection can you get than to have an army of angels living, breathing, and working around the one thing that can kill you? Never mind the fact that no one knows where they are exactly. Only the archangels themselves."

"So how did our charming little friend come

across one?"

I shook my head. "I have no idea, but I know one thing."

"What's that?"

"If he had it then something bad must be happening up there."

CHAPTER SIX

Ronin

As we talked about the dagger and the possibilities of how the vampire ended up with it, the tension between us slowly dialled down a few notches. I would dare say that she even began to realise I wasn't a threat.

All I knew was that I couldn't take my eyes off her. She was stunningly beautiful. If Heaven's angels all looked like her, I couldn't wait to die. When the conversation dried up, I decided to ask her some personal questions.

"How long have you been hiding out here?" I asked, surveying the abandoned cemetery around me.

"Years. But I've been gone for a couple of months. I've been back about four hours," she replied. "Do you have any idea how much I've missed my bed?

Then that buffoon came and ruined it."

"Where have you been? Do you have any idea how much of a legend you are?"

"No," she said, a sad smile taking over her pretty features. "I didn't know anyone even knew about me being on Earth."

"Oh, yes. We're all taught about you from a very young age. Every hunter I know has always dreamed of meeting you."

She gave me a curious look and smirked. "Why? I'm really not that fascinating."

I opened my mouth but didn't know what to say. Why were we all taken with the idea of her? "I guess because none of us have ever met an angel. Sure, we have stories about you guys passed down the generations, but we've never actually seen one of you. Plus, some of us think you're going to be the salvation."

That made her laugh. The noise was like music to my ears. "Salvation? You do know why I'm down here, right?"

"Yes. You told God and Lucifer to stick their petty argument and refused to pick a side."

"Well, it didn't quite go like that. It was more a case of I didn't agree with either of their opinions. This was my punishment."

"To float around Earth for eternity?"

She nodded and sighed. "Pretty much. Cursed to loneliness forever. The only thing that keeps me busy is helping the human souls pass over." She shrugged her shoulders. "Kept me busy I should say. I don't really do that anymore. Not unless I feel like it. So, I stay here, chilling out and wasting my eternity away."

"I'm sorry he disturbed you. I had no idea where

he was running and of course, even less of an idea I would find you in here."

Her face suddenly lit up, her golden eyes glazing over with wonder. "Do you live around here?"

"No, I'm about two hours away."

Her eyes dulled over, and her shoulders sagged. I'd just popped her joy like I'd stuck a needle in a balloon. "Oh."

"Why did you ask?"

"No reason," she said, sighing.

"There must have been some reason behind your question. I don't bite."

She eyed me for several seconds and then replied, "I was only going to ask, if you were local that is, if you would perhaps give me a guided tour of the city. I've always wanted to see this place properly but have dreaded meeting all of the other creatures down there. I figured you would know where to avoid."

This was a golden opportunity if I'd ever been presented with one. "I'm here for a few days and I've always wanted to look around this place, especially the French Quarter."

Life filled her eyes with such vigour, it took my breath away. Nodding enthusiastically, she said, "Yes. That looks like one amazing area for sure. It's so beautiful. I've only ever passed over it—" she pointed up "—when I'm flying, but I want to spend some time there. I'm really drawn to this part of the world for some reason."

"How do you feel about looking around it together? I really don't think you need to worry about any creatures considering." I pointed at the pile of ash at her feet.

Silence. She stared at me, blank and impassive.

Seconds ticked by. I started to break out in a nervous sweat. Had I crossed a line? Was this going to be the end of our brief meeting?

"Together?" she said, breathing out as she said the word.

I nodded. "Just an idea. No pressure."

"You know people, regular humans, can't see me, right?"

"I figured, seeing as you've never been spoken of."

"You're going to look like you're talking to yourself if you walk around with me."

I shrugged my shoulders. If looking crazy meant I got to spend some more time with this incredible angel, I didn't give two hoots. "I don't care."

She tilted her head to one side. "Really?"

"Really. I don't care." I took a breath and swallowed the lump in my throat. "I'd love to get to know you better."

"I don't even know your name."

"Ronin," I said, holding my hand out.

She hesitated but then took it. The instant our skin connected, the world around us seemed to fall away, leaving only us stood in the centre. Our eyes locked once more, and a bright white light started emanating from her being. It flooded outwards, covering me and encircling us both.

Through my fingertips I could feel her heartbeat pulsing through my skin. Hot pins and needles flooded my arms, spread through my shoulders, and then cascaded down and through my body. I felt like I'd been transported to another universe. It was so surreal.

Her eyes filled with wonderment and amazement, glowing more and more golden with each moment.

Her irises seemed to move and swirl with colour, hypnotising me into staring at her even longer.

She took her hand back. The second our skin disconnected, the entire thing vanished like someone had flicked a switch. I found myself gasping for breath and looking around me to make sure I was still on Earth.

"What was that?" I said, slapping a hand over my chest.

Staring at her hand like she'd just grown it, she stayed silent for a good minute or more. "Impossible," she breathed. "Absolutely impossible."

"What is?"

She looked at me again, except this time, when our eyes made contact, I could hear her heartbeat in my head. "I need to go."

With that, she spread her wings and took off, almost blowing me off my feet with the draft she left behind. All I could do was watch as the beautiful angel soared into the skies above me, leaving me alone and totally confused.

ANGEL OF THE CRYPT

CHAPTER SEVEN

Makeysha

It couldn't be true. It couldn't. What I'd just experienced with the handsome hunter, Ronin, was something that was not only impossible, but illegal. That kind of thing only happened to an angel when they found their soulmate. Only three counts of angels finding their soulmates had ever been recorded—and they were angel on angel couples, the only way soulmates could ever be.

This guy was human. Mostly, anyway. That was illegal. If I was ever going to piss God off even more, pursuing Ronin would be the way to do it. My heart hammered inside my chest, pounding against my ribs. Then I remembered how it had felt to feel his pulse beating in time with mine.

For the first time in my miserable existence, one brief moment had seemed to click everything into place, like a jigsaw puzzle. Ronin had lit up my world, if only for a minute. But I couldn't indulge. I had no option but to leave, to save both of us.

If any one of the angels caught a whiff of what had just happened, he'd die. They couldn't afford a glitch in the Universe that allowed an angel and a human to be together. He was a threat and he would be eliminated.

Even as I flew through the starry skies, putting distance between us, my heart was already aching to be with him, my body craving for that delicious electricity that filled my very essence when we touched. I wanted to turn around and go back, just to calm the screaming of my soul if anything.

Determined to resist, I flew for a good hour, fighting with myself, throwing options around in my head for every scenario possible. Each one ended with dire consequences for him. Maybe it was just because I hadn't had a decent conversation with anyone for years, perhaps that's all this was. Everything else was in my head.

Conversation wouldn't end with his death so that would be ok. After all, God and Lucifer couldn't banish me here without expecting me to ever speak to another soul again.

I convinced myself that enjoying a good chat would be fine, so I turned around and flew, as fast as I could, back to my abandoned cemetery. As I approached it from overhead, I expected to find the graveyard empty and to have to search the city for him. To my amazement, he was sat in my crypt, leaning back on my bed with his feet crossed at the ankles, totally chilling out.

As I came in to land, I flapped my wings more than normal, creating a stir in the peaceful place. His amber eyes were burning bright and fixed solely on me as he stood in the doorway.

"Figured you'd come back," he said, a wry smile tugging at his lips. "This bed is far too comfortable to leave."

Just being within feet of him had my body trembling in anticipation of our next touch. I wanted to feel that wholeness again, feel our hearts beating as one, revel in the delicious heat that enveloped me when our skin met.

"Do you have any idea how dangerous it is for us to be near one another?" I said, my breaths coming short and shallow.

He pursed his lips and then nodded. "I had a little chat with a friend whilst you were gone. I'm guessing that we're not supposed to be soulmates?"

My breath caught in my throat. He knew. How did he know? "Who's your friend?"

"A witch down in the French Quarter. She's who I came to see, why I'm even here in the first place. Her name is Wanda. She's really knowledgeable about all this stuff."

I looked at the unicorn dagger laid on the bed next to him. "Can she help us with that little mystery?"

"Maybe."

"Can you take me to her?"

My request was simply because I couldn't be around him and a bed and be able to trust myself. I hadn't had sex for two thousand years. That was a long time by anyone's standards. To then have what was apparently my soulmate suddenly appear in my life made all of that so much more difficult.

Up in Heaven, angels took partners with whom they enjoyed intimacy. We were only allowed one partner, so it wasn't like a 'free for all' or anything, but it was a well-accepted fact that intimate relations were a necessary part of keeping the soul at peace.

Obviously, since I'd been banished to Earth, intimate relations were out of the question, unless I fancied doing so with Lucifer's creepy crawly creatures. I'd had no trouble in ruling that out as an option.

"Yes," Ronin replied, breaking my train of thought. "I can take you to her." He moved towards me, bringing the dagger with him. "Maybe we can have a night tour of the French Quarter afterwards?"

As he stood in front of me, mere feet away, my heart rate tripled. "Yes," I said, clearing my throat. "That would be nice."

He stepped forwards and grabbed my hand. My soul flooded instantly with light. It beamed out of every pore, wrapping him up in it. Everything around us fell away, paling into insignificance as only the two of us mattered at the centre of our own universe.

Our hearts beat as one, our eye contact connecting our souls together. He reached for my other hand and grasped a hold of it. I expected the feeling to intensify but instead, I found our minds linking to one another, our thoughts travelling between an invisible neural pathway.

This is incredible, he said, his deep voice echoing around my mind.

I could see, in my minds eye, the bright white train tracks that united our minds. It stretched, like a long tendon, from my head to his, and back again. It throbbed with energy, its rhythm matching that of our pulse.

"Ronin," I breathed. *"We mustn't. If the angels see or feel it, they will kill you."*

He flashed me a dazzling smile. *"I would die a thousand deaths just to experience this again."*

My breath caught in my throat. This dude was smooth, that I had to give him.

"As smooth as Galaxy chocolate," he said, laughing and giving me a cheeky wink.

I broke our connection and narrowed my eyes at him. "Stop that," I said, my cheeks filling with heat. "I am entitled to my privacy."

He grinned. "I'm sorry."

"I haven't had this much interaction with anyone for two millennia. You should be thankful I'm not a savage beast."

He laughed at me. "Let's go see Wanda."

I reached for the unicorn dagger and swiped it from his hands. "I'll keep a hold of this, thank you."

"So untrusting."

I snorted. "You think?"

"Are we walking there or can you carry me somehow?"

I burst out laughing. "Do I look like some kind of packhorse?"

He opened his mouth but faltered for several seconds. "I think it's in my best interests if I don't answer that question."

"Good answer, smooth dude."

He grinned at me. "I'm guessing we're walking then?"

I sucked in a deep breath. "I'm sure once we've touched a few more times, this whole thing will calm down. I have an idea."

"Why does it sound like you're unsure of this 'idea'?"

"Because as far as I know, only angels can do it. Although, technically with your hunter talents, you're part angel anyway."

"What is it?"

"Angels can teleport if they know where they're going."

"Ok. But you don't know where Wanda is."

"No, but you do. And our minds can link."

He lifted an eyebrow and gave me a sceptical look. "That sounds like it could be an epic fail."

"It could well be."

"And if it is?"

I shrugged my shoulders. "Then we probably burn up and die or explode into a million tiny stars."

"You're joking, right?"

I pointed up into the clear night sky, thousands of glittery stars shining down on us. "You don't seriously think that stars are dying planets, do you?"

His mouth dropped wide open. "I think we'll walk."

I giggled. "I'm joking."

"I'm still more comfortable with walking."

"Chicken shit."

He widened his eyes and said, "What did you just call me?"

"Chicken shit."

"I've been called many names over the years but never have I ever been called a chicken shit."

I grinned. "First time for everything, smooth dude. Now, pack your little girl panties away and try this out with me."

"I was actually thinking the walk might be an ideal

opportunity for us to talk a bit more. You know, get to know each other and all of that."

I rolled my eyes. "Where is Wanda's place? The address?"

"724 Dumaine Street."

By the time he'd spoken the words, I had a hold of his hands, channelling his visual memory of Wanda's place into my mind. I took a deep breath and called my powers back to the surface. The warmth from my magic combined with the heat from touching Ronin shot my temperature through the roof. I felt like a walking volcano that would erupt at any moment.

In my mind's eye, I took hold of Ronin's memory and channelled my focus into it, willing my magic to take us there. The ground beneath my feet started trembling and shaking. Ronin squeezed my hands, uncertainty flickering through his amber eyes.

"We'll be fine," I said, giving him a smile.

Before he could respond, everything stopped moving, becoming still and silent once again. I let go of him, the light around us vanishing the second we stopped touching.

"Holy moly," he breathed, looking around him. "You did it!"

I studied my surroundings, noticing the grey building in front of me. Two green double doors were firmly closed, but a wooden sign that read Historic Voodoo Museum swung back and forth steadily, no doubt disrupted by our sudden arrival.

"It worked!" I said, thoroughly excited by the news. "Wow. I can't believe it worked."

Ronin shot me a filthy look. "You mean you genuinely didn't know if that would work or not?"

"I did tell you."

"You said you were joking."

"About the stars, yes."

"Wait," he said, frowning. "Which part about the stars? That we would explode into millions of them or that they're not dying planets?"

I grinned. "I'll leave you to mull over that one."

He didn't get a chance to say anything then as one of the green doors opened revealing a short, petite woman standing in the open doorway. Yellow light flooded the room behind her.

She covered her mouth with a hand and dropped down into a curtsy. "I can't believe you're real. Please come in."

I went to her and placed a hand on her shoulder. "Don't be silly. I'm not royalty. Far from it."

"But still," she said, looking up at me with big brown eyes. "You're from a higher place and have powers we can only dream of. You should be treated with the greatest respect."

I smiled. "Perhaps you can put in a good word with God for me then."

She stood up and moved aside, allowing me to walk into the small room. I scanned around the artefacts adorning the walls, impressed she had such a vast collection. Over my time here, I'd become accustomed to humans and their wide variety of cultures and traditions. The tribes who practiced voodoo were among the most fascinating though.

"This is incredible. You've been far and wide to collect some of these." I turned around and gave her a smile. "Is there anything you're missing?"

Wanda blushed. "I've never managed to find a complete Louvre Doll. It's the one thing I wish I could add to the display here."

"Consider one found," I replied. "It would be my pleasure."

She gasped, tears filming over her eyes. "What can I give you in return?"

"Just your knowledge. As you well know, I've been a little out of the loop for the past couple thousand years. Ronin here happened upon my graveyard because he was chasing a vampire. This vampire, somehow, had this in his possession."

I revealed the unicorn dagger to her, holding it out on the palm of my hand.

"Oh my goodness," she said, inhaling a sharp breath. Her hands flew to her mouth. Shock flashed through her eyes. "It's true. It's all coming true."

"What is?" I asked.

"There are tales, we thought they were nothing more than whispers, of these daggers having been stolen from Heaven and scattered upon the Earth. Some angels, so it is said, tired of the war and having humans unfairly caught in the middle. The stories say that these angels decided to level the playing field, enable us to better defend ourselves, and so they stole these sacred weapons and threw them down to Earth."

My eyes widened. "So the other six are somewhere on Earth?"

Wanda nodded.

"We have to find them. Before anyone, or anything else, gets a hold of them."

"That might be more difficult than you think," Wanda said, her voice becoming a breathless whisper.

"Why?"

"The rumours are that Lucifer already has five."

ANGEL OF THE CRYPT

CHAPTER EIGHT

Ronin

Who knew that an innocent two hour drive to see a witch about a spell would have thrown my life into such turmoil. In a matter of hours, I'd stumbled upon the legendary angel, an ancient weapon, and a dangerous situation involving none other than Lucifer himself.

"Why does Lucifer want them all?" I said, frowning. I ran a hand through my hair and let out a breath I didn't realise I'd been holding.

"Because he can destroy all the archangels. Without the archangels holding Heaven in order, Heaven will fall into chaos," Wanda replied.

"No," the angel said, making me realise I still didn't know her name. "Lucifer wants the power. Only he and God would be strong enough to contain all that energy." Her golden eyes stared off into the distance as realisation hit her. "He wants to take down God."

"How do we stop him?" I said, adrenaline already trickling through my veins.

She looked down at the dagger in her hand for several seconds. "What if we don't?"

"Are you insane?" I said, not believing I'd just heard those words. "What the…why…what…why would you even say that?"

She shrugged her shoulders. "What has God ever done for me? He threw me out of Heaven like a piece of trash because I didn't agree with his opinion. Lucifer and all of his believers, too. What is that if it's not a petulant child having a temper tantrum? Why would I want to help save someone like that? Maybe he needs taking down a peg or two. Lucifer is the only one who can do that."

Wanda folded her arms across her chest and nodded. "I have to say I see her point, Ronin. Sometimes even a God needs reminding of their position. It's only because humans follow him that he has power. If humans didn't believe in him, who would he be?"

"The angels believe in him, well, half of them anyway," my angel said.

"If they see him crumble, they will change their opinions," Wanda replied. "What is your name, my love? I don't believe I know it."

"Makeysha."

"That's a beautiful name."

"Thank you."

"Ma-key-sha," I said, sounding the name out. "Do you spell it how it sounds?"

She nodded.

"I like it. It suits you." I gave her my best smile, briefly wondering when I could be close to her again.

Heat flushed through her cheeks before she turned her attention back to Wanda. "This isn't right though, is it? I should want to protect God, surely?"

"Look at it with cold hard facts," Wanda replied. "You had an opinion that was different to two supreme powers. They both shut you out of their realms as punishment. You shouldn't just be wanting to go after God here."

Makeysha lifted a dark eyebrow and grinned. "You're right. I like you, Wanda. I think we're going to be firm friends."

"Whoa," I said, holding my hands up between the pair of them. "Steady on now. Rewind. Just what exactly are you suggesting here, Wanda?"

"This war between God and Lucifer has gone on for two thousand years, with us and our beautiful planet caught in the crossfire. Neither of them have considered us in their petty, bitter feud. The only reason you hunters exist is because some of God's angels blessed a group of humans with their powers. They obviously knew that at some point, God would withdraw all angelic powers, leaving the earth to be overrun by Lucifer and his demons."

"Yes…" I said, motioning with my hand for her to continue.

"God didn't care about leaving us to perish to all of Lucifer's evil. Lucifer, on the other hand, uses us as nothing but pawns to get back at God. He revels in torturing humans and this planet for the sole reason of hurting God. What if we took that power from both of them? Forced them to sit up and listen and take notice of what their pathetic argument is doing?"

"That sounds like a very dangerous game. Never mind the fact that five of those daggers are currently in Hell with Lucifer, no doubt guarded by a million of his wretched creatures."

Wanda tapped the side of her nose and grinned. "That is where I come in. If you're up to the task, if you want to do this, I can help you."

I sat down on the stool I'd sat on a mere few hours ago. My head was spinning. How the hell had my life turned into such a train wreck with what was supposed to be a simple 'Thanks but no thanks' meeting?

Makeysha came over and knelt down in front of me. "There's no pressure on you to take part in any of this."

I looked down at her, noticing for the first time her bare shoulders and perfectly round breasts peeking out of the top of her dress. Her eyes had captured all of my attention up to this point, but I now had other focal points to enjoy.

"Eyes up, wise guy," she said.

I chuckled. "I'm not even sorry."

She lifted an eyebrow, a quirky smile tugging at her pink lips.

"What happens to us?" I said. "If God and Lucifer make up or one of them dies. What happens to us hunters? Do we keep our powers or do we die? Do Lucifer's creatures die or will he keep making them?"

"I don't know," Makeysha said. "They're questions we don't know the answers to."

"Actually," Wanda said, holding up one of her index fingers. "I can make an educated guess."

Makeysha turned around, looking at the little

witch holding all the answers.

"Your powers are a part of your soul—you were born with them remember. They can't take them without removing a part of your soul, so unless they're going to massacre the entire hunter community, I think you're pretty safe."

"What about Lucifer's lovely creations?" I said.

"I don't know what he'll do. He may keep them hidden from God as an insurance policy in case anything like this happens in the future, or he may destroy them all. It's impossible to say."

"What's the likelihood of them two patching things up anyway?"

"Small. They're both egotistical maniacs in their own right," Makeysha replied.

"So what's the point in us taking these daggers back if they're not going to kiss and make up?"

"To make them realise they can't keep all the power and put Earth in the middle."

"Ok. And where exactly do we keep these things once we get them, if by some miracle, we manage to retrieve them that is? Where are we going to hide anything from two superpowers?"

Wanda pursed her lips and stared off into the distance for several minutes. "I could merge all of them together to create one big dagger. One thing is easier to hide than seven."

"Any other options?"

"Makeysha, is there anything to stop more of these daggers being made?" Wanda asked.

"Yes," she said. "Unicorns are sacred in Heaven. Only when a new archangel is crowned can one be sacrificed to create a dagger. Pegasus feathers are shed all the time, so they're not hard to come by."

"Then we could hide them inside unicorns," Wanda said, a big grin taking over her small face. "The perfect definition of hiding in plain sight."

My mouth dropped wide open. "Are you forgetting the teeny tiny matter of how the hell we're supposed to get anywhere near unicorns?"

"They're known to come down to Earth, more frequently than you think," Makeysha said. "On a full moon, they come down to drink from a specific place—the axis mundi."

I blinked several times. "The what now?"

"The axis mundi," Makeysha said. "It's the connection between Heaven and Earth, kind of like an umbilical cord between a mother and child. Unicorns are nothing but purity. Under the strength of the lunar light, they come to drink from Mount Olympus to keep their pureness intact. Living in Heaven alone can't fulfil their souls."

"Mount Olympus?" I said. "There's nothing to drink on Mount Olympus."

Makeysha smirked. "Not to the human eye, no. But there is a lake there. Its waters are so clear and crystal blue, you can see to the bottom of the ocean. No human would be able to perceive its beauty hence it's hidden from them. Also to stop them ruining it."

"Ok," I said, clapping my hands together. "This should be a walk in the park. All we have to do is ask Lucifer for the five daggers back, find the missing one, then catch seven unicorns on a full moon at Mount Olympus and stuff sacred, ancient daggers inside them. Piece of cake."

Giving me a sympathetic smile, Makeysha said, "It's ok, Ronin. You don't have to do this."

"I get the feeling you're going to do this regardless

of what I do?"

She nodded. "The fact these daggers are out of Heaven is a huge risk. I can't sit on something like that. No one should have that power but they're all too wrapped up in this war to see it themselves."

"So you're going to make them hate you a little bit more?" I asked, admiring her tenacity.

"Not exactly going to hurt my feelings, is it?"

I leaned forwards and resisted my urge to touch her. "Why do you care so much about what happens to this world and all of the people in it?"

"Humans only exist because God wanted them to. How is it right that he then allows them to be used and abused by his greatest enemy? I'm an advocate for what's right which is something both he and Lucifer couldn't understand. If either one of them uses those daggers to enhance themselves, Earth will be obliterated."

"You don't have to do this," I said. "No one said it was your problem."

"They didn't say it wasn't either. I can do something here." She sighed and placed a hand on my knee. Sizzling tingles heated my leg through my jeans. "Do you believe in Fate? Everything happens for a reason and this has happened to me tonight for a reason. I'm meant to do something."

I reached out and cupped her cheek with my hand. The room around us filled with bright white light. Everything fell away, leaving just the two of us once more.

"I didn't believe in fate until I met you," I said.

She smiled at me. "Smooth," she whispered. "I'll let you have that one because I like it."

"Are you ready to save the world?"

"Yes," she said. "So long as you're there at the end of it."

"With my smooth moves? Of course I will be."

When she laughed, it was like music to my ears. Joy and pleasure spread through me like wildfire. This morning I'd been a single man, resisting an arranged marriage. Now I had a soulmate and the fate of the world resting in my hands.

What could possibly go wrong?

CHAPTER NINE

Makeysha

"**F**irst things first," I said, turning to Wanda. "How do we find out exactly where these daggers are?"

"Lucifer's creatures," she said. "It's the only way. Bring me one and I will extract the information."

Ronin grinned. "I can get any information you want."

Wanda smiled. "I can do it without killing them."

"Fair play," Ronin said, chuckling.

"Any particular creature you have in mind as being the best bet?" I asked.

"Stay away from magical creatures. So no warlocks, wizards, or witches. It will make my spells ten times harder. Go for a vampire or werewolf."

"Where's the best place to find them?"

"There's an abandoned graveyard about three miles outside of the city. They all seem to come and go from that central point. My guess is it's a portal of some kind."

My jaw dropped. "Odd Fellows?"

"Yes," she said, frowning. "How did you know?"

"Because that's exactly where our vampire was when he bumped into me, with this." I waved the dagger at her. "See what I mean about Fate?" I said, looking at Ronin.

"I would hazard a guess that he was about to go and deliver that to the Prince of Hell," Wanda said. "Shame you killed him. He could have been useful."

I pursed my lips and sighed. "Had you ever seen him before?"

Wanda shook her head. "I didn't see him. Ronin?"

He shook his head. "I've never seen him before. Doesn't mean you might not recognise him though. Makeysha—can you do your weird mind link thing with Wanda to show her my memories?"

"I don't know…I've never heard of it being done before."

"If you're open to it," Wanda said. "I can use a ritual to see your memory."

He hesitated, looking back and forth between me and Wanda. "Voodoo? You want to do voodoo on me?"

Wanda grinned. "Yes."

"Is there any other option?"

"Not unless you're great with a sketch pad."

Silence fell as he fought an internal war. About a minute later, he sighed. "Alright, fine."

Wanda shot up and started rifling through her draws. Her whole energy buzzed with positive energy and excitement. I suspected she was looking forward to this.

"You'll be fine," I said, giving Ronin a reassuring smile.

"Are you going to give a dead man one last kiss?"

I burst out laughing. "That was not so smooth."

"Man's gotta try."

"Keep trying, wise guy," I said, grinning. I loved his sense of humour.

Wanda spread various small tubs and glass bottles over the wooden counter. Then, she reached behind her and plucked a mirror out from a small space between the edge of the counter and the wall.

"Ronin," she said, pointing to the space in front of the mirror. "Come and sit in front of the mirror please."

Worry creased the edges of his eyes, but he did as she asked. Wanda pulled out several incense burners and sticks, and then six candles. She arranged the candles around the mirror and then started opening the tubs and bottles, sprinkling bits of powder over the candles.

"Can I ask what you're doing?" I asked, curious about all of this.

"Sure," she said, talking as she carried on with her ritual. "I have powdered dragon's blood and nutmeg that I'm tipping onto the candles, which I'll then light. The nutmeg helps with hallucinations and the powdered dragons blood purifies the air."

She finished dressing the candles and proceeded to light them.

"Next, I have a dried mint leaf and a ginger root, which Ronin is going to place on his tongue and hold there. They help charms and spells work faster. Then

I'm going to dip the incense sticks into this dragon's blood…" she held up a small brown bottle with a liquid inside "…and burn them. The natural form of dragon's blood, when it's burned, allows for people to shape shift."

"Shape shift?" Ronin said, his eyebrows shooting up in alarm.

"Yes," Wanda replied, settling a hand on his shoulder. "I'm going to stand behind you and watch you in the mirror. Once my spell has been cast, you need to remember that vampire's face. Your face will then morph into his, enabling me to see who you saw."

"My face will turn back though, right?"

Wanda laughed. "Yes. It'll last a matter of seconds, if that. Now—" she held up a dried mint leaf and a small chunk of ginger root "—hold these on your tongue. Do not swallow them."

Ronin stuck his tongue out, allowing Wanda to place the two items on his tongue. He gently took his tongue back into his mouth and sat stock still on his chair. Wanda dipped the incense sticks into the red/purple coloured dragon's blood and then lit them. She began chanting words in Latin and moved to stand behind Ronin.

I watched fascinated, as the room filled with a smoky fog and the rich scent of burning dragon's blood. When Wanda finished chanting, the room fell into an eerie silence. Then, as the streaks of smoke drifted in front of the mirror, Ronin's reflection started to morph into the ugly face of the vampire I'd met hours earlier.

His fingers clawed at his knee as panic seemed to win over him. Wanda gasped, a hand flying to her mouth.

"Oh my," she said. "It can't be."

She rushed forwards and blew all the candles out but left the incense sticks burning. She ordered Ronin to spit out the mint leaf and ginger root, which he gladly did.

"What's wrong?" he said, screwing his face up like he'd just tasted something disgusting. "Have you got a drink? That was gross."

Wanda handed him a bottle of water from her purse then sighed. "That vampire was none other than Lord Melrose."

Ronin cocked an eyebrow. "The mythical figure people likened to Count Dracula?"

"The one and only."

"None of my community have ever seen him. He's as much of a myth as what Makeysha is."

"I think it's safe to say, at this point, that anything you ever shrugged off as a myth is now a distinct reality."

"That was Lord Melrose?" I asked. "He really didn't live up to the hype."

"The fact he's involved means that dark and powerful forces are gathering together to help Lucifer's quest. It means that this mission just reached another level of dangerous." Wanda sighed. "Is there any chance you didn't kill him?"

"I incinerated him," I said. "I'm afraid Dracula dude is long gone."

"The thing is, without him, we have no idea where he got that dagger from, let alone where to start looking for the other one," Wanda replied, sighing.

"Have you heard of any other old creatures mysteriously reappearing lately?" I asked.

"Yes!" Ronin said, jumping up from his stool.

"There's an old werewolf who we thought had died centuries ago. The Whitstable's swear blind they saw him on a hunt a few weeks back."

"Where was that? What made them think it was him?"

"He had an easily recognisable tattoo on his forehead. He's the only one that bears it because he's the original creation. They were in Arizona, near the Grand Canyon."

I gasped. "Oh my goodness. That's where we fell. When God tossed us out of Heaven, Lucifer and his angels were falling towards a huge mouth in the earth. That's where it was. Hell's mouth is the Grand Canyon."

Ronin's jaw dropped. "You're sure?"

"Very sure."

"That makes sense," Wanda said, clapping her hands together. "Only the oldest of creatures could withstand walking through the mouth of Hell to deliver these to Lucifer."

"Well, that makes this a thousand times easier," I said, folding my arms over my chest. "No need to go hunting."

"Why's that?" Wanda said.

"We simply stake out the Hellmouth and wait for dagger number seven to show up."

CHAPTER TEN

Ronin

She had a good plan, I'll give her that. My only concern was that we didn't know what exactly would show up.

"What other old creatures do we know of?" Wanda asked. "We have Lord Melrose, who was a vampire. This werewolf…what's his name?"

"Bryn," I replied.

"Lord Melrose and Bryn. I know Melrose was old but was he a First Creation?" Wanda asked.

"Yes," Makeysha said, her eyes lighting up with excitement. "All we need to do is figure out the other First Creations and track their whereabouts. Has Bryn been seen since he went to the Hellmouth?"

I shrugged my shoulders. "I have no idea."

"Is there a way to find out?"

"Not without catching a werewolf and 'extracting information'," I said, grinning.

"What other First Creations were there?" Wanda asked.

"Lasander, King of the Elves," I replied, ticking them off mentally in my head. "Imani, the first witch. Caesar, the first wizard. And The Twins."

"The Twins?" she asked, raising an eyebrow.

"Warlocks. The first of their kind and the only twin warlocks ever to be born. Lucia and Kaspar."

"Lucia, Kaspar, Imani, Caesar, Lasander," Makeysha said, counting them on her fingers. "Plus Melrose and Bryn. That's seven creatures. One creature for each dagger..." she gazed into the distance, as if she was putting a jigsaw back together "...why wouldn't he just use one creature to gather them all?"

"Maybe because of the time it would take?" Wanda asked.

"No," Makeysha said. "I think the creatures are staying in Hell with the daggers."

"Why?" I asked, trying to figure out Lucifer's game play. "He has thousands of minions down there to protect them."

"All of which would be useless against any significant power. But his First Creations? They're a different story. I think he's going to use them to attack the archangels. Save his own hands getting dirty." She gasped and put her hands to her mouth. Her golden eyes filled with fear. "Oh my. He's going to absorb each dagger. He's not going to use one dagger on all of them to gain the power, he's going to use one dagger per angel."

"Does that make a difference?" I asked.

"Yes," she said, nodding frantically. "If he takes in one dagger per chakra area, he could definitely harness all that power. No questions asked. His power would be tenfold and evenly spread throughout his being."

"He'd be unstoppable," I said, figuring out the ending.

Makeysha nodded.

"Right. Let's hit the road. Time to go to Hell."

***

Whilst I'd been all fired up and ready to rumble, I hadn't considered that the Grand Canyon was over fifteen hundred miles away.

"Can you teleport us there?" I asked Makeysha.

"Have you ever been?"

I shook my head. "But you fell there, when you fell from Heaven?"

She sighed. "That place would have changed a lot since I last was there. I need a recent visit to work with, like within the last few months or a year."

"Oh. I can't help. I'm sorry."

She smiled. "It's ok. It looks like we're taking a road trip."

"I'll come too," Wanda said, smiling.

"I think it's best if you stay here, Wanda," I said. "Not only will you be safer, but you can let us know if anything untoward happens around that portal. Wait a minute. The portal in Odd Fellows, will that be a direct link to Hell or just to the Hellmouth?"

"Just to the Hellmouth," Wanda replied. "But there's no reason you two couldn't use it. It's basically just a doorway. It'll save you a long drive."

"Can you help us?" I asked. "Figure out how to use it?"

"Need you ask?" she replied, laughing.

We took my SUV and drove the three miles to the abandoned cemetery so that Wanda had a way to get back to hers once we'd gone. I took a selection of weapons from my backseat and tucked them into my waistband. I figured I'd be having to travel lightly.

"You can take your backpack," Wanda said. "If you need all of it."

I grinned and grabbed a hold of the black bag. "That makes life a lot easier."

Wanda opened the wrought iron gate that both myself and Melrose had jumped over hours earlier. A simple flick of her wrists and it swung on its hinges like a hurricane blew it open. Sometimes I envied the easy life of a witch, having energy and power at their fingertips. Other times, I was glad not to have the responsibility of it.

"I will start tracking down the whereabouts of the First Creations, see if I can figure out who you should be looking out for," Wanda said, stalking up and down the aisles of the cemetery. "Unless of course they appear before I have an answer for you."

"Thanks, Wanda," I said, glad that she was so eager to be involved. "I really appreciate you wanting to help."

"It's my pleasure. I don't get too much drama these days so it's nice to have a change."

I laughed and followed her down one of the pathways. To my left, the outer wall of the cemetery loomed over us, rows of wall vaults lining the white bricks. Wanda homed in on one in particular.

"Here," she said, passing her hand over its solid

face. "This is it."

"Are you expecting us to climb into that?" I said, screwing my face up in confusion.

Along the massive white wall, dark grey stone separated the rows and columns of final resting places. It reminded me of an oversized noughts and crosses board. The space where the bodies had been pushed through couldn't have been much more than two-feet square. An aged bronze plaque had been screwed into the centre of the 'headstone' Wanda was focused on.

Luci Ferstar. Born January 1666. Sadly passed away December 1666. Always in our thoughts.

Makeysha giggled. "He couldn't have been much more obvious if he tried."

"Luci-fer-star," I said, shaking my head and smirking. "Nice. Was this place even around in 1666?"

"No," Wanda replied. "This cemetery wasn't even founded until 1849. Considering the intellect of the average vampire, it's no wonder he had to leave obvious clues."

"So how does it work?" I said, curious.

"Well, you know that Lucifer's creatures carry their own EMF signature?"

I nodded. "Yes. We've used detectors before now to hunt them."

"Well, bronze is an excellent conductor for EMF. When they enter the field, the doorway will open for them immediately."

"But of course, we can't open it because our bodies don't give off the correct EMF signature," I said, looking at Makeysha.

She nodded. "Thanks for the explanation."

Wanda placed her hands on the plaque and closed her eyes. Everything fell silent. After several seconds, she started whispering strange Latin words in a hushed voice. Another minute or so passed, then the bricks behind the plaque cracked open, spilling out a bright orange streak of light onto the pathway.

The sliver of light grew wider and taller, morphing into a huge archway. Wanda stepped back and smiled. "There you go. Simply walk through it and you'll find yourselves at the Hellmouth."

Makeysha glanced at me. The smallest trickle of worry flickered in her golden eyes.

"Come on," I said, holding my hand out to her. "Let's go hunting."

She took a breath and then shook her head. "Probably a good idea if we don't touch. A bright white light appearing in the middle of the Grand Canyon might attract some attention."

"They're an hour behind us over there, time wise," Wanda said. "Just bear that in mind."

I lifted up my left arm and adjusted my watch. "That means we're time travelling, technically," I said, grinning.

Makeysha tilted her head to one side and smiled. "You're a bit of a geek at heart, aren't you?"

I couldn't help but laugh. "My answer depends on whether you like geeks."

"I might do," she said, smirking. "I might not. We'll see."

We stood side by side, just out of reach of the orange light. "Ok. On three."

Makeysha nodded.

"See you soon, Wanda. One. Two. Three."

We both stepped into the orange doorway. Heat bit at my skin. Seconds passed by. Just as the searing pain became too much to bear, the light around us vanished, leaving us stood in the middle of the Grand Canyon.

I looked around us, squinting against the darkness in an effort to see something.

"Here," Makeysha said.

She clicked her fingers and produced a ball of soft white light. Holding it in the palm of her hand, she hovered her other hand over it. The ball doubled in size. She gently pushed it out into the vast expanse of darkness and blew over it with a long breath.

The light moved away from us, slowly moving around our environment. It revealed nothing but jagged cliff edges and empty space.

Makeysha uncurled her wings and lifted herself off the ground by a few feet. She drew the ball of light back to her by simply holding out her hand. Then she soared above me and cast the light down on the rocky surface we'd been standing on.

Light flooded all around me, enabling me to see the exact predicament we were in. And it wasn't good. We had landed on a rock face that stood in the middle of a U-shaped cliff.

"I know this," Makeysha said. "It's Horseshoe Bend, and it hasn't changed one bit. I could have teleported us here after all."

"Little late for that but thanks," I replied, wondering what the hell we were supposed to do.

"We are literally in the Hellmouth." She pointed down at the water. "The water is there as a passage through to Hell."

My eyes widened. "What are you saying? That we've got to go swimming to get to Hell?"

"Yes," she replied, smirking. "Is that a problem?"

"I'm not a fan of water."

"Awww, don't worry. I'll hold your hand."

I sighed and frowned. "How do we get down from here?"

I looked behind me to see the landscape rolling out before me. This cliff edge was still connected to a main piece of rock, but it was a good mile or more before it spanned out, let alone allowed for a way down.

"Well, the obvious way."

"A long walk it is then. Or are you going to fly me?" I grinned and wiggled my eyebrows at her.

She laughed. "No, the obvious way is straight down."

"I'm sorry. What now?"

"You've got to gain enough air speed to hit thirty feet into the water. Only then will the Hellmouth open."

"I'm sorry. What now?"

She floated back down to stand beside me, a cheeky grin all over her beautiful face. "Not a fan of high diving?"

"I'm not a fan of dying."

"Oh come on. Not a lot can kill a hunter, you know that. You'll be fine."

"Elderberry juice, anything made from ivory, pomegranate—"

"Alright, wise guy. I don't think you're going to find any of that down there, are you?"

"I don't know if hunters can die from high jumps, but I'm pretty sure I don't want to be the one to test the theory."

"Ronin," she said, making her voice all husky and sexy. A shiver ran down my spine. "I thought you were a big, brave man, not afraid of anything. And now you're telling me you're scared of a little jump?"

Heat flushed through my body. "No," I replied. "I'm not afraid…I'm just assessing the health and safety aspects of it beforehand."

She giggled and placed a hand on my chest. Stepping in to me, she whispered, "Are you being all geeky again?"

My heart leapt into a new rhythm. Her lips were only inches from mine. Damn, I wanted to kiss her. If the world fell away when we touched, what would happen if we kissed, or more?

"I might be," I replied. "If you like it, I'll carry on."

She moved her face closer, so our noses were almost touching, and whispered, "I think it's adorable."

Adorable? What the hell? As much as I wanted to seize the moment and kiss her right now, I couldn't tame my male ego enough to tolerate being called adorable.

"Did you seriously just call me adorable?"

"Maybe," she said, licking her lips. "Why? Don't you like it?"

"Do I look like a cute bunny?"

Giggling, she wiggled her fingers in front of me and said, "I could make you look like one if you wanted."

I couldn't help it. I laughed. "No, thank you. And if you ever turned me into anything small and furry, I'd never speak to you again."

"What about big and furry?"

I frowned. "What is big and furry?"

"Cows, some large dog breeds, horses, bison—"

"I swear down, Makeysha, stop talking right now."

She grinned. "Or what?"

"Or I'm going to shut you up."

"Oh really? And how will you do that, wise guy?"

"Keep talking and find out," I said, lowering my gaze to her lips.

The second she opened her mouth, I pressed my lips to hers.

CHAPTER ELEVEN

Makeysha

His lips were so soft. His kiss was so demanding yet tender, it took my breath away. He wrapped his arms around me, drawing me further into his warm, head-swirling world. A gentle wave of love and peace washed over my soul, bathing me in serenity. Fuzzy tingles, like pins and needles, crept through my body, awakening long forgotten desires.

In my mind's eye, I could see the link between us, buzzing and alive with energy. This was so exciting and yet so surreal. How had my luck changed so drastically? Whatever Fate had decided to bring into my life, if it was this good, I didn't care. This, right here, made the last two thousand years totally worth it.

Ronin, we should be watching out for the creature, not

kissing.

In my head, he chuckled, then replied, *So break it off then.*

As much as my head screamed at me to stop, my heart wanted something different. I wanted to keep this enchanting connection between us and never let it go. I could feel my soul blooming deep within me, showering me in the delightful sensation of being complete for the first time in my life.

"This seems like the butt of a good joke. An angel and a hunter kissed on the edge of a cliff..."

I froze upon hearing that voice. A calm yet authority ridden female voice that chilled me to my bone. I'd heard that unnerving tone before. And it only belonged to one person.

Tearing myself away from Ronin, I glanced to my left to see none other than Lucia, the female Twin. An ethereal white glow emanated from her, lighting up the immediate area around her. Her tall, slim figure was perfectly highlighted, along with her wavy long locks, the mix of browns, reds, and blonde all mingling together into a hypnotising blend. Her skin-tight white silk dress clung to every part of her, making her look the epitome of lethal beauty.

"Who the hell are you?" Ronin said, frowning at her.

"Lucia," she said, offering her hand to him. "Pleased to meet you."

"I don't think I can extend the same courtesy," he replied.

"Such a shame. A strong, handsome man such as yourself. We could be great friends." She winked at him then licked her lips.

I glared at her, resisting the urge to scratch her

onyx coloured eyes from her head. I'd managed to escape coming face to face with a warlock for two thousand years. Now I find my soulmate, I also find some powerful biatch drooling all over him. That just about summed up my life.

"I don't think so," Ronin said.

He stared back at her, a muscle in his cheek twitching. Sweat broke out on his forehead. I started to panic.

"You have some resilient mental shields," Lucia said, narrowing her eyes at him. "I'm impressed. Considering you're human and all."

Without even thinking, I reached out and wrapped my hand around Ronin's wrist. Light beamed around us when we touched, but it seemed less vibrant. Our minds connected, giving him extra strength from me. Lucia's presence looming on his mind was like an awful migraine bearing down pressure on his brain. I could feel his walls struggling to hold the heaviness of her power.

He started shaking, the effort of holding her off becoming more and more difficult. Worry climbed inside my chest like ivy. I had to do something drastic. I called my magic up, anxiety churning in my stomach.

My magic was powerful, but I had no idea what it was truly capable of. The most I'd used it for to this point had been teleporting us to Wanda's and cleaning up my crypt.

My bed. I'm not going to get to sleep in my bed.

I shook my head, dispersing the thoughts of my fluffy dreamland. I closed my eyes, and in my mind, pictured a golden shield standing in front of us, taking all of Lucia's energy. Ronin suddenly gasped for air, his breathing laboured and heavy.

When I opened my eyes to look at him, we were stood behind a huge golden shield. It was vibrating from Lucia's focused powers bearing down on it. I could feel the pressure on Ronin's mind had lifted, leaving him ok but short for breath from the physical exertion she'd pressed upon him.

"You can't stop me, Angel," Lucia yelled. "I'm more than a match for your whimsical powers."

"Take me on then," I shouted back. "One on one, leave the human out of it."

The shield stopped vibrating. I'd caught her attention enough for her to cease her assault on us; for now.

"An angel and a human who are soulmates. This is priceless information."

I narrowed my eyes at her. "And who exactly are you going to give that information to?"

"Well, I know Lucifer would be very interested in that. Especially as you're damned to an eternity of loneliness. What must be going on in the Universe for this to happen?"

That was a question I was also wondering. "And what is he going to do with it? It's hardly news of the century, is it?"

"Ahh, that's where you're wrong," she said, stepping forward with a sinister grin on her face. "This is news. Big news. THE biggest news we've had for a long time."

I gulped down the ball of fear lodged in my throat. "And why is that?"

"How often do soulmates happen? Not very."

"It's two souls reconnecting. What's so dramatic about that?"

She took another step forward and clasped her

hands together in front of her. "It's kind of like a lunar eclipse, don't you think? You know how the humans get, going all crazy over such a simple occurrence. They think it's something special, something magical. Seeing two soulmates come together is no different in our world."

I laughed at her. "You expect me to believe that? That you simply wanted to see two souls finding one another? I'm not an idiot, Lucia, so please don't treat me like one."

"Well, there was one other thing," she said, flashing me a big grin. "Apparently you're indestructible. Immortal, if you will." She cocked her head to one side and folded her arms over her chest. "I wanted to test the theory."

"Alright," I said, smirking. "You're on. If I don't die, I get that dagger."

I pointed to the unicorn dagger hanging from the belt around her middle. The thick black accessory she was wearing to accentuate her hourglass waist looked like it came with the weapon attached to it. It was all part of her perfect looks that enabled her to capture the most suspicious of prey; warlocks fed exclusively on human souls.

"Makeysha," Ronin whispered. He widened his eyes and glared at me.

"It'll be fine," I replied. "Trust me."

"I don't know about that," Lucia said. "That seems a little too easy for my liking...standing there and taking my attempts at death is a lot easier than fighting for something you want...if you want it, why don't you come after it? Then we'll see if you can die."

I grinned. "Let's go."

"Makeysha!"

I flicked my wrist at Ronin. I only meant to motion for him to go away, but my magic actually flung him back twenty feet, leaving us both shocked.

"You have no idea what you're even capable of, do you?" Lucia said.

"Should make it easy for you to kill me then, shouldn't it?"

"Are you sure you're ready to die, Angel?"

She uncurled her arms and held her hands out at her sides, palms facing up. A football sized ball of whirling black energy appeared over each hand, pulsing with menace.

"Bring it on, bitch," I said, grinning.

A malicious grin spread over her face. Without further hesitation, she threw one of her dark energy balls at my head. On instinct, I put my arms up in front of me. The mass of magic hurtled towards my face. Around six inches out, it stopped and splattered out like a giant paintball.

Beaming from my arms was a bright white wall of power, now covered in dark magic. The black mixed in with the white and turned my magic a murky grey.

What the...? What does that mean?

My eyes widened as over the course of several seconds, all traces of the grey slowly dissolved into white. My magic wall grew brighter and bigger, its shining brilliance almost blinding.

"What *are* you?" Lucia said.

If I didn't know better, I'd swear blind I heard her voice trembling.

"You know what I am."

"No...I've killed dozens of angels before you. None of them have done that."

I didn't know how to take her words. Was she

baiting me to lower my shields so she could blast me or was she genuinely concerned about fighting me? I briefly debated if I could hurl her magic back at her and somehow give her a taste of her own medicine.

As I thought this, the colour of my magic wall started to change again, turning grey. Then, as if time was being rewound, all of Lucia's black magic gathered back into a football sized ball. I blinked and the dark energy was suddenly rushing through the air, right back at her.

She lifted her arms and threw her remaining ball of magic at it, no doubt trying to deflect its course. It didn't work. All it did was merge with the ball I'd unwittingly thrown at her and double in size.

Lucia thrust her hands down towards the earth. Wine coloured energy blasted from her palms and within a second, she'd encased herself in a globe of dark power. The ball I'd thrown at her sliced straight through her shield and hit her square in the chest.

She shrieked, I guessed from shock and surprise, but then as I watched, I wondered if fear was a part of it. The ball I'd thrown back at her exploded over her body, covering her perfect white dress in dozens of tiny black spots. I continued to watch in fascination as the spots grew larger, reaching out to each other like long, spindly fingers.

Lucia looked down at herself and started frantically trying to wipe it off, but the more she touched it, the quicker the energy reacted. In less than ten seconds, Lucia was wrapped up in a coat of black magic. She looked at me, panic streaming through her dark eyes. The magic crept up her neck like jungle vines, then slowly climbed over her face like spidery black veins.

She stared straight at me as it took the last few inches of her face, then seeped into her eyes. When she blinked, her black eyes turned milky white.

I was dumbfounded. Shocked. Speechless.

"Makeysha," she said, her voice now light and airy. "Please accept my sincere apologies. Consider me at your service."

My mouth dropped wide open.

Then she curtsied.

My mind was totally blown. I glanced over at Ronin, who stood staring at the suddenly obedient Twin in total shock.

"What the…?" I said to him.

"I'm lost," he said, audibly gulping. "I'm way out of my depth here."

"You and me both."

"What on earth do we do with her?"

I shrugged my shoulders. "Damned if I know." I looked back at Lucia and decided to try my luck. "Lucia, if you're at my service, please hand me the unicorn dagger you have."

Lucia nodded. Staring straight ahead the entire time, she fumbled with the weapon attached to her belt. When she finally released it, she placed it on the palm of her left hand and then walked towards me with her hand outstretched, like it was an offering. She had a warm smile on her face the entire time which chilled me more than when she grinned like an evil maniac.

She stopped two feet away from me and then bowed. I hesitated as I reached out to take the dagger, wondering if at any moment she would suddenly snap out of this trance and kill me in a heartbeat.

When my fingers wrapped around the delicate handle, I snatched it away, scared she would pull some clever move at any moment. I threw it to Ronin and stood before Lucia as she rose back to her full height.

This was it. She would pull some kind of stunt now, I knew it.

"What would you like me to do next, Makeysha?" she asked.

I looked over at Ronin who shrugged his shoulders as he tucked the unicorn dagger inside his jacket pocket.

"I think we need to speak to Wanda," I said to him. "Because I have no idea what's going on."

He nodded and came over to me. "Let me call her, see what she says."

"Can't we just go and see her? It would be a lot easier."

He looked at me and then at Lucia. "Can you teleport three of us?"

"I…I don't know actually…all we can do is try, right?"

"Are we likely to lose your new follower if it goes wrong?"

I shrugged my shoulders. "No idea."

He cocked his head to one side and frowned. "Are we missing a trick here?"

"Why?"

"If she's now your obedient little slave, why don't we send her into Hell to get the other daggers?"

"Look at her," I said, motioning a hand up and down in front of Lucia. "She hardly looks like the same evil Twin they'll all be expecting."

"Can't you do something to make her look like the normal Lucia again?" he said, waving his hand through the air.

"I don't know. I honestly don't know what I did

to do this to her, let alone anything else. I'm not feeling particularly confident about my magic at the moment."

"Can we at least question her about what to expect down there?"

"Yes, I think that's a good idea. Let's go back to Wanda, regroup, interrogate the warlock, and figure out our next move."

He grinned and took hold of my hand. The area around us lit up at our touch, but again it seemed duller than before. "Is that supposed to be happening too?"

"The light getting dimmer?"

He nodded.

"I don't know. Looks like Wanda is going to have a long night answering all our questions."

Chapter Twelve

Ronin

Back at Wanda's, things seemed even more chaotic than before. We appeared on the street right as she was locking up the museum.

"Jeez, what are you doing back here?" Her eyes fell on Lucia and she gasped. "Oh my goodness. What is she doing here?" She took a step forward and peered at the entranced warlock. "What have you done to her?"

"I don't know," Makeysha said. "That's why we were hoping you could help."

"Come over to the house," Wanda said, walking briskly across the street. "Let's sit down comfortably and talk through what's going on."

Hurrying across the street, we followed Wanda

inside her home. It was a modest two storey Creole townhouse that had one centrally positioned front door. It looked like the house had been split in two with each side of the house having one set of French doors on both the upper and lower levels. The upper storey was framed with a wrought iron balcony, in typical Creole style, yet the fact it didn't reach across the entire width of the house was slightly unusual. An arched window sat in the central space above the front door.

As we walked into the hallway, a set of stairs lay straight in front of me. Looking up, they split left and right, an oak handrail lining the edge of the stairs and the hallways upstairs. To my left and right were two identical oak doors.

"This used to be two apartments," Wanda said, motioning for us to head left. "I bought both but only use this side. I haven't had the time yet to turn it back into one house."

My questions answered, I opened the oak door and held it for the ladies to enter first. When I followed Lucia in, I found myself stepping back in time. Everything in here was historic French colonial era. High ceilings, two gothic chandeliers, aged wooden furniture, shutters for the windows—it was stunning.

"This is gorgeous," Makeysha said, wandering around in amazement. "It's truly like I've stepped back in time."

"I tried to keep everything as original as possible," Wanda said, sitting down on an antique dusky green leather sofa. "Except the sofas. I had to compromise for comfort on that one, although I think these fit well with the rest of the décor. Some of the rooms have been turned modern but I am going to turn them back."

Makeysha nodded and sat down on the identical facing sofa. A dark wooden coffee table separated the two sofas with a magnificent fireplace overlooking the cosy setting from the right.

Lucia sat down next to Makeysha, silent and seemingly lost in her far away gaze. I took the seat next to Wanda, wondering where to start.

"First things first," Makeysha said. "Ronin and I…every time we touch, the light that shines from us seems to be getting dimmer. Is that anything to be worried about?"

"No," Wanda replied, smiling. "That's a good sign. It means you're connecting, your bodies are getting used to one another. Gradually, it will disappear altogether."

Makeysha glanced at me and gave me a warm smile. Her golden eyes glowed with happiness. My hands itched to be touching her again, to feel her heartbeat in rhythm with mine, to see our minds connecting. I felt like a lovesick teenager addicted to nothing but good feelings.

"That's good," I said, needing to talk to break my train of thought. Wanda didn't need any PDA's right now. "Next question. What on earth has happened with our evil friend here?"

"Can you tell me exactly what happened?"

I looked to Makeysha, figuring this would be best coming from her seeing as the pair of them had been in some sort of magical powers fight before it happened. As Makeysha talked Wanda through our odd scenario at the Hellmouth, I struggled not to wander off into thoughts of our kiss. Damn, I wanted to do it again.

After listening to the replay, Wanda frowned. "So, you had a fleeting thought of giving her a taste of her own medicine?"

"Yes," Makeysha said. "But literally as in 'Wouldn't it be cool if I could somehow throw her magic back at her'. That was it."

"And then the magic that you'd absorbed came back out and went at her?"

Makeysha nodded.

"Wow. Ok." Wanda turned to me and smiled. "You know how I have to perform a ritual to marry hunters so their powers pass from one family to the other?"

I nodded.

"That's what's happening here. Except it's not needed any intervention. It's simply happened all on its own."

"How have I helped Makeysha throw Lucia's magic back at her?"

"Part of your supernatural talents are influencing things, right?"

"Yes…"

"Well imagine that magnified tenfold, no, fifty-fold. That's what happened. Her angelic powers have amplified any talents you're passing over."

Excitement rushed through me. "So that will work both ways? As in her angel powers will pass to me, too?"

"I don't know," Wanda said, patting my knee with a sympathetic smile on her face. "Angelic powers require a strong body to hold them. It could very well destroy you."

"*What?*"

Both Makeysha and I said it at the same time. We

exchanged a panicked look.

"How do we stop it?" she said.

Wanda shook her head. "I honestly don't know. I can make some enquiries, ask around, but I don't have any answers for you now."

"But…but how long will it take? For our powers to fully transfer from one to the other?"

"The more you touch, the quicker it will happen. When the light, you know the one that shines from you both?" We nodded. "When that stops shining, the process is complete. Then it's anybody's guess. You never know, your body as it is, Ronin, could be more than capable of holding the power you will gain from Makeysha. It's not like this has ever happened before for anyone to compare it to. This is a complete unknown."

"That makes it so much better," I said, dryly.

"Will there be any signs we need to watch out for?" Makeysha said. "Anything that might indicate if he's…" water glazed over her eyes "…if he's, you know, not going to make it?"

"I don't know, honey, I'm so sorry. At a best guess, if it's going to happen, it will happen within minutes of the unification being complete. But then, because he's technically supernatural, he could be fine for days and then suddenly it might happen."

Makeysha looked down and said nothing.

"Are we talking, like, instant explosion here?" I asked, curious about my impending doom. "Or a slow, painful death?"

"Again, best guess, probably an explosion. Like the rumours about archangels and these daggers. It would be like a pressure cooker building up inside you."

"Speaking of daggers," I said, reaching inside my jacket. "Here is number two."

I pulled it out and laid it on the coffee table in front of Wanda.

"You managed to get it?"

"She handed it over," I said, nodding my head towards Lucia.

"She what?"

"Makeysha asked for it, when Lucia was all, you know, like this, and she offered it to her. With a curtsy."

Wanda raised her eyebrows and picked the dagger up from the table. "I'll put it with the other one, which by the way, is very safe." She tapped the side of her nose and grinned. "As for Little Miss Evil here, I'm certainly intrigued. I think the mix of both of your magics, as in yours and hers, Makeysha, has somehow overruled her natural tendencies. Kind of like a flu virus hitting a human."

"So it won't last?" I asked, eyeing Lucia with caution.

"I can't say for sure. Again, it's not like this has ever happened before. We're in unchartered territory here."

"Will it go away as quickly as it happened, or will it fade?"

Wanda shrugged her shoulders. "I have no idea, Ronin. I'm sorry. For all we know, this could be permanent."

I nodded and sighed. "Great. So we have a hypnotised warlock who may or may not turn back into an evil biatch at any moment, and Makeysha and I finding one another could in fact result in my explosive death because her powers might be too much for my body. Wow. What a trip this has turned out to be."

"I'm sorry, Ronin," Wanda said. "But it's not like anyone planned this. All I can do is hope and pray for you."

"Don't think praying is going to do much good," I said, chuckling. "Fraternising with one of God's angels? The one he cast out of Heaven? Yeah, I can see that going down well."

Wanda smirked. "You know what I mean. It was just an expression."

"Seeing as Lucia is compliant and eager to please, shall we ask her some questions?" Makeysha said, wiping her eyes with the back of her hand.

My heart clenched at seeing her upset. I wanted to reach out to her, hold her, tell her it would be ok, and we'll get through it, but I couldn't. Not unless I wanted to speed up the clock to my possible untimely death.

Wanda nodded. "Sounds like a good idea. I'll let you take the lead."

Makeysha offered her a small smile. "Lucia," she said, shifting in her seat slightly so she faced the evil Twin. "Can you tell me what you were doing with the unicorn dagger please?"

"Of course, Makeysha. I was on route to deliver it to Lucifer."

"And how many daggers does Lucifer have in his possession?"

"Three. Mine would be the fourth."

We all exchanged looks of hope. This was good news.

"And what happens when you arrive in Hell with the dagger?"

"I don't know for certain, but I can tell you what my brother told me. He was the first to arrive."

"Is he still down there?"

"Oh yes," Lucia replied. "Lucifer has set up seven different realms for each dagger. Each realm is guarded by the creature who brought it."

Makeysha's face drained of all colour. "And what is the purpose of these realms?"

"They're tests, like trials. He created them with the purpose of luring the archangels to retrieve them."

"Why does he want to lure the archangels to Hell?"

"To kill them. Without them, Heaven will fall into greater chaos. There will be no one to guide the angels, except God, and he can't manage all of them."

"Is he going to kill the archangels with the daggers?"

"Yes. Then he will drain their blood, ready for his ascension."

"Ascension? What do you mean?"

"To become the ultimate divine being, he must drink the blood of all seven archangels, then absorb the daggers that killed them."

Makeysha grimaced. "How will he absorb them?"

"Through a ritual on the next blood moon. It will open each of his chakras. He will absorb one dagger into each chakra in order to achieve his goal."

"And what is his plan after his ascension?"

"To throw God into Hell for two thousand years. Take Heaven back."

Makeysha sighed. "Ok. So what happens when you arrive in Hell with the dagger?"

"According to my brother, the Hellmouth has been modified to seek out our unique aura's. It delivers us straight to Lucifer's chambers. At that point, he then directs us to the realm we will be staying in with the dagger."

"Do you know anything about the realms?"

"A little. I know what one I will be guarding."

"And which one is that?"

"Treachery."

"Treachery?"

"Yes."

Makeysha sighed. "Lucia, what do you mean?"

"Research Dante's nine circles of Hell. You will find your answers."

It was my turn to pale. I literally felt the colour wash out of my face. "But you said Lucifer only created seven realms?"

"Yes," Lucia said. "Lucifer picked his seven favourite circles and based his realms off of those."

"Marvellous," I whispered to myself.

"Lucia," Makeysha said. "Do you know which realms are already guarded?"

"My brother is guarding gluttony. I believe Imani is in greed, and Bryn is in lust."

Wanda rushed out of the room. "I'll be back in a minute. I'm just fetching a book."

Excellent. We know who is already down there, I thought.

"Do you know where the remaining creatures are?" Makeysha asked. "The ones that still have to bring the daggers to Lucifer?"

"Lord Melrose is in New Orleans. Lasander went to Canada. Caesar was sent to Mexico, I believe."

Makeysha smiled. "Lucia, thank you so much. You've been a great help."

"No problem, Makeysha. Is there anything else you would like me to help with?"

"Not right now, no. Thank you, Lucia."

The evil Twin pressed her lips together and resumed her robotic pose.

Wanda burst through the door carrying a huge book. It must have been as thick as it was long. Easily A4 sized, the small woman struggled to balance it on one hand as she closed the door behind her.

"Ok, the nine circles of Hell are levels that souls are sent to based on their sins during life. Think of the seven deadly sins with a couple of extras thrown in."

"We only have Lasander and Caesar to catch," Makeysha said. "One is in Canada, the other in Mexico."

"Ok, good. Although we don't know how long ago they were all sent off. They could be anywhere by now."

"The realms already guarded are gluttony, greed, and lust." Makeysha took a deep breath. "What are we facing to go into those realms?"

"You can't be serious?" I said, not believing what I was hearing.

"How else do you suppose we get them? I don't think they're going to hand them over as easily as what Lucia did."

"Well, can't you just blast them with whatever you did to her?" I said.

"That was her own magic mixed with mine," she said. "What options does that leave me with for a werewolf? Or a witch? I could possibly take Kaspar down the same way."

"But you took down a warlock and made her your bitch," I said, trying to calm my rising panic. "And now you're telling me you can't take out a werewolf and a witch?"

"Calm down," she said. "I don't know what I'm

capable of. It's not like we needed to use our powers in Heaven, and other than a bit of spring cleaning, I've not used them at all since I've been down here."

I pointed at Lucia and said, "But look, Makeysha. That's what you did. With barely blinking. What could you do if you tried?"

"We don't know what that is," she replied. "There are so many variables going on here, you can't possibly pin it all on my magic. There's no way of knowing. Anyway, we have other more important things to worry about."

"Such as?"

"Figuring out what we're going to face in Hell in those realms, and also where Caesar and Lasander are."

"Here," Wanda said, her eyes still focused on the book. "I've got something." She traced her fingers over several lines of text. "In the circle of gluttony, souls are subjected to laying in vile slush created by a never-ending icy rain. The slush symbolises their personal degradation and overindulgence in food, clothes, and other worldly pleasures. They're blind and unable to see others around them, which represents their selfishness and coldness in life."

"That doesn't sound too bad," Makeysha said. "Just means getting a little dirty. I can handle that."

I raised an eyebrow and waited for Wanda to continue.

"Lust," Wanda said. "Those in the second circle are souls who were overcome by lust. Their punishment is to be blown violently back and forth by strong winds, preventing them from finding peace and rest. The strong winds represent their restlessness and desire for pleasures of the flesh."

Makeysha shrugged her shoulders. "See?" she

said, looking at me. "So far we've got bad weather. You just a fair-weather hunter, wise guy?"

I smiled at her. I had to give her credit for her tenacity at least.

"And greed," Wanda said, still skimming her finger over the sentences of small text. "Souls in this circle are divided into two groups—those who hoarded possessions and those who indulged in spending. They are punished by being forced to push great weights, namely boulders, with their chests, which symbolises their drive for fortune."

"That's good," Makeysha said, nodding her head. "Some bad weather and some heavy weights. I can do that."

"You're not doing this alone," I said. "I'm coming with you."

"You can't possibly, Ronin. We can't risk touching. If I get stuck or need help, you're going to have touch me to help me, and we both know what that means."

"And if you get stuck and you're alone, then what? You'll die. If this is a choice between you dying and me dying, then I'm going to choose me every time."

She sighed and gave me a sad smile. "And I would choose me every time, Ronin. I'm old. Way older than you can ever imagine. You're still so young, you've got so much life ahead of you."

"A life that won't be worth living without my soulmate."

"Ronin, you didn't even know you had one until about six hours ago. Don't act like it's suddenly something you can't live without."

I stood up and walked over to her. I knelt down on the hard-wooden floor and took hold of her hand.

Our connection immediately resumed, light shone from both of us, our hearts beat as one, our minds linked.

Makeysha tried to take her hand back. "Ronin, no…let go."

I gripped her harder and shook my head. "No," I said. "I'm not letting go. Don't you get it? If you die, this part of my soul will die too. I can't live a life knowing I had something so fantastic and let it walk right back out without so much as a fight. How could I ever be with anyone else, knowing that this is the true feeling of being with someone? This is the feeling of being complete and being with your other half. I'm not letting that go."

"You'd find someone else, Ronin. A soulmate isn't the be all and end all."

"No, you're right. But how could I ever accept anything less than this now I know what this is? I'm not prepared to live a sub-par life because you're scared of what might or might not happen."

"You're asking me to be a part of your death and I won't do it. You're asking something of me that I can't do." Her eyes swam with tears. "Please don't make me kill you because that's essentially what you're asking."

"We don't even know that that's going to happen," I said. "I'm strong. Wanda's already told me I'm some sort of throwback and have more angelic powers than a regular hunter. Take a chance. Take a risk. I promise you, it'll be fine."

"Don't make promises you can't keep, Ronin."

"I'm not. Whatever powers you give to me, I can handle them. Look at me. I'm hardly a scrawny geek, am I?"

She laughed and squeezed my hand. "I want to believe you, I do, but I'd rather live a life apart knowing that you're still alive, than have a few short days with you and kill you."

I let go of her hand and cupped her face with both of my hands. "Listen to me. I'm not going to die. And you know what? I'd rather die in a few days if it means I get to experience the true meaning of being with a soulmate in the meantime. Ninety years of being half fulfilled and lonely is nothing compared to a few days of complete bliss with my true other half, my missing half."

"Awww," Wanda said. I looked over my shoulder to see her hand over her chest. "Ronin, you're so sweet."

I'd totally forgotten she was there. I squashed the rising heat of embarrassment and focused back on Makeysha. "Don't shut me out because you're scared for something I'm not."

"But what if you do die? Then I'm left to an eternity of loneliness because you wanted your few days of being 'complete'. You might die happy, Ronin, but I'd continue to live, miserable and missing a piece of me."

I sighed and dropped my eye contact. My eyes landed on Lucia. Something stirred deep in my memories. "Makeysha," I said, letting go of her face and taking her hands. "Do you remember what Lucia said to you before your fight?"

Her brow creased together, then she shook her head.

"She said that we're apparently immortal, indestructible, remember? She said she wanted to test the theory on whether you could die."

"But she's killed angels before…"

"Exactly, which means she was talking about the fact we're soulmates. Soulmates are immortal."

Her golden eyes lit up. "Oh my goodness, you're right!" She grabbed my face with both hands and kissed me so hard, I thought she was going to imprint my teeth into my lips. "Ronin, you're a genius."

I grinned. "Well, it comes with the geek territory."

ANGEL OF THE CRYPT

CHAPTER THIRTEEN

Makeysha

Thanks to Ronin's excellent memory, my mood lifted a thousand levels. I was curious though, why Lucia thought we were indestructible. I'd never heard that before.

"Lucia," I said, turning to face her. "What made you say that we're immortal?"

"It's a known fact. My mother was torn from her soulmate when God and Lucifer opposed one another. Her immortal status remains intact though."

I thought back to the three immortal couples I knew of in Heaven. None of them had been in my castle so I hadn't ever really gotten to know any of them. I could feel their names whirring around in my memory somewhere but couldn't quite grasp them.

"And you're sure? That soulmates are indestructible?"

"Oh yes," Lucia said, the ghost of a smile pulling at her lips. "Once two souls have been fully reacquainted, they're impossible to pull apart. Except, of course, for differences in opinion tearing the heart to pieces instead."

"If they're soulmates," Ronin said, frowning. "Shouldn't they have the same thoughts and opinions?"

"Oh no," Lucia said. "Quite the opposite. It would be like having a coin with two sides the same otherwise. What one soul is missing, can be found in the other, and vice versa. Like a two-piece jigsaw puzzle."

"Lucia," I said, licking my lips as I chewed over her words. "You said 'once two souls have been fully reacquainted, they're impossible to pull apart'. What did you mean?"

"Physical bodies get in the way of souls fully reconnecting on the first touch. Of course, over time, holding hands and such empowers the connection, but it won't ever complete it. That can only be done by uniting physically. At that point, the soulmates become immortal."

My heart skipped a beat. "Uniting physically?"

"Yes," Lucia said. "Through inter—"

"Yes, yes, yes, I get it. I just can't believe what I'm hearing."

I glanced at Ronin who was grinning from ear to ear. "So, we've got to have sex in order to save my life. And I didn't even make it up."

I narrowed my eyes at him. "Don't go getting excited, smooth dude, we've still got plenty of light left between us yet."

"Why wait, hmmm? No point in pushing me to the brink of death is there?"

I raised an eyebrow. "Why don't you keep talking and see where you end up?"

"I'm just saying," he said, chuckling. "If there was ever a reason to have some bump and grind, now is it."

"Bump and grind?"

"Yes, you know—"

"I know what you mean, Ronin. I'm just in shock that my soulmate could use such a phrase. Totally tasteless."

He grinned and winked. "I can assure you, tasteless I am not."

"Ewww. So rude. Good things come to those who wait, wise guy."

"Well, if you wait too long, all this sexy might be gone. Then what would you do?"

I smirked. "I'm sure I could bump and grind my way through eternity."

The amusement on his face disappeared instantly. It was almost like I'd pressed a button to activate the glaring stare of an unimpressed Ronin.

"That's not funny," he said.

"Is it not? I thought it was far more amusing than your lame lines."

"Hey, I'm dying here. I'm desperate."

I fixed him with a deadpan stare.

"No, no, no, no, no," he said, holding his hands out. "I didn't mean it like that."

Inside, I was giggling, but I maintained a poker face, for the purpose of my own enjoyment. Wanda laughed behind him but kept her eyes on the ancient book still open on her lap.

"Desperate? Nice. I'll remember that."

"I didn't mean it like that," he said, grabbing one of my hands. "You know I didn't."

"No, I don't. I barely know you. Which is exactly why, impending death or not, you're not getting your 'bump and grind'."

He sighed. "This must be a first...lack of sex killing a man..."

I grinned and gave him a playful shove on his shoulder. "I'm not saying it's off the table, wise guy. Just that you've got to earn it."

His golden eyes lit up with joy. "That sounds like a challenge." He twisted his lips into a mischievous grin. "A challenge I can rise to."

I giggled at his bad innuendo. "You keep making bad jokes like that and there won't be anything to rise to."

"Where it concerns you, there's always something to rise to."

I burst out laughing. "Ten out of ten for cheese, but I like it."

He gave me a cheeky wink. "Like it enough to kiss me?"

"Maybe," I said, grinning. "I'm still deciding."

"Guys," Wanda said. "I hate to interrupt but I need to point something out."

I glanced over at her. "What's up?"

"Lucia said the Hellmouth is coded to their unique aura's. That leads me to believe you can't just go waltzing straight in there."

"Shoot," I said, mentally cursing myself. "You're right. I completely forgot about that."

"Lucia," Wanda said, looking over at the bewitched Twin. "Can anyone pass through the

Hellmouth."

"Oh no," she replied, the same chilling, robotic smile painted on her face. "Your aura has to be coded into it. All of Lucifer's creations carry the same mark in their aura that the Hellmouth recognises."

"What happens if you try to enter without this specific thing in your aura?"

"You burn up and die."

Wanda raised an eyebrow and looked at both me and Ronin. "That could be a problem. It kind of gets in the way of the whole dagger mission."

"There must be something we can do," I said, wondering if my magic would be able to assist in any way. "Their auras were coded in so there must be something that can be done to allow me in."

"And me," said Ronin.

I narrowed my eyes at him but decided to have that discussion later. "Can we somehow disguise ourselves with Lucia's aura or follow her in or something?"

Wanda shook her head. "No. I would have to find a way to either trick it into accepting your auras or coding yours into it."

A sense of urgency started to climb inside me. "But we need to get those daggers. Now."

"No," Ronin said, shaking his head. "We don't. They're not going anywhere. And we have two of them. Nothing can be done without all seven. Lucia, can anything be done without all seven daggers?"

"No. All seven daggers are needed to complete Lucifer's ascension."

"See?" he said, smiling at me. "Chill out. We don't need to go into this at breakneck speed."

"But we can't just sit here doing nothing, Ronin.

The world is literally at stake here."

"We're not going to," he said, standing up. "We're going to go and do what we both said we wanted to do."

I frowned. "What's that?"

"Tour the French Quarter."

I smiled. "I would love to, but it feels rather inappropriate to go on some tourist adventure whilst Lucifer is plotting the end of the world as we know it."

"Why don't you both get some sleep for a few hours?" Wanda said. "I will, too. Then, in the morning, when we're all refreshed and thinking straight, we'll sort a plan for how we can get you past the Hellmouth to save the world."

"Ok," I said, sighing in defeat. "I might have a different perspective on things after a decent sleep." I stood up and smiled at Wanda. "Thank you, Wanda, for everything. I'll come by around ten a.m.?"

She frowned at me. "Where are you going?"

"To my bed. In Odd Fellows."

"Don't be so silly. You can take the other side of the house. There's no point in you sleeping in some abandoned graveyard when I have a perfectly good bed here."

I faltered, not really knowing what to say.

"And he can stay too," she said, nodding her head towards Ronin.

My cheeks burned with heat. Ronin grinned at me. "Don't even think about it, wise guy," I said.

He let go of my hand and held his hands up in a surrender sign. "I wasn't going to say a word."

"You didn't need to. That grin said it all."

Wanda laughed. "Once I'm asleep, nothing wakes me up."

"Trust me, Wanda. There will be nothing going on to wake you up."

Ronin pouted and looked at me with puppy dog eyes.

"I've lasted this long, smooth dude, I don't think a few more weeks is going to hurt," I said.

"Can't blame a guy for trying."

I shook my head and turned to Wanda. "Thank you, Wanda, for the offer of staying here. If you're certain, I'd love to accept."

"Of course I am. There are three bedrooms you can choose from on that side. The master bedroom has an en-suite, but there is a main bathroom at the back of the house, too."

"Thanks, Wanda." I looked at Lucia and sighed. "Lucia, I'm going to show you the room you will be staying in."

Lucia stood up and stared at me. As I ventured out of the living room and up the stairs, I wondered how I could ensure she wouldn't escape whilst we were all sleeping. Should I tie her to the bed? Would the door lock? Or considering her new compliant state, would a simple instruction of 'don't move' work?

I heard Ronin saying goodnight to Wanda before his footsteps then followed me up the stairs. My heart leapt into my mouth and nerves churned around in my stomach. I wanted him, of course I did, but just because he was my soulmate, it didn't mean I was going to lose all respect for myself by jumping him the first day I met him. Even if his life was at stake.

Turning right at the top of the stairs, I opened the first door I came across to discover it was the main bathroom. It looked to be in keeping with the rest of the house, but as I looked around the modest sized room, I realised it was actually more 'shabby chic' than French colonial. However, the casual rustic look fitted really well.

"That's the bathroom, Lucia," I said, turning around to find her stood inches from me. I jumped back in surprise. "Do you need to use it?"

"No, thank you, Makeysha."

Ronin locked eyes with me briefly and we exchanged a look of confusion before moving on to the next room. A single room was behind the next door, its walls painted in a pale blue colour. A white wardrobe sat against one wall, whilst a matching dresser stood next to it. The bed was a simple plain divan with pale blue sheets. I resisted the urge to shiver at the coolness emanating from the room.

"Lucia," I said, standing back from the open doorway. "This will be your room. Is this ok?"

She stepped into the room and glanced around before sitting on the bed. "Yes, thank you, Makeysha. It's lovely."

"Ok. Get some sleep," I said, briefly wondering if she could sleep. "And we'll call for you in the morning. If you need the toilet, the bathroom is right next door."

She nodded before climbing under the duvet. Laying flat out on her back, she pulled the covers up to her chin and just laid there, staring at the ceiling. I looked at Ronin and raised my eyebrows.

"Creepy mofo," he said, his brow creasing together as he stared at the evil warlock.

"As long as she stays like this, I couldn't care less," I said, closing the door. "Do you think I need to put a lock on the door?"

"How is she going to use the toilet?"

I shrugged my shoulders. "I don't know. I could

put a block up at the top of the stairs that will stop her from going down them?"

"Are there any potential repercussions from it?"

"Not really. Except it'll block Wanda off from this side of the house."

"I don't see that being an issue. She said it used to be two apartments."

"Don't you think its rude though? To do that in someone else's house?"

"Makeysha, she's not stupid. She knows we've got to be careful with Lucia. It's only for a few hours, not forever."

I pursed my lips and sighed. "Yes, I suppose you're right. Don't really have much choice unless we want a hypnotised warlock running around the streets."

"Technically, that's a paradox," Ronin said, giving me a cheeky smile. "If she's hypnotised, she won't do anything but what you tell her."

I smirked at him. "Are you going all geeky on me again?"

"Maybe," he said. He reached out and grabbed my waist, pulling me in close. Heat sizzled my skin from our contact. It kind of made me glad that the clothes were in the way to lessen the connection slightly. "Depends if you like it."

"Hmmm," I said, running my index finger down his t-shirt. I could feel the hard chest hiding beneath, making me rethink my determination to make him wait. "It's kind of cute."

"Cute?"

"Yes…"

"Do you remember that conversation we had about 'adorable'?"

I giggled and wrapped my arms around his neck. My forearm nestled against the smooth skin of his neck, lighting us up in an instant. I ignored what it meant, wanting to savour the moment instead of worrying about everything else. "Maybe…"

"Well, cute falls in the same category as adorable."

"Does that mean you don't want to kiss me?"

"Oh no," he said, grinning. "Quite the opposite. I'm more than willing to kiss and make up."

I burst out laughing. "Nicely done. I think you almost deserve a kiss just for that comment."

He grinned at me and curled his arm around my back. "I think that's the best news I've heard all evening."

"Better than finding your soulmate?" I teased.

He laughed. "I know you're trying to catch me out here and I'm not falling for it."

"Me? Never."

"Anyway," he said, smirking. "My soulmate offering me a kiss is definitely a step up from finding her."

"Oooo, now that's smooth. That definitely earns a kiss."

He wasted no time in leaning in for a passionate embrace. The second our lips met, I felt a surge of excitement coursing through my veins. Heated, fuzzy tingles shot to every part of me. My mind whirled with the instant link between us growing stronger and stronger. Pure bliss settled deep in my soul, soothing all my worries away in a millisecond.

When he opened his mouth and deepened the kiss, I basked in the new wave of pleasure that soared my soul to new heights. The two millennia I'd been alone were worth every second if this was my reward.

I'd never felt such calm and happiness nor wanted someone so much either. My body ached for him, but I was not going to give in. Yet.

The slow stroke of his tongue against mine stirred my core, lighting me on fire. Within seconds, a slow, sensual kiss turned into a frantic, passionate embrace that threatened to break down every last bit of my determination.

I pulled away, breathing heavily. "Steady on, wise guy. Remember what I said."

"I made a bet with myself I could make you give in," he said, grinning at me.

"I'm sorry to say that you're going to lose."

"I reckon a few more kisses like that and you'll be like butter on hot toast."

I raised an eyebrow. "Oh really? Someone is awfully self-confident."

"Is that a problem?"

"It depends if you're confident in all areas of your life."

He ran his tongue over his lips and smirked. "Well, why don't you find out?"

I laughed at him and pushed him away. "I will do. Soon enough."

"Damn it," he said, chuckling.

"Do I need to shut you out of this side of the house for the night?" I asked, smirking.

"You wouldn't dare."

"Try me."

"I'm trying to."

I giggled. "Alright, enough now. Go and get the bed warm whilst I seal us up."

He wiggled his eyebrows at me and all but ran into the master bedroom at the front of the house. I loved our banter and the naughty innuendos he seemed so natural at responding to almost everything with. As I created a solid wall of impenetrable magic, I couldn't wipe the smile from my face. Life had never been so good.

CHAPTER FOURTEEN

Ronin

When Makeysha came into the bedroom, I cut the cheesy jokes and the flirty lines. The last thing I wanted her thinking was that I was some sort of sex pest. The fact I was still single and had only ever been with two girls in my life should be enough to calm anyone's worries about my sexual intentions.

The room had been decorated with a pastel yellow theme making everything seem light and airy. Seeing Makeysha's raven black hair against the pale colour was a stark contrast that only highlighted her beauty even more. I couldn't take my eyes off her.

"All sorted?" I asked, as she closed the door behind her.

"Yes. We're sealed away in half of the house with

an evil warlock who may or may not turn back to her former state at any moment."

I grinned. "Just the kind of thing that helps me sleep easy."

She walked around the large room, her footsteps silent against the aged wooden flooring. Sitting on the sturdy wooden bed, she sighed.

"My bed was so much comfier."

"That's because you made it out of magic. I'm afraid you're going to have to slum it with plain old human furniture tonight."

She smirked at me. "What did you think I'd been sleeping on before?"

I frowned. "Fluffy white clouds?"

She laughed. "No, I'm afraid not. I've been sleeping wherever I thought looked comfortable enough. I learnt a lot about where to sleep, believe me."

"Do you actually need sleep?" I asked, curious.

"Yes and no. If we can't sun gaze, it definitely helps recharge us. Otherwise, we just cat nap here and there. We don't need a solid eight hours like most humans. Although, up in Heaven, it was lights out every night at ten-thirty and up at the crack of dawn. We fell into routines where sleeping that long became the norm."

"Do you miss it? Heaven?"

"Sort of." She sighed and stared off into the distance, a wistful gaze spreading through her golden eyes. "I don't miss the regimented way it runs. The freedom I have now is great and I love it, but the loneliness? That gets to me. Except for when we went to bed, we were always around other angels. Being on my own was the hardest thing to adjust to."

"Have you not spoken to anyone over the years?"

"Not really. I've come across creatures here and there, most of them not so nice. A few humans have been able to see me, they were all hunters, but I would disappear before they could get a real good look and confirm what they'd seen."

"What made you run? From the hunters?"

"I don't know," she said, shrugging her shoulders. "I knew angels had abandoned humans and I didn't want them to blame me for the other angel's actions or think I was some sort of saviour or going to help in some way. I just wanted to be left alone."

I smirked. "What you mean is you wanted to wallow in self-pity?"

Her mouth dropped open as she looked at me, gobsmacked. "How rude."

"Tell me I'm wrong."

She pursed her lips. "So what if I wanted to? My entire world had been turned upside down because I'd done nothing but be true to myself. Yes, I wanted to feel sorry for myself. Is that so bad?"

I sat up and reached for her hand. "I never said it wasn't. I wasn't judging you or anything and I'm sorry if it came across like that. That wasn't my intention."

She squeezed my hand and sighed. "Let's just get some sleep. I'm tired. I tend to get cranky when I'm tired."

"How are we…" I cleared my throat "…doing this? Are we staying clothed, sleeping head to toe…?"

"Head to toe?" she said, laughing. "What are we, teenagers?"

"I'm just trying to be the gentleman and make sure I don't cross any boundaries."

"After all your tacky innuendos earlier?"

I grinned. "It was only a bit of banter."

She giggled. "I know. If you can promise to keep your hands to yourself, then I'm sure we can manage to sleep at the same end of the bed."

"Scout's honour," I said, saluting. "Cross my heart and hope to die." I realised after I said it, what I'd said. "Actually, no I don't…"

Makeysha burst out laughing and stood up to peel the duvet back. She waved a hand over herself, turning her black dress into a sheer white floor length nightgown. The way it clung to her curves made my heart race instantly. I swallowed the lump in my throat and tore my eyes from her.

"I'm afraid I can't do that," I said, taking my t-shirt off.

"I can give you a pair of cute pj's if you want?"

I tossed my top onto the floor and looked at her. She was grinning from ear to ear. "I think I'll pass. I can already see 'Hello Kitty' running through your mind."

Giggling, she dived under the covers. "Actually, I was thinking of 'Peppa Pig'."

"You dare and everything I say will be cheesy innuendos."

"Ok, you got me."

I stood up, secretly jumping for joy when I noticed her eyes wandering down my exposed torso. I believed firmly in modesty, but I knew I had a good body. Having a job like mine meant I had to be fit or it would cost me my life. It had been years since I'd had a woman look at me with such hunger. It made me feel good and I wanted to give her the same feeling—when she would let me that is.

"You ok if I sleep in my underwear?" I asked,

resting my hands against my belt.

"So long as the mouse stays in the house."

I raised an eyebrow. "Mouse?"

Her lips were twisted up into a wicked grin. "Yep. Mouse stays in the house."

"You know those conversations we had about cute and adorable? Referring to my manhood as 'the mouse' needs to go in a 'taboo' category like those."

She laughed and shuffled down under the duvet so only her face was visible. "Come on," she said. "I'm waiting for my peep show."

"You've spent all night telling me how, despite my life being on the line, we're not doing anything sexual, and then you tell me you're waiting for a peep show? And you women wonder why us men can't figure you out."

Her smile grew into a dazzling grin. "I'm no normal woman. Besides, there's nothing wrong with window shopping before committing to buy."

I couldn't help but laugh. What an analogy. "What the…? Did you seriously just say that?"

She nodded and pulled the duvet up over her mouth to stifle her laughter.

I undid my belt, wiggled my hips from side to side, then took my pants off, giving her a goofy, super quick strip show. Her eyes gleamed with joy and the smile never fell from her face. When I'd finished, and all I had on were my black briefs, she raised an eyebrow.

"Maybe not so much a mouse as a—"

"Don't," I said, holding up a hand. "Don't even finish that sentence. Not unless you're going to call it something really manly."

"Manly? And what would you consider a manly name for it?"

I shrugged my shoulders. "I don't know something…something that instils fear like…Hercules or The Rock or The Destroyer."

She laughed. She laughed so hard she cried. Tears flowed down her cheeks as she doubled up on her side, crippled with laughter. I stood staring at her for several minutes as I tried to process what was so funny.

"Please tell me you weren't seriously suggesting those as names."

"Well," I said, folding my arms over my chest. "They're all better than 'the mouse'."

"Really not," she replied, in between splutters of laughter. "How about we just leave it nameless for now?"

"Nameless? That's worse than calling it 'the mouse'."

"How is it?"

"Because then it's like it's not even worthy of having a name."

She giggled. "I'll name it after I've…played with it."

"So until then it's just, what?"

"The same thing it's always been up to now."

I pouted at her as I pulled back my side of the duvet. "You definitely killed whatever dirty thoughts I had about sharing a bed with you."

She snuggled into my side and laid a kiss on my chest. "Then my work is done."

I chuckled to myself as I held her against me and closed my eyes. The light emanating from our contact illuminated my eyelids, a painful reminder chasing me into peaceful dreams that my time was limited, and my life was being held in the hands of an angel.

CHAPTER FIFTEEN

Makeysha

I woke the next morning, surrounded by light. Sunshine streamed through a gap in the thick curtains, highlighting a streak across the king-size bed. The majority of it, however, was shining from me and Ronin. We were still cuddled against one another in the exact same position we'd fallen asleep in.

How cute, I thought, then giggled when I remembered Ronin's reaction to the word cute.

Ronin stirred beside me, breaking our contact when he moved to stretch. I shuffled away and sat up, admiring the view of his perfectly chiselled abs partially covered by the duvet. It was a picture-perfect sight to wake up to.

As he yawned and stretched his arms, I couldn't help but watch how his biceps flexed. Sculpted arms had always been a weakness of mine. Ronin's were just perfect. Not too big and not too small. I wanted to feel them, squeeze them, kiss them…

I shook my head, dispersing my naughty thoughts away. Perhaps sharing a bed with him hadn't been the best idea in the world. Being around him was seriously weakening my determination to not sleep with him 'just because'. I was starting to understand female humans and their love of sex toys.

Given the two thousand years I'd gone without a single stirring of desire, it was a relief to know that something in that region still worked and hadn't gone stale. I knew once I had sex again, it would be like popping my cherry for a second time and I'd be ravishing him at any chance I got. In the midst of everything else going on, it was a partial reason as to why I wanted to hold off for as long as I could. The world mattered more than my sexual wants and needs.

"I think I saw some drool slip out of the corner of your mouth," Ronin said, snapping me from my daydreams.

My eyes widened and heat flushed my cheeks as I dabbed a hand to each side of my mouth. When I realised he was joking, I narrowed my eyes at him and gave him a playful shove in the shoulder.

"Not funny," I said.

"It is from where I'm sitting. You can touch if you want to, you know. I don't bite."

"Are you trying to kill yourself even quicker?"

He gave me a playful wink. "I know you'll come to my rescue before it gets that far."

"You're awfully self-confident."

"No, I just trust in my soulmate."

I shuddered as he said the word 'soulmate'. It still sounded so surreal. "Pulling out all the smooth lines already? My, I'm in for a treat today, aren't I?"

"You certainly are because I'm taking you for a tour of this beautiful city."

"Ronin—"

"No. There's nothing we can do until Wanda figures out how to get us into the Hellmouth."

"Yes, there is. We need to be hunting down Lasander and Caesar."

"Why? Why should we waste precious energy on that when we know where they're going?"

"Because of the realms, Ronin. Do we really want to be going through two more that we don't have to? It makes sense to stop them at the Hellmouth like we did Lucia." It suddenly dawned on me then that I hadn't been to check on her. "Lucia. Oh crap. What time is it?"

I threw the bedcovers back and ran out of the room, not even bothering to wait for Ronin's response. I sprinted down the hallway and burst through her bedroom door. When I saw her laid in bed, in the exact same position as when I left her hours ago, I breathed a sigh of relief.

Ronin padded up behind me in his underwear. "Happy now?" he said.

I balked at him. "What are you doing? Are you forgetting she tried to seduce you? Go and put some clothes on."

"Aww, sweetie, this is all for you, don't worry. Besides, I don't think she's registering much at the moment, is she?"

"That's not the point," I said, lowering my voice.

"Anyway, you're distracting me, walking around like that. Get dressed."

He chuckled and shook his head as he ambled back to our bedroom.

"Lucia," I said. "You can get up now if you like."

She sat bolt upright and stared straight ahead. "Thank you, Makeysha. May I please go to the bathroom?"

"Of course. You didn't have to wait for me."

"I prefer for you to know where I am at all times."

Folding the corner of the duvet back, she swung her legs out of bed and stood up, shoulders square. With her milky white eyes and generally brainwashed demeanour, she reminded me of a possessed human. I shivered and stepped out of her way as she came towards me.

I went back to Ronin, frowning. "What are we supposed to do with her whilst we're out?"

Buckling his belt up, but still topless, he smiled. "Let's have a chat with Wanda. See what she has to say. What's the time?"

I looked around the room for a clock and found an antique bronze piece with roman numerals mounted on the wall next to the window. "Ten a.m."

"Loads of time," he replied. He bent down and picked up his shirt. "Want a final look before I put my shirt back on?"

I smirked at him and waved a hand over my nightgown, turning it back into my black corseted dress. "I'm good, thanks."

He chuckled to himself and pulled his t-shirt back on. "Do your clothes wash or something when you do that?"

"No. They're brand new."

"So you have a new dress every day but it's always the same one?"

"Is that a problem?"

"No…I was just asking, nothing more, nothing less."

"I know what I like," I said, shrugging my shoulders. "I've grown quite fond of black in my time down here and I like the support the boning in the corset gives me."

"You don't need to explain yourself to me, Makeysha. I'm not judging you."

I pursed my lips and chewed on his words. "Do you think I should try a different colour?"

"You try whatever you feel like trying. You're a woman with the world in her hands."

"Literally."

"I didn't mean that," he said, closing the gap between us. "I meant you're capable of doing anything you want to."

He stopped in front of me, our feet touching toe to toe. I reached for him and slid my arms around his neck. "You are smooth today. I like it."

Smiling, he leaned in and brushed his lips over mine. It was such a soft, sweeping glance, goosebumps sprung up all over my body. Just as I thought about kissing him back, a nagging feeling of being watched irritated my mind.

I turned to my left and jumped in surprise. Lucia stood in the doorway, robotic, motionless, and her face nothing but a blank picture.

"Lucia," I breathed. "Please don't sneak up on us like that."

"I'm sorry, Makeysha. I just thought I should let you know that my brother is attempting to communicate with me telepathically. He knew my deadline for retrieving the dagger and is aware I've missed it."

I muttered a curse under my breath and regretfully released my hold on Ronin. "Deadline? You had a deadline for taking the dagger to Lucifer?"

"Yes," she said. "We all did. Lucifer gave us explicit instructions not to arrive before or after our designated time. Only at that specific time."

I frowned, confused. "Do you know why?"

"It's to do with the complexity of creating the realms. He staggered our arrivals so he had time to prepare each realm."

Bingo. "Do you know Lasander's and Caesar's deadlines?"

"Yes. Caesar is due in two days at one a.m. Lasander two days after at two a.m."

I glanced at Ronin and gave him a broad smile. "Doesn't it feel like the universe is working with us?"

"It certainly feels like we've had a truck load of luck for some bizarre reason."

Something pinged to mind about Lucia saying Lucifer needed a blood moon. "Do you know when the blood moon is?" I asked Ronin.

"I don't...but I bet Wanda does. Unless your freaky friend there knows."

"Lucia, when is the blood moon?"

"Six days time. Two days after Lasander's arrival. Lucifer will perform the ritual at three a.m."

I sighed and smiled. "Of course he will."

"Three a.m.," Ronin said. "The Devil's Hour."

"He's so obvious it's sickening," I said, shaking my head. "At least we have a timeline now. This is turning out to be a great day and we haven't even left the house."

"Don't forget what she initially told you," Ronin said, his face taking a serious edge. "They know she's not there."

"Which means they're going to come looking for her." I stomped my foot on the floor. "Dammit!"

"Lord Melrose has also been noticed as missing," Lucia said. "Would you like me to respond to my brother?"

I hesitated for a moment. "Are they sending someone to come and look for you?"

"My brother will potentially be released from his duties to gather the rest of us."

"This is perfect," Ronin said. "Then there's only two of them to worry about if they're all up here."

"Do we get her to respond to her brother?"

"No," he said, shaking his head. "If there's no response then he'll come looking for her."

"But he won't know where to come looking for her."

"He'll find her. He's a warlock, and not just any warlock either, remember. Trust me, we're best off playing this one silent."

I nodded as nerves churned around in my stomach. He had a point. If we allowed Lucia to send a message that she was in trouble, he would want details; details we wouldn't want her to give. He would know something was up. If we played total radio silence, he would fear the worse and come for her without even thinking about a potential trap.

"We need to speak to Wanda," I said, grabbing Ronin's hand and pulling him towards the door. "Maybe she can trap him. If we have these two on side, the others will be a piece of cake."

Lucia moved out of the way, allowing us to take the lead towards the stairs. The shimmering purple wall of magic I'd created hours ago was still holding firm. I waved my hand over it, dissolving its presence like an eraser over a board.

We headed downstairs, Lucia following behind like a loyal dog. Ronin opened the living room door, allowing us to pass through first. I walked in and saw Wanda on the sofa, flat out on her back, several open books spread all around her. Soft snores filled the air.

"Awww," I said, waiting for Ronin to come into the room. "I don't want to wake her."

"Well, she kind of needs to wake up, really," he replied, pulling his lips into a thin line.

Just as he said that, Wanda rolled onto her side, but unfortunately, didn't have enough room left on the sofa. She fell onto the floor, promptly waking up. Looking around her a little startled, her brown eyes settled on us for a brief moment before her cheeks turned bright red.

"I'm so sorry," she said. "Have you been there long?"

"No," I said, struggling not to laugh. "We've literally just walked in."

She put a hand to the back of her neck and rubbed at it. "Going to have a sore neck today."

I walked over to her and knelt down in front of her. "Here," I said, moving my hands towards hers. "Let me help."

She moved her hand, giving me room to place my hands on her small neck. I placed both hands on the back of her neck, next to each other, and closed my eyes. With my mind, I called my magic up, and imagined it as all shades of green flowing through my body and into my hands. Then, I pictured it streaming out of me and into Wanda, encasing her in a wonderful green glow.

After several seconds I stopped and moved back. "Is that better?"

She looked up at me and moved her head from side to side. "Like magic," she said, grinning. "Thank you so much."

"My pleasure." I offered her a hand to help her stand up. "We've got a little update for you."

She took my hand, then with her free hand pointed towards a dark framed doorway at the other end of the room. "Coffee," she said. "I need coffee."

Ronin headed towards it, a big grin on his handsome face. Lucia stood in the living room doorway, looking slightly confused.

"Sit down on the sofa, Lucia," I said. "Would you like a drink?"

"Just some water please, Makeysha," she replied, gliding towards one of the sofas.

I headed towards what I presumed was a kitchen, Wanda striding ahead of me, no doubt desperate for her caffeine fix. I heard mugs clinking around and presumed Ronin was also keen for a drink.

As I walked through the doorway, my eyes fell upon the most gorgeous kitchen I'd ever seen. It was clearly new but had been designed to fit the French colonial era. White cupboards tinged with dark smudges gave a fantastic aged look. The fancy iron handles, all twisted into intricate designs, blended beautifully with tasteful decorative edgings around the doors.

A white marble topped island took centre stage, a fresh fruit bowl sat in the middle and overflowed with a variety of delicious fruit. Three low hanging gothic style chandeliers basked the room in a yellow glow. A large window to my left, covered with a white lacy netting, opened the room up, making it seem so much bigger than it really was.

"This is incredible," I said.

"Thank you," Wanda replied, walking over to the far side of the room. "I spent a lot of money having this designed. My favourite room in a house is always the kitchen so I spared no expense when I did this up. My bank account is still recovering."

I laughed. "Look at it though. Worth every cent."

"Definitely," she said. "At this rate though, it will take me a century to do the house up to the same standard. Still, it keeps me out of trouble."

We both laughed as we waited for Ronin to empty the coffee pot into three mugs.

"You like coffee?" he asked, a quizzical look on his face.

"Yes. It's not good for us. It's a bit like chocolate for humans, but I can't remember the last time I had some."

"How do you like it?"

"Black. Straight out of the pot."

"No cream?"

I shook my head.

He filled a plain white mug to the brim with the dark, tarry substance and then passed it over to me. I took it from him and immediately lifted it to my nose, inhaling the rich aroma of freshly ground coffee.

"This is gorgeous," I said, looking at Wanda.

"I have to have the best coffee," she said, taking her mug from Ronin. "I don't buy it from stores—that stuff is disgusting. I have a contact at a coffee roasting company. As soon as he's roasted the beans, he calls me, and I go down and take what I need."

"You can certainly tell the difference," I said, taking another sniff of my treat. "I need some water for Lucia."

Ronin nodded and filled a tumbler glass up with some tap water. "Shall we head back in there?" he said, motioning his head towards the living room.

We all migrated back to the sofas and sat down in comfortable silence as we took our first few sips of delicious invigoration.

"What's new then?" Wanda asked, setting her mug down on the coffee table.

"Kaspar has been attempting to contact Lucia. They know she's missing. Apparently, all the creatures had a specific deadline to be at the Hellmouth for," I said.

Wanda raised an eyebrow. "What about Melrose? Do they know about him yet?"

I hadn't even thought about him. I turned to Lucia. "Lucia, are they aware that Lord Melrose is missing also?"

"Lord Melrose was running late. Lucifer was extremely displeased. It meant that he would be arriving not much before my deadline. My brother did not mention him not arriving."

Turning back to Wanda, I said, "Perhaps they still think he's running late. Regardless, Kaspar is being relieved from his duties to come and find Lucia."

"Which means another evil warlock running around?" Wanda visibly shuddered. "I'm not too fond of the thought of that."

"We had an idea," Ronin said. "If you could come up with a way to trap him, we have the two most powerful First Creations. The rest will be easy after that."

"She's easy," Wanda said, pointing at Lucia. "There's no guarantees Kaspar can be turned the same way. We don't even fully understand what Makeysha did to turn her like this in the first place, let alone replicating it."

"Surely there must be some sort of voodoo thing you can do to him to give a similar effect?"

"I can have a look through some books, but I can't promise anything."

"Looking is enough," Ronin said, giving her a warm smile. "If you can't find anything, I'm sure Makeysha can do something if pressured."

I raised my eyebrows. "Oh really?"

"Look what you did last time. If Kaspar hurls some magic at you, chances are something like this will happen again, right?"

I shrugged my shoulders. "I have no idea. Magic isn't predictable. Never mind the fact it could affect him in a completely different way."

"Ok," he said. "Well for now, I say we leave Kaspar in the capable hands of Wanda here." He turned and looked at Wanda. "If you can't find anything then we'll rethink things from there. In situations like this, we can't afford to waste time thinking and planning for problems that may or may not arise. Things could change in a heartbeat at any given moment."

I nodded. "Ok. We'll go with that for now. If you're happy, Wanda?"

"Sure. Sounds good to me."

"Right," Ronin said, clapping his hands together. "If you're ok with it, Wanda, I would like to take this beautiful lady on a tour of the city. Are you happy to babysit our hypnotised warlock whilst we're gone?"

Wanda eyed Lucia with suspicion for several seconds. "I think so. Provided she doesn't suddenly turn back into her evil normal self."

"I think it's safe to say if she was going to turn back, it would have happened by now," I said. "If this magic didn't have a permanent hold on her, there's no way it would have held her this long if it was only temporary."

Wanda eyed Lucia for several seconds then sighed. "Ok. I agree. Go and enjoy yourselves before the hard work starts."

I gulped down the rest of my coffee and stood up, feeling as energised as a puppy. "Thanks, Wanda. I really appreciate it." I turned to Ronin and held my hand out. "Come on then, smooth dude. Dazzle me for the day."

ANGEL OF THE CRYPT

CHAPTER SIXTEEN

Ronin

With the blood moon being only six days away, I figured today would be our one and only chance to really enjoy some time together. I knew Wanda wouldn't take long to figure something out for us to get into the Hellmouth and I also knew that Makeysha would be getting twitchy to do something other than relax and enjoy doing things together.

As we strolled out of the front door, holding hands, I decided we'd head down towards the river and take a leisurely walk along its banks so we could chat without fear of distraction or interruption.

"So where are you taking me first?" Makeysha asked, flashing me a smile.

"To the river. I thought we could take a romantic

walk along the banks and gaze into the disgusting brown waters."

She laughed. "I'm sure it's beautiful in its own right. You humans have a habit of only focusing on the negative aspect of things, rather than appreciating the positives."

A cool breeze slid down the street, bringing with it a pungent stench of stale liquor and urine. I screwed my nose up and coughed, trying not to choke on the overpowering mix of disgusting smells.

"What is that?" Makeysha asked, her eyes watering. "It stinks."

"Bourbon Street is behind us—" I pointed to the street running across the top of Dumaine Street "—it's pretty infamous for its smells."

"That's really gross. Please tell me we're not going there?"

I grinned. "Technically, we should. It's part of the whole French Quarter experience."

"I think I've just experienced it," she said, giggling. "Come on." She tugged at my hand. "Before another gust of wind chokes us to death."

We made a hasty retreat towards the Mississippi river. As we put more and more distance between us and Bourbon Street, thankfully a wide variety of pleasant smells enveloped us as we made our way to the river's edge. Freshly baked goods, roasting coffee beans, the sweet scent of jasmine and small trees—it was all a perfect mix to truly embrace us in the arms of a bustling city with plenty to offer.

"I almost feel like a tourist," Makeysha said, inhaling a deep breath. "If the world wasn't about to end, I'd dare say I could almost call it a holiday."

"When we met last night," I said, remembering

for some odd reason what she'd said to me hours ago. "You said you'd only been back four hours. Where had you been?"

"I took a trip," she said, grinning. "I decided to do some sight-seeing. I wasn't gone long. Only a couple of months."

I raised an eyebrow. "A couple of months? That is a long time."

"Maybe to you humans. But to me, it's like a week or something. Time really isn't relevant to angels."

I hadn't ever considered that option. It was an interesting point. "So where did you go?"

"All the typical places most tourists go. Stonehenge, the pyramids, the Mayan temples." She shrugged her shoulders. "The usual."

"That sounds like quite a trip."

"It was good. I felt a little guilty though."

"Why?"

"Because my job is to help souls pass over and I've abandoned that duty for the last few years in pursuit of my own happiness."

"Don't be so hard on yourself. Has Lucifer come up here and told you to get back to work?"

"No."

"Then I wouldn't worry about it." I squeezed her hand in an effort to reassure her. "If you're going to be stuck down here then you may as well enjoy the world, right?"

She smiled at me and lifted our joined hands to her mouth. Then, she brushed a soft kiss across the back of my hand. "Thank you."

"For what?"

"For trying to make me feel better. Being an angel means we have to be totally selfless but the more time

I've spent on my own, wallowing in self-pity—" she smirked at me, making me grin "—the more inclined I've become to do things that make me happy, but at the same time, it makes me feel bad. Does that make sense?"

I chuckled and nodded. "You, my lady, are a total paradox."

"I presume, being a geek and all, that you like such things?"

"I do indeed," I said, taking our hands to my mouth and gifting the back of her hand with a tender kiss.

"Can I take your picture?"

The sound of a male voice interrupted our moment. I turned to the sound of the voice and saw a young man in his early twenties with short fluffy blonde curls and a face covered with freckles. A camera hung around his neck, the lens on it big enough to knock someone out.

"Sorry?" I said, not understanding why he wanted a picture.

"What you did there, kissing her hand, the way you looked at each other was just incredible. It was perfect for a picture of a young couple in love." He offered me his hand. "Sorry. My name is Dale Chambers. I work for the local newspaper. I love capturing shots of unique things in our city and I'd love to include you two in it."

I took hold of his hand and gave him a firm handshake. "Sure, no problem." I turned to Makeysha. "You good with that?"

Makeysha stood staring at him, open mouthed, shock filtering through her golden eyes. "You...you can...you can see me?"

Dale frowned and gave me a curious look before looking back at Makeysha. "Err…yes, Ma'am."

She turned to look at me, tears filling her eyes. A broad smile spread over her pretty face. "He can see me, Ronin." She gasped. "Of course. The transfer…" she motioned a hand between us "…of our pow—"

"Shhh," I whispered. In my mind, I said, *"Don't freak the human out."*

Her cheeks flushed red as she stifled a giggle. "Sorry," she said, turning back to Dale. "I've spent a long time being invisible to people."

Dale gave her a sympathetic smile. "I know exactly how you feel. I've been bullied, ignored, and ridiculed all of my life. It's something I've just learned to accept now though."

Makeysha reached out and wrapped her hand around his forearm. "I really hope that changes for you. And soon."

I watched in amazement as reels of rainbow coloured energy rolled off her and surrounded Dale. When she released her hold on him, his whole body seemed to glow with a renewed energy. His cheeks gained a new shade of pink, and he stood taller and squared his shoulders.

"Thank you," he said. "I hope things change for you soon, too."

Makeysha smiled at him. "Would you still like to take our picture?"

"Yes, please. As you were when I saw you."

I lifted our hands to my mouth again, gazing into Makeysha's glorious golden eyes as I did so. She looked back at me, warmth and compassion pouring from her soul. I swept a kiss over her smooth skin, revelling in the moment.

A distinctive click sounded through the air, telling me that Dale had indeed got his shot. I looked at the young man to see he was already greedily scrolling through his camera's memory.

"Wow," he breathed, turning around so we could see the photo. "This is stunning."

I had to agree with him. The background behind us, all of the different coloured Creole style buildings, gave the perfect setting to a picture of a young couple who were happy and the epitome of being in love. Both of us smiled not just with our mouths, but with our eyes, and the way my lips puckered up to kiss Makeysha's hand was the perfect vision of a lover's kiss, even if it was only to her hand.

"You two make a stunning couple," Dale said. "Thank you so much for this." He fished out a card from his back pocket. "If you want a copy, swing by my office in a couple of days and I'll print one off for you."

"Thank you," Makeysha said, taking the card. "It's a lovely picture. We'll see you soon."

Dale nodded before scurrying off towards a café on the other side of the street. Makeysha pushed the card down her cleavage before motioning towards the river.

"Shall we?" she said.

"Did you just put that card in between your boobs?" I asked, struggling not to laugh.

"It's not like I have any pockets."

"You only had to ask," I said, grinning. "I bet he would have had a heart attack if he'd seen where you put it."

She laughed and resumed walking towards the river. "Maybe. They're only breasts. They're really not that fascinating."

"That's because you're not a guy."

Shaking her head, she continued laughing. "If you say so."

"You got a surprise or something for me down there then?"

She frowned, then giggled. "No," she said, giving my shoulder a playful slap. "I meant if you say so to them being fascinating."

I grinned as we carried on ambling towards the river bank. "What did you do to him? When you touched him?"

"Nothing much," she said, shrugging her shoulders. "I just changed his aura and his energy so people would take him more seriously. I gave him a bout of luck, if you like."

"A bout of luck? You can do that?"

"Yes…why?"

"That's amazing. You've potentially just changed that guy's life with a brief two second touch. Do you have any idea how huge that is?"

"For him, yes. For me, not so much."

"How so?"

She pursed her lips for several seconds. "Think of it like rescuing animals. You can't save them all, right? You can't possibly change the whole world, but you can change the world for one animal at least. That's all it is. I've changed his world, but it's not affected mine in any way. If I rescued a stray dog, I changed the world for that dog, but not for me."

"That's a really odd comparison but I get your point. Do you not feel anything about the fact you've just changed his world?"

"No. I've just done my job, that's all."

"Your job?"

"Yes. Part of my angelic duties, aside from the soul's thing. I've selflessly helped him in his life. It's just part of what we do."

"So why don't you help everyone?"

"It's not that easy or that simple. First off, not everyone deserves a lucky break. Second of all, we have to like them as a person and want to help them. If we change someone's life and they do something horrific like murder a bunch of schoolkids, that comes back on us. We should have noticed they were a bad soul."

"I get it. So you see into their soul, so to speak?"

"That's exactly it. Well, their aura at least. Dale was full of joy and positivity, despite having been bullied, ignored, and teased for all of his life. That's a special person right there who deserves some divine intervention."

"You're amazing," I said. My heart clenched as I said it and my body ached to wrap her up in my arms and kiss her until the world melted away underneath us. "I can't believe my life has changed so much in less than twenty-four hours."

"In all honesty, neither can I. I've never been this lucky. I can only guess Fate has a part to play in this which makes me curious as to where exactly it's going."

"You speak of it like it's a person," I said.

"Fate is a woman. She split herself into three parts, ergo more commonly known as 'The Fates', but she's actually just one woman."

"Ergo."

"Yes. It's Latin for 'therefore'."

I smirked. "I know what it means. It's just been a long time since I heard anyone use it in a conversation."

"I've had a long time to study different languages. They fascinate me."

"You fascinate me."

She looked at me, her cheeks flushing pink. "You're going to have to quit the smooth dude routine whilst we're out in public."

"Why?" I asked, chuckling.

"Because not many people are keen on couples kissing in public."

"I know the perfect place we can kiss," I said, picking up the pace.

I rushed us down the street, ignoring the fact that we should be soaking in the different shops and sights to see. My head was solely focused on reaching that river and the peaceful banks where I knew there were benches to sit on so we could relish in each other's company.

We crossed the street, heading towards a water fountain feature with men playing instruments stood in the centre of it. The stone figures were all doing different things from playing a trombone to holding an umbrella. It was a pretty feature but didn't hold my interest more than getting Makeysha to myself and indulging in kissing her.

Running up a set of grey stone steps, we hurried across a car park and over a railroad crossing. Green grassy banks stretched to the left and right of us. A smooth path lay ahead, enticing us to walk along it. The Mississippi river extended out in front of us in all its glory for what seemed like miles. Along the path's edge, wrought iron benches sat every few feet, offering the perfect seating to enjoy the view. Dotted along the river banks were green gothic style lamp posts every twenty feet or so.

"I bet this is gorgeous at night," Makeysha said. "With all those lights lit up and the river lapping away at the banks."

"We could always come back tonight," I said, already feeling the romantic setting she'd hinted at.

"Let's see what the rest of the day brings first. We don't know if Wanda is going to have any problems and will need us."

"Such a pessimist," I said.

"No," she said, smiling. "I just don't want to be disappointed when my hopes and dreams are shattered."

I headed to the right down the path, thankful that not many people were around yet. Another hour or so and this place would be thriving with life. We strolled along, hand in hand, in a comfortable silence for a couple of minutes. Makeysha, to my left, continuously stared out across the bay.

"Isn't it just beautiful?" she said, her voice almost a breathless whisper.

"Brown water? Sure."

She giggled and shook her head. "No," she said. "Ignore the colours. Just look at the scenery. The open landscape, the rolling clouds, the fresh air, the peace and tranquillity being out here…it's just incredible." She pointed to the other side of the river at Algiers Point. "There's a whole other world happening over there. Don't you think that's amazing?"

I considered her point for a moment. "I guess it's kinda cool in a weird way that there's a bunch of people over there, going about their day, completely oblivious to everything around them." I sighed and then said, "Right now, as we stand here, someone is dying, someone is being born, someone is getting good news, someone else is being told something awful…don't you think that's odd?"

Makeysha nodded, a beaming grin across her face. "Within one huge world, there's millions of other little worlds, all interacting and colliding together, that as a whole, affect the big world. Life is incredible."

I squeezed her hand. "You're right. It is."

"Shall we sit?" she asked, pointing to an empty bench.

I led us over to it and sat down. The wrought iron was cold, even through my jeans. Makeysha huddled up next to me and I naturally slipped an arm around her. She let out a wistful sigh and then placed her head on my shoulder, gazing out over the peaceful scenery before us.

"How could anyone want to ruin this?" she said.

"What do you mean?"

"Lucifer. How could he want to let anything destroy this world? Why did he have to create such wicked creatures to wreck everything?"

"I guess his hatred for God supersedes anything and everything else. When you're so focused on something, nothing else comes into the equation."

"It's sad. I feel sad for them."

"Why?"

"Because they were such good friends. Now, it's just all turned so bad, it's sour and beyond repair. It shouldn't have to come to the point where innocent lives are in danger because of some ancient petty fallout."

"I agree, but unfortunately, that's the way it is."

She sighed and lifted her head. When she looked at me, her golden eyes were swimming with warmth and joy. "But there is one good thing."

"What's that?"

"If they'd never fallen out, angels wouldn't have come down to Earth…and you wouldn't exist."

I gave her a cheesy grin. "Now look who's coming out with all the smooth lines."

She laughed. "It must be you influencing me."

"I wonder what else I can influence you to do."

"Ha, nice try. Shut up and kiss me, smooth dude."

CHAPTER SEVENTEEN

Makeysha

We stayed on the bench for a good hour, sharing tender kisses and looking out over the river. The more time I spent with Ronin, the more rested my soul felt and the more hope filled my heart that maybe my life was going in a great direction at last.

The trials and tribulations that lay ahead of us were nothing but a speck in the back of my mind at this point. If Ronin insisted on coming through Lucifer's realms with me, which I had no doubt he would, then we would need to be as bonded as possible to stand any chance of surviving.

Some bad weather and heavy weights were a real lightened version of what I knew in my heart of hearts lay waiting for us.

"Come on," I said, standing up. "We're not seeing much of the city sat here. Time isn't our friend at the moment." I looked around me, wondering which way to head, when I caught sight of a building. My heart stopped dead. "Oh my goodness."

"What?" Ronin said, jumping to his feet. He whirled around, following my line of sight. "What's wrong?"

"That building…the cathedral…we have to go there, now."

"Ok, sure. Is there something I should know?"

Twenty feet or so from our bench was a set of steps leading to a rail road crossing. I ran towards it, dragging Ronin with me. As I reached the steps, the view of the cathedral opened up, the trees that partially blocked it before no longer in my line of sight.

"That's Gabriel's," I said, rushing down the steps.

We hurried across the wooden planks of the rail road crossing and across the car park. A tall white wall stood at the end of the car park, steps to the left and right taking us back up to what I thought was street level. I headed up the left-hand set, taking two at a time. We reached the top, enabling me to see the cathedral once again.

My heart hammered inside my chest. "It's an exact replica of the castle, my castle, in Heaven."

Various benches and potted plants were around me, everything neat and well cared for. A monument of an old cannon sat to our right, the words 'Washington Artillery Park' scribed into the front of it.

Ronin looked at it with interest, but he didn't understand my urgency. "We can come back later," I said. "I have to get inside that cathedral."

166

"Ok," he replied, turning his attention from the old piece of artillery. "But at least tell me why."

"Remember I said that the unicorn daggers were kept inside our castles?"

Ronin nodded.

"I don't think they were. At least not in Gabriel's case. I think he built this cathedral on Earth and hid it in there."

"So…"

"That means that the dagger we took from Lord Melrose is Gabriel's—Lucia said he was sent to New Orleans, remember? I didn't even think to look at each dagger to see which one belonged to who. If I get inside that cathedral, I can communicate with Gabriel."

"What exactly are you going to say to him?"

"I need to tell him what's going on. He won't have a clue. If he knows, then he can send help."

"You mean come down to Earth, him and all the other archangels, which is exactly where Lucifer wants them?"

"Earth, Heaven, it makes no difference to Lucifer. He'll get them one way or another."

He fell silent and allowed me to lead him away from the artillery park. We found another set of steps, leading back down to the street. Two lanes of busy traffic were in front of us, and on the other side of the street, dozens of horses and carts were lined up along the roadside, eagerly awaiting their next tourists to take around the city. I was almost tempted to indulge the romantic notion of going for a ride in one, but my focus on Gabriel's building was too great.

We waited for what felt like an eternity for a gap in the traffic. When one finally came, we dashed across the road, squeezing in between two waiting carriages, and power walked into the scenic park beyond.

Beautiful black wrought iron railings lined the park's boundary, complete with four intricately decorated lamp posts that also served as gate posts. A sign to the right read, 'Jackson Square'. In the centre of this neatly landscaped park stood a huge metal statue of a man on a rearing horse.

"That's gorgeous," I said, looking at the impressive feature with the cathedral as its background. "It's beyond words."

"It is quite something," Ronin said, gazing up at it as we neared its towering height. "But then again, so was that man."

I looked at him out of the corner of my eye. "Are you serious?"

"Yes. If it wasn't for him, the British wouldn't have retreated from New Orleans. In thirty minutes alone, the British lost two thousand men. Jackson lost barely a hundred. That deserves recognition for sure."

"Are you completely forgetting what he did to the Natives? You do know about the Trail of Tears, right?"

"Of course I do, I'm not an idiot. His conduct in one area of politics shouldn't belittle what he achieved in other areas. If he hadn't forced the British to retreat, could you imagine how different this place would be today?"

"Yes. And if he hadn't forcibly removed thousands of American Indians from their land, land that they'd lived on and cultivated for generations, could you imagine how different the country would be today?"

"That's a fair point, but the man still deserves to be honoured for what he did here."

I snorted. "Ok, so if I murder someone, but then

rescue a homeless dog, does that make my murder any less of a crime?"

He chuckled. "No, not at all. But they're completely unrelated incidents that say different things about you as a person. Besides, it's not like Jackson did it all on his own. White Americans all had the same attitude towards the Natives. They all wanted their land."

"But they were pushed and led by Jackson."

"So you think it wouldn't have happened if Jackson hadn't led them?"

"Perhaps not as violently as it did, no. And maybe not even on the same scale. Jackson viewed himself as above the law—that much is clear from his response to the Supreme Court's ruling. When you have someone as ignorant and arrogant as that trying to lead a movement, why would you oppose him when even the law can't control him?"

Ronin nodded. "Ok. You may have a point, I'll give you that."

I smirked. "I think we just had our first disagreement."

He lifted my hand to his mouth and kissed the back of it. "No…we shared a difference of opinion in a calm, intellectual discussion."

I burst out laughing as I tugged him towards the cathedral. "Smooth."

Wearing a goofy grin, he followed me past Jackson's aged monument and towards the cathedral. Beautiful white stone, black pointed roof turrets, and a demanding presence to it, St Louis Cathedral was a building that commanded attention.

"So how are you going to contact Gabriel exactly?" he said in a hushed voice.

"I just need to find the harp, then I can call him."

"The harp?"

"Yes," I said, dragging us towards the open door. "Each archangel has their own instrument that they excel at playing. Within each castle in Heaven, there is one of these instruments in the communal hall which when played, calls the archangel straight back to their castle. It's kind of like an emergency call. It must only be used in the direst of circumstances."

"What makes you think there will be one of those in here?"

"I just know there will be. Gabriel is a fantastic logician. He'd have put a fail safe in, just in case."

"But what if he hasn't?"

"I know he has."

"But—"

"Don't even say it," I said, pushing through a crowd of people milling around the outside of the door. "Stop being such a pessimist."

"Can I say I told you so when we don't find it?"

I turned to look at him and grinned. "Only if I can say the same when we do find it."

We stepped inside and both in unison we said, "Wow."

This cathedral was amazing. A vast open space lay before us, a perfectly polished black and white marble floor gleaming under the bright lights. Rows and rows of wooden pews, interspersed with fantastic white columns that supported an upper level balcony area either side of the cathedral. Stone ornamental angels stood at the back of the seating, almost like a gateway to the wooden seats beyond.

The ceiling was painted with intricate artwork detailing angels and God, its bright colours a stark contrast against the white background. At the very far end of the church was a centrepiece of an altar, almost to the point of being a shrine. I looked around me, my mouth open in admiration. This stunning piece of architecture was nothing short of Gabriel's work. Above the doors behind us, on the balcony level, sat an organ, its pipes promising nothing but sweet music.

"This is incredible," Ronin said. "Is it anything like the one in Heaven?"

"Very nearly as good," I replied, wondering where he would have hidden the harp. "I dare say he came here himself and painted this. He's quite the painter."

I scanned the space around me, looking for something, anything, that screamed out to me. Next to the large, solid pulpit, stood a table dressed in a white tablecloth. A donation bowl sat in front of an angel statue—an angel playing a harp.

"There," I said, rushing towards it like my life depended on it.

Ronin mumbled something under his breath as he followed me. I was going to wait until Gabriel appeared before I gave him my 'told you so' speech.

An old couple stood in front of the table, picking loose change out of their purses and putting it in the donation bowl. I needed them to move away so I could touch the harp in my own space. Once Gabriel answered my call, an invisible shield would fall around us, keeping anyone on the inside of it from the eyes of the human world.

We stood behind them, and as patient as I am, even I couldn't stop myself from foot tapping as they fussed over giving their money. After what felt like an age, they moved away, shuffling together as they discussed what to have to eat.

"Finally," I said, eyeing up the harp.

Ronin smirked at me but said nothing.

I reached out and with my right hand, wrapped it around the harp. I stroked my index finger along each of its fake strings. My body started vibrating, my angel powers humming through my veins. The harp warmed in my hand. A blinding beam of light shone straight down on us. Excitement coursed through my veins.

Glancing behind me, I saw a shimmering wall, invisible to anyone but supreme beings, surrounding the table and us. This was it—Gabriel had heard my call. I looked back up at the light and gasped as a shadow came into view at the very top of the light.

"He's coming!" I said, squeezing Ronin's hand. "I can't believe this has been here all this time. I could have contacted him so many times before now."

"Better late than never," he said, squeezing my hand back.

As the shadow took the form of an angel, falling closer and closer to us, I felt like screaming with joy. Tears welled up in my eyes. I hadn't realised quite how much I'd missed Gabriel until now.

The shadow became a body. The distinct white angel clothes came into view, glowing golden eyes, strong sinewy forearms, a broad muscled upper body, and then the handsome face…

I gasped.

The archangel landed before me, but this was not Gabriel.

"Makeysha," he said, his deep voice booming through my head. "It's been a long time."

My mouth dropped open. "Apnastin…"

CHAPTER EIGHTEEN

Ronin

"**T**he one and only," the angel replied. A sickly-sweet grin spread over his broad face. "I'm glad to see you haven't forgotten my name." He stepped forwards and reached for Makeysha's free hand. "I always felt like we had a connection."

Makeysha stepped back. My heart rate quickened, and worry flooded my gut. My hand tingled like I was being stabbed with thousands of hot pins. I realised then that Makeysha's overwhelming emotions were flowing into me through our connection.

"Easy, buddy," I said, taking a step in his direction. "I think you're scaring her."

Golden eyes settled on me, ablaze with surprise,

then annoyance. "Who are you?"

I immediately bristled. I didn't care for his tone at all. "Someone you need to worry about if you upset Makeysha."

He titled his head back and laughed. When he looked at me again, an amused smirk danced at the corners of his mouth. "And what exactly do you think you're going to do to me? You do know who I am, right?"

"I know you're an angel, yes."

"I'm all but considered an archangel, *hunter*, so I suggest you watch your attitude."

"'All but considered'? So you're not an archangel?"

Apnastin clenched his jaw. A muscle in his cheek began twitching erratically. I think I hit a nerve. "I deserve to be," he said, his voice cold and snappy. "I nearly was…"

His eyes glazed over as his memories clearly became a reality in his mind. I let him revel for a few minutes and then said, "Where I come from, nearly is only halfway and halfway is nowhere."

Makeysha stifled a giggle and clenched her hand. Apnastin's eyes were alight with burning ire in an instant. "You arrogant little human. How dare you mock me? Do you have any idea of the power I have at my very fingertips? I could make you disappear with one click of my fingers."

I shrugged my shoulders. "Go on then. Do your worst."

"Whoa, whoa, whoa," Makeysha said, stepping in between us. "This is getting out of hand." She let go of my hand, severing our connection. The sickly nausea feeling I'd had before still remained in my stomach, swirling around like a washing machine. "Apnastin, why are you here?"

"Because you called for me," he replied.

"No…I called for Gabriel."

A malicious smile spread over the angel's face. "Gabriel is a little…tied up at the moment."

My stomach dropped. My heart did a triple beat. With my hand still tingling like crazy, despite our skin no longer touching, I realised that our soulmate bond was only strengthening.

"Apnastin," Makeysha said, dropping her voice to a quiet, calm tone, as if she was talking to an upset child. "What has been happening? Where is Gabriel? And the other archangels?"

"A lot has happened since you left, Makeysha. I was offered my trials, for a chance to be an archangel. Do you know how gruelling they are? I thought I wouldn't survive some of them, but I did, I made it. And do you know what they did? When I reached the end and they all voted on whether I should join their ranks or not, they all turned me down. Every single one of them. I went through all of that and they turned me away."

Makeysha gave him a small smile tinged with sadness. "I can understand how that must have upset you, Apnastin. But they must have had their reasons."

"They said because I had fourteen lives and they all had below ten that I would be the odd one out and not see by the regular ranking angels as being worthy of archangel status. They said I wouldn't be taken seriously."

"But I thought the limits were set at fifteen?"

"Yes, they were. Not now. Now they've been 'adjusted' to ten or less."

"That's ridiculous."

"Exactly!" He reached out and grabbed her hands, cradling them in his. "I'm so glad you agree with me. I knew you would." Tears glistened over his eyes. "I wish I'd come to see you before now. I debated it nearly every day."

"So what's happened?"

"Well, I put them in a position where they had to take me seriously," he replied, snorting in disdain. "I spent years figuring out where they had hidden their unicorn daggers and one by one, I found them and threw them down to the one place I knew not one angel would dare venture."

"Earth."

He nodded. "Except, by the time I figured out where Gabriel had hidden his, he'd moved it—here. It took me a long time to find this place but when I did, boy was that a feather in my cap."

I couldn't help but think what a huge douche this guy was. He had some serious narcissistic issues, and then some.

"So where are the archangels now?" Makeysha said, her voice rising in panic.

"Up until a few days ago, they were still running their castles like nothing had happened. But with the blood moon coming, I need them prepared for Lucifer's return so they're currently sitting out the next few days, bound by ropes of Nephilim hair in the Pegasus fields."

Makeysha gasped. "Apnastin, no. You're working with Lucifer?"

He raised an eyebrow and gave her a look that implied she was stupid. "Well, yeah. No one else was going to take me seriously but I knew he would. Once

I let him back into Heaven, I'm going to have a seat at his side even higher than if I'd made it as an archangel."

"He's using you, Apnastin. He will kill you once he's finished with you."

"No, he won't. I've saved him. I've given him a door back into the kingdom he rightfully belongs in."

Makeysha shook her head vehemently, her black curls swinging from side to side. "Apnastin, you can't. You must stop this. Don't do this over some silly archangel trial."

Streaks of red flashed through his eyes. "'Some silly archangel trial?' I almost died, Makeysha. And you know how hard it is for us to die. I had to collect sun flakes. Do you have any idea how difficult that is? Let alone trying to tame a minotaur or navigate a maze of mirrors with a Medusa running around inside. They need to realise that I am capable of much more than they think I am, and they need teaching a lesson."

"Lucifer is going to kill them," Makeysha said.

"I know." He shrugged his shoulders. "And?"

"That's not teaching someone a lesson. That's murder."

"So were those trials."

"Don't make this any more difficult than it needs to be, please."

"I'm not…but you are. I know you have one of my daggers. I need it returning to Lucifer immediately."

"Where is God?"

"Shut himself away in the Gardens of Eden. Haven't seen him for years. With the archangels missing, the clans are wandering around, aimless and lost." He pulled Makeysha's hands towards his chest, yanking her into him. "And this is all because of me.

Don't you see how powerful I am? You don't want to be on the wrong side of me."

"Apnastin," she said, wriggling her hands free from his grip. "This is wrong. You need to release the archangels and cease your communication with Lucifer immediately."

"No can do," he said, shaking his head. "I need my dagger back, Makeysha."

Makeysha shook her head and stepped back. "That's not happening."

"If you don't give me that dagger, you can consider yourself at war with me."

"Then so be it." She glared at him with everything she had, her golden eyes were glowing with furious determination. "I'm not letting you take out an entire world because of some stupid grudge."

"What world?"

"This world," she said, opening her arms and motioning around her. "Lucifer wants nothing more than to destroy Earth to get back at God."

"So what if he does? We're so much more powerful than these stupid little critters anyway. There's no point in them at all. They're nothing but an ant farm, something for God's amusement."

"They're living breathing beings, Apnastin. They have a right to life just like anything else."

"Unfortunately, Makeysha, in war, there are always casualties. Collateral damage if you will. It just so happens that this world is caught in the middle of a powerful war. What is it they say here? Shit happens?"

"The statue."

The words rang through my mind like a church bell tolling the hour.

"What?" I replied.

"The statue. Break the statue. It will send him back."
"What?"
"NOW!"

A wave of urgency pushed me into action. I surged forwards, bumping into Makeysha. She fell into Apnastin, knocking him off balance. I grabbed a hold of the golden statue and smashed it against the white brick pillar behind it.

Apnastin shouted, "No!" as a violent gust of wind sucked him back up into the heavens. Makeysha snatched a hold of my hand and cast a bubble of pink magic around us. I watched, in awe, as people stood pointing and staring at the broken statue that had somehow smacked itself against the bricks and shattered into hundreds of pieces. A couple of people even ran from the cathedral screaming the devil was here.

"We're invisible in this," Makeysha said, motioning at our bubble of magic. "I didn't see a quick-thinking way out of that one."

"Instead dozens of people are wondering how a statue broke itself?"

She smirked. "It'll give the 'ants' something to think about."

I chuckled at her as she led me out of the beautiful building. When we reached the doors, she merged us into the back of the tour group currently exiting the cathedral. With one wave of her hand, our invisible shield was gone, and we were back in plain sight again.

"Oh," I said, pouting. "That could have been so much fun."

She giggled. "Unfortunately, it takes a lot of energy to keep one of those up."

"Maybe we can find a use for it in the future," I

replied, grinning and winking.

"I don't think I'd have the energy to do that and *that*," she said, giggling. "I'd be all drained out within minutes."

"Hey, two minutes is all I need to show a girl a good time."

She spluttered with laughter. "Wow. A whole one hundred and twenty seconds of passion. I am such a lucky woman. How can I ever thank the Universe enough?"

"I don't know…but you can thank me with one hundred and twenty kisses if you like."

"Oh really? And why would I do that?"

"Because I've just spotted our third dagger."

CHAPTER NINETEEN

Makeysha

I gasped. "Where?"

"Our tour guide isn't quite so human. Which means he probably just saw our whole interaction with your lovely angel friend back there."

The incident with Apnastin had left me reeling. I'd never in a million years have considered him any kind of threat. He seemed so genuine and true in the few weeks I'd known him before everything happened. The fact he was behind part of Lucifer's plan had slotted some jigsaw pieces into place. Now I knew Lucifer was being handed the archangels on a plate, things just got a whole lot more complicated for us.

I looked over the twenty or so human heads in front of me, focusing on the tour guide. He seemed human enough—at a glance. His aura was tinged with the grey edge of a regular human, his appearance also that of a regular human, but his eyes gave him away. As he turned around to smile and wave at his herd of tourists, the sun shone into his eyes, highlighting the emerald green energy hiding behind them.

"Lasander," I whispered. "Sneaky boy."

Ronin shrugged his shoulders. "He's just doing what elves do best—hiding in plain sight."

"And hypnotising a load of people to follow him to their deaths."

"Creature's gotta eat."

I looked at him out of the corner of my eye. "Since when are you a creature sympathiser?"

"I'm not," he said, grinning. "I'm just saying he's doing what he does best."

"Well, at least it's not a bunch of kids," I said, sighing. "It could be worse."

Ronin looked at me and frowned.

"The Pied Piper of Hamelin," I said, smirking. "You're looking at him."

Ronin's mouth dropped open. "No…really?"

I nodded. "He still uses his flute now and again."

"How do you know that?"

"Because I can hear it. Wherever he is, if he plays that supernatural instrument, I can hear it. It's almost like I'm being warned so I can do something about it."

"Have you ever tried?"

Sadness and shame clenched my heart. "No…there comes a point where you have to understand that the circle of life does indeed have to play a part. This world is seriously over populated. Tragic things are sometimes the natural way of cleaning that up. When we ascend to Heaven, it's one of the first things we learn to understand. There has to come a point where we can't interfere and sometimes, we have to let things play out."

"I get that, but creatures aren't natural."

"No…but they've fit into the ecosystem as if they are."

"If that's the way you think then why are you so concerned about Lucifer?"

"Because killing all or most of this world is just plain wrong. Population control for a natural order of life is exactly that—a part of life. The Universe will have written into their soul journeys that that's an experience of death they must have, so it happens."

"Following an elf to their deaths is a part of their soul journey?"

"For some, yes. For others, being eaten by a shark is an experience they must have or dying peacefully in their sleep. It's whatever the Universe feels that soul needs in order to move on from this realm."

He fell silent as we continued following the tourists across the street towards a cute looking café. A big neon sign blinked above the door with 'Hamelin's Café' in a rainbow of bright colours.

"Nothing like being obvious is there?" Ronin said, chuckling.

"Like you said—hiding in plain sight."

"I'm curious," he said, folding his arms over his chest. "How is he going to explain the disappearance of twenty people from his café?"

I smiled. "He's not. Inside that building there will be music playing over a sound system, much like any other place these days. Unfortunately, what those poor people don't realise is that the music will slowly infiltrate their sub conscious, so over the course of the next seven days, they will all die in different ways. However, because Lasander's music will be deep within them, their souls will call to him when they pass. Then it's just a matter of going around and cleaning up."

Ronin visibly shuddered. "Eating human flesh...I can't even..." he started retching "...it's disgusting."

I giggled at him. "He probably has the same reaction to you eating vegetables. They are 'of the land' remember. When you bury someone, where do you think they...go?"

"But that's different."

"How is it?"

"Because..."

I gave him several seconds to continue, but he didn't. "When a body...decays, it does so into the earth. Mother Nature is effectively soaking back in what she gave out all those years ago. When Lucifer made the elves from the land, he technically made them walking, talking versions of Mother Nature."

His eyes wandered off into a far away place as he thought about my words. I could see him trying to work it out—another Circle of Life.

"Think of it like this," I said. "When a bird is alive, it eats ants. When the bird dies, the ants eat the bird. It's—"

"The circle of life."

I nodded. "Cruel, I know, but that's the way it is. Death is an ugly truth, whilst Life is a beautiful lie."

He looked at me and smiled. "I like that. That's really...poetic."

As we neared the café, delicious smells of freshly baked bread and warm cookies enveloping us, I realised we had no plan of action.

"What's the idea here?" I said, watching Lasander open the door for his new victims.

"He's here for a reason," Ronin said. "And I presume it's to do with Lord Melrose."

"He will know we're not human."

Ronin nodded. "I figured. I'm curious to see what he's going to do when we reach the door."

"You don't actually want to go in that place?"

"I will if I have to, but I don't think it'll get that far."

As the crowd in front of us thinned out and we neared the smiling King of Elves, I soaked in his appearance. He hadn't changed one bit over all the years I'd known of his existence. He still looked as fresh and youthful as the day Lucifer set him free upon the Earth. Of course, back then I hadn't known quite how important he was. To me, he was just another dreadful creature to avoid at all costs.

Tall and slim, he stood a head above the humans. His long straight silvery hair shone like a piece of jewellery under the sun's bright rays. His clothes were a mix of dark green and brown, complete with rigger boots. He looked like he'd just finished a day's hunting out in the back country.

"Well, well, well," Lasander said as we stood in front of him. "If it isn't an angel and a hunter. Quite the story."

His silky-smooth voice coated me in warmth. Had I been human, he would have soothed me into relaxing around him in an instant. It was easy to see, with that hypnotising voice and those sparkling eyes, how humans fell prey to him within seconds—especially females.

"King of the Elves in New Orleans," Ronin

replied. "Now that is also quite the story. You're supposed to be in Canada."

Lasander's eyes glistened with joy. "My duties in Canada are very much complete. I'm ahead of schedule so I thought I'd make a quick pitstop to ensure I have a good meal once my next job is complete."

"Ah," I said, smirking. "You mean guarding one of the realms that Lucifer created?"

He narrowed his eyes at me. "What do you know of that?" he said, his tone clipped and curt.

"More than you realise. Hand it over, Lasander, and I promise I won't hurt you."

Tipping his head back, he let out a slow chuckle. "I'm afraid if you want that dagger, dear Angel, you will have to kill me first."

"That's not a problem," I replied, crossing my arms over my chest. "I've already killed one of you."

He sucked in a deep breath. "I sincerely hope for your sake that you are telling some sort of joke."

"Unfortunately, I'm not."

"Do you have any idea what Kaspar will do to you?" he said, hissing like a peed off snake. "He has the wrath of a thousand demons at the best of times, let alone when a shamed angel has killed his twin sister."

I grinned. "Oh, Lucia is very much alive. Just for the record, I'm really not too worried about Kaspar. I've fried bigger fish."

Lasander lifted his lips into a wry smile revealing two rows of pearly white teeth. "I love your bravado, but you must be mistaking me for someone who can't see your aura and your lies."

I snorted. "I'm an angel—I don't have one."

"Oh, but you do, Sweetness. I'm guessing it's

something to do with your part human soulmate here."

My head swirled. I hadn't even considered the negative effects that being paired with a human could have. The delight at people being able to see me had completely overruled my mind and the fact that other things would be going on. Ronin hadn't had an aura when we first met, but I guessed our strengthening connection was quickly changing that. How though, I wasn't sure.

"Where's the dagger?" Ronin said, taking the heat off me for a moment.

"You mistake me for someone who is intimidated by a part human part angel abomination." He leaned forwards and lowered his voice to a sinister murmur. "Do you know how many of your kind I've *enjoyed* over the years? There's something about the tinge of angelic power that makes your flesh so much sweeter." He ran his tongue over his lips and straightened back up. "I could snap your neck with the flick of my wrist, *hunter.*"

"You don't scare me," Ronin said, his voice nothing but menacing. "I suggest if you value your life, you hand it over and leave."

Lasander turned his head to look at me, effectively severing his conversation with Ronin. "So if you didn't kill Lucia, who did you kill?"

Still reeling from the possibility that I wasn't as invincible as I thought, I answered on autopilot. "Lord Melrose."

Silence hung in the air for several seconds. Lasander held an excellent poker face but his aura fell into clouds of murky grey. He was confused as to what to do next. "So I presume you have his dagger?"

"Now that would be telling."

"Don't treat me like a fool," Lasander replied.

"Yes," I said, giving him a sly smile. "I have his dagger."

Lasander pursed his lips. "And Lucia is compromised?"

"I never said anything about her."

"You said she's very much alive which means you know more about her than what you're letting on."

"You elves are sometimes too intelligent for your own good," I said.

"If you have compromised one of the Twins, then I may have to rethink my position."

I raised my eyebrows. Well, this was a turnaround. "What exactly are you saying?"

"If Lucifer isn't the only power in play here, his security isn't what he declared it to be."

"Basically," Ronin said, a wide grin spreading over his face. "You're more concerned about saving your own ass."

"Elves are survivors," Lasander replied. "We go with where the best odds lay. If you have killed Lord Melrose and somehow compromised one of the Twins, Lucifer's guarantees of a risk-free mission are nothing but empty words."

"And you think we're going to trust you? Just like that?" I said. "We have two daggers. Lucifer still has more than we do."

"Without all seven, Lucifer has nothing. It's an all or nothing deal. If you have the ability to intercept his plans this early on, then his assurances mean nothing to me and the odds of him fulfilling his dreams are becoming slimmer with each passing second."

"And you want to be on the winning side of the fence."

"Of course. It's common sense. The best way

to—"

"Survive," Ronin said. "We get it. We're only going to even consider your quick change of sides if you hand over what we came for."

Lasander reached into his back pocket and pulled out exactly what we were looking for—the third unicorn dagger. Not trusting this guy one bit, I stepped back, more than cautious of the weapon he was offering on an open hand.

Ronin swiped it from the King's long, slender fingers and stepped back. "We're going to put this somewhere safe. I suggest you stay here. If we have questions, we will expect you to answer them."

"Of course," Lasander said. "I plan on going nowhere."

We backed away but I kept an eye on the sly elf, just in case he tried something, but he didn't. That had been far easier than expected. What the hell was going on?

ANGEL OF THE CRYPT

CHAPTER TWENTY

Ronin

For what had started out as such a beautiful day, it had quickly turned into something unnerving and obscure. It seemed that this looming apocalyptic event would follow us around like a dark shadow until it was fully dealt with.

I felt bad for Makeysha. All I'd wanted to do was let her relax and enjoy our time together. I wanted to get to know her better and I wanted our bond to strengthen as much as possible before we ended up in the realms of Hell.

Now, she was facing the reality of being part human, which greatly reduced her chances of survival against the tests waiting for us in Lucifer's twisted realm. As much as I joked about us becoming intimate, I didn't want to take anything away from what it should mean. It shouldn't be anything but two souls connecting, but the rate things were changing it was soon going to mean life or death for the both of us. I didn't want to jump into bed with her for the sake of it—I wanted it to be as right as she did. After all, you only get one first time with someone.

"Back to Wanda?" I said, glancing back over my shoulder at the Hamelin Café.

Makeysha nodded.

Seeing Lasander scoot inside his building, I began to wonder if he was being genuine. We hurried back to Wanda's, arriving in less than ten minutes. I burst through the front door and stopped dead in my tracks. Makeysha bumped into me as I'd blocked the entire doorway with my abrupt stop.

"What the…?" she said, as she peered over my left shoulder.

In front of me was Lucia, on her knees, scrubbing the wooden floor with a soft bristle brush and a bucket of soapy water.

"Have we stepped into a real-life version of Cinderella?" I whispered.

"Please be careful," Lucia said, looking up at us. "The floor is wet and slippery. I would hate for you to slip and fall."

Makeysha stifled a giggle.

Wanda came flying through from the living room doorway, her hair sticking up in all directions. I raised an eyebrow at her pink sweatpants and grey tank top.

"Oh hi," she said, waving her duster at us. "Just doing some house chores. I didn't expect you back so early. Everything ok?"

I held up the unicorn dagger. The tin of polish and the duster Wanda was holding clattered to the floor.

"Oh my," she said, rushing forwards. "Where did you get that?"

"Lasander. He handed it over quite freely."

"And," Makeysha said. "We know that Lord Melrose's dagger belonged to Gabriel. Can we see it and Lucia's to figure out which three we have?"

Wanda's mouth fell open. "Sounds like you've had quite the day. Let's have some coffee whilst you fill me in."

"The daggers," Makeysha said. "Can you fetch the ones we already have?"

"Of course," Wanda replied, giving her a warm smile. "Bring me up to speed first and then I'll get them."

Several minutes later, we sat on the sofas with steaming mugs of coffee in hand. Wanda listened intently as we told her what had happened with Lasander.

"I have to say, I'm not surprised. Elves are sly and loyal to no one but themselves. He obviously feels that we have a winning hand here. This is really good news."

"It's not though, is it?" Makeysha said. "Even though Lucifer needs all the daggers, the fact we have three of them only means he's going to come after us with a greater vengeance. For all we know, Lasander is filling him in on what we do and don't have. I don't trust him."

"You're right not to," Wanda said. "He will turn on you just as quickly as he has done Lucifer. But you can guarantee one thing—whilst he's on your side, you can bet he's weighed the odds in your favour."

"Even if we retrieve all seven daggers," I said. "Lucifer is still going to come after us. He's always going to be intent on carrying out this crazy plan of his."

"If we have all seven, that's a lot of hassle. Combined with the fact of where we're going to hide them, he has no chance of ever getting his grubby hands on them," Makeysha said, giving me a reassuring smile.

"You think Lucifer is worried about 'lots of hassle'?" I said.

"If he even discovers where we've hidden them, he's not going to risk his life, seven times, by going after them," she replied.

I scrunched my face up in confusion. "Have I missed something here?"

"Why?"

"Why would going after seven unicorns be life threatening for him?"

"Because they're guarded by pixies."

I raised my eyebrows. "Of course they are."

Makeysha narrowed her eyes at my flat deadpan response. "Did I not mention that before?"

"Does this look like the face of a man who knows that deadly flying miniature ninja's protect the thing he's got to slit open to hide a sacred weapon inside of?"

She grinned at me. "I would say no."

"Pixies," I said, sounding the word out for my own sake. "Pixies protect unicorns. Of course they do. Do you know how much I hate them damn things?"

"Why? They're an excellent ally if you can get them on side."

"The key word there was 'if'."

"Leave them to me. We'll be fine."

I took a swig of my coffee and then asked, "Have you ever been stabbed by a pixie? Or rather, a swarm of pixie's?"

"I can't say that I have," she replied, giving me a sly smirk.

"You do know that some hunters are allergic to the toxins they have laced their tiny little weapons with? And they've died within minutes."

"Are you allergic to their toxins?"

"No...but I suffered some seriously disturbing hallucinations after being attacked by a horde of them. I was out of it for nearly a week trapped in my own living hell. That is not something I wish to revisit."

"Awww, poor baby." She wrapped a hand around my forearm and gave me a playful smile. "Don't worry. I'll protect you from the nasty little pixies."

"You're not funny."

Wanda giggled into her coffee mug. "I think you're missing a key point there."

"What?" I said.

"Pixie's are lethal to *all* living things—including supernatural creatures. Lucifer isn't excluded from that judging from what Makeysha has just said."

My brain kicked into overdrive. "So we could use them to what? Keep him at bay or something?"

"Better. Lock him inside Tartarus."

"Whoa," Makeysha said. "Now that's a big step."

"But it would work, and we would never have to worry about him coming after those daggers again."

"Surely the fact that the pixies protect the unicorns would be enough," Makeysha replied. "What's the point in going through all the extra trouble?"

"Security. As long as he's free, there's always a

chance he's going to come after the daggers again. If you lock him away as well as hiding the daggers in the unicorns, then it's like an extra layer of protection. It's the fact he's got to get out of Tartarus and then face a pack of pixies."

"If he gets out of Tartarus, a load of pixies isn't going to faze him," Makeysha replied.

"That's a fair point. But they are still capable of killing him?" Wanda said.

"If they make enough contact with him, yes. I personally know of three angels who have died from pixie attacks. It's one of the hazards of catching a unicorn, unfortunately."

"What makes you think you can deal with them?" I said.

"I saved their Queen from death a very long time ago. They are less hostile towards me than others, but they are very untrusting creatures. If I make one wrong move, they will attack me."

"Don't they have like a secret love or something?"

"Like what?"

"I don't know…like horses love carrots and apples and dogs love prime cuts of beef."

"Lavender," she said, a warm smile lighting up her golden eyes. "They're always wearing lavender in some form. That's their thing."

"So give them a bunch of lavender as a sweetener."

She gave me a look of disbelief. "They live in lavender fields."

"Oh."

"Yes," she said, lifting an eyebrow. "However, lavender juice is something they struggle to make because of the processes involved. That could be a way in."

"Lavender juice?" Wanda said, rubbing her chin between her thumb and forefinger.

Makeysha nodded.

"I can make lavender juice real easy."

"This could work," Makeysha said. "But I do feel like we're making ourselves more work than necessary."

"I think it would be good to have it as a back up plan. You know, keep it in mind," I said. "We have no idea how the next few days are going to turn out. It could be our only option."

"Ok," she said. "Plus, the lavender juice will come in handy for getting close to the unicorns."

"Speaking of unicorns," I said, holding up an index finger like I was back in class. "How the hell are we supposed to get anywhere near them? Let alone hide something inside them?"

"Well, it's a little bit tricky. You have to look them in the eye. Once you do that, they will instantly become calm and docile. The problem is getting them to catch your eye. They will do everything to avoid it."

I wasn't quite sure how a horse could avoid someone's eye contact, but my knowledge of horses didn't extend past knowing they had four legs, a head, and a tail. To me, the fact they had a horn protruding from their forehead made them nothing more than a horse with a horn. I found myself wishing I had some sort of an affinity with animals so I could guarantee neither of us would be impaled by an angry unicorn.

Then I had a dawning realisation. "Caesar!" I shouted, jumping to my feet in excitement. "If we find Caesar and get him on side, we can use him to control the unicorns."

Makeysha looked up at me and grinned.

"Please tell me a wizard's power will work on a sacred animal?" I said, trying to quash the rising hope inside me.

"It certainly will."

"Then surely that's all we need to do—he's our answer."

"I knew there was a reason the Universe tied me to you," she said. "Good call."

"So how do we find Caesar?"

Wanda cleared her throat. "I might be able to help with that."

"Really?" I said. "How?"

"My father was a wizard…I inherited some of his abilities."

I sucked in a deep breath. "Wanda…how did you…why…are you sure?"

"Very much so. He had to leave home when I was just a little girl, so I don't remember much about him, but every now and then I get glimpses of him through the eyes of an animal. It's almost as if they're trying to let me know that he's still alive and he's ok."

Cross-supernatural species breeding was a strictly off-limits area. The fact that Wanda even existed and had lasted on the earth as long as this was something of a miracle. No one knew why Lucifer didn't permit cross-breeding, just that any hint of it was rapidly stomped out and the offspring destroyed.

"How have you…survived all these years?"

"Oh, I'm not alone," Wanda said, smiling. "There are scores of us. Those who perished lacked the help of a witch or the essence of witch DNA. Thankfully, we had enough knowledge and support around us to hide ourselves from Lucifer and his demons."

Wanda was quickly turning out to be a treasure chest of information. "Is there some way you can connect with other wizards or something then?" I asked.

"No, but I can project an image of him out into the minds of animals. When they respond positively, I simply lock on to their geographical location."

"You make it sound so easy."

"It is."

"It sounds complicated to me."

"I promise you, it's really not."

"Do you need anything?"

She shrugged her shoulders. "Just the usual. Map, candles, incense sticks, and some blood."

I raised an eyebrow. "What blood?"

"My blood. The fact we share abilities means we're connected, even though its remotely."

It all sounded difficult and way out of my depth. "When can you do it?"

"I can do it now."

I sat back down and wrung my hands together. "Well, only if it's not too much trouble."

"Nothing is too much trouble for you, dear."

I smiled at her. "Thank you, Wanda. You have no idea how much I, we, appreciate this."

Makeysha stood up and gave us both a flat smile. "I'm going to take a walk. I need some time to myself."

Something deep in my gut wrenched tight. "Is that a good idea?"

"I'll be fine. There's just so much going on, I need time to digest it all and think things through. Come at it all from a different angle."

Every instinct screamed at me to keep her by my side, but being the gentleman I am, I respected her wishes for some privacy. "If you need me, you call me straight away."

"I will, but I'll be ok." She stepped forwards and took my hand. *"Don't let that dagger out of your sight."*

I arched my eyebrows in surprise. *"What? Why?"*

"Just promise me. Please?"

"Ok…are you sure you're ok?"

"Yes. I just need an hour or two in my own space."

She leaned forward and pressed a light kiss over my lips. Then, in the blink of an eye, she was gone.

CHAPTER TWENTY-ONE

Makeysha

Well, my strange little scenario just became a whole lot more complicated. I teleported myself back to my homely crypt and my divine bed. As I collapsed into the lightweight fluffiness, I let out a huge breath and imagined all my worries leaving my body at the same time.

It hadn't ever crossed my mind, up until about half an hour ago, that Wanda might not be the innocent, helpful witch that Ronin and I took her to be. Men weren't as perceptive as women when it came to two-faced situations or passive aggressive circumstances. However, the tight-lipped smile she gave when I asked her the second time for the daggers didn't go unnoticed. It was a warning not to go there again.

Then when she admitted that she's an illegal cross-breed that even Lucifer won't tolerate, the alarm bells started ringing. I'd heard, in my time in Heaven, that even soulmates can learn to shield their thoughts from one another. All they had to do was mentally envision a wall around their minds and all of their personal musings being kept inside it. I'd spent the last half an hour willing this to be true and controlling my surging doubts behind a cast iron mental shield. Other than my last words to Ronin just now, it appeared to have worked.

I needed some time and space to figure out what to do if my growing suspicions were true. Whilst I'd spent all of my time alone on earth, I hadn't been immune to whispers and rumours going on in the supernatural world. I'd merely chosen to ignore it all and carry on in my own little bubble.

Cross-breeds were exactly as Wanda said—there were scores of them, and the survivors were either part witch or had the help of witches. That made things difficult. What exactly a small army of cross-breeds would want with seven archangel daggers was beyond me—at the moment. The way things were playing out, falling nicely into place, made me wonder how much of this Wanda had orchestrated.

I'd lived in this abandoned cemetery for years. Admittedly, I'd kept myself to myself, but it made me wonder if Wanda knew I'd been here all along. Had she called Ronin here on purpose? Had she even somehow made sure Lord Melrose was in the right place at the right time? Everything just seemed like a massive coincidence. One seed of doubt had unravelled a spiral load of conspiracies and possibilities.

Regardless of what Wanda had or hadn't forced to happen, the question still remained of what to do and the best way to go forwards from here. I stared up at the ceiling of my cosy crypt and closed my eyes for the briefest of moments.

***

I opened my eyes to find myself in a lavish garden. A grey path stretched out before me. Neatly trimmed knee-high privet hedges lined the walkway. Blooming trees arched over the path from both sides, their scores of colourful flowers filling me with joy and wonder. Reds, yellows, pinks, and purples dotted around me in various different forms from roses and lilies to amaryllis and orchids. Everything was vibrant and overflowing with beauty and life.

Glancing around me in awe, I saw nothing but the long footpath I'd seemingly appeared in the middle of. As far as my eye could see, this particular scenery repeated itself for miles, nothing but a sea of colourful nature.

"Hello, Makeysha."

I turned around at such a rate, I nearly fell over. Stood a few feet in front of me was God. The dark hair I'd last seen him with was gone, his trademark sunshine yellow hair back in place. His golden eyes burned brightly but they seemed tinged with sadness. He looked…tired.

"Oh!" I said. "H…hi."

"I understand you may be a little surprised to see me after all this time."

"A little?" I folded my arms over my chest. "I

think that's the understatement of all time."

He lifted his arms and motioned around him. "I've brought you to the only safe place I knew we could have this discussion."

Something clicked into place in my mind. Apnastin had told me where God was. "The Gardens of Eden."

"The one and only."

"Is this it?" I asked, pointing at the single path.

"No," he said, a small smile lifting the edges of his mouth. "This is merely one walk I'm very fond of. Perhaps another time I will take you on a complete tour, but our time here is limited so we must be quick."

"Why are you suddenly acknowledging me after all this time? You threw me out of Heaven. Now you want to chat?"

"I need your help."

I snorted. "*You* need *my* help? What could I possibly do for you that you can't do for yourself?"

"Heaven is in a state of chaos. It needs a leader. My time has long since passed. Since Apnastin revolted, no one will even listen to me."

"So you've what? Shut yourself away in here? That's not what a leader does."

"I've lost my edge. I'll admit that. The angels can sense it and they won't listen to me. Lucifer is running riot, plaguing Earth with his demonic creations. I'm expected to act on it, but I can't...I don't know what to do. You...you're not afraid to stand up for what you believe in, regardless of the cost. I don't have that in me. I was so angry all those years ago, all I could see were the qualities you were lacking instead of the qualities you have."

His compliments were lost on me. Too little, too

late. "If you don't know what to do, what exactly do you expect me to do?"

"The right thing."

I screwed my face up in confusion. "What is that supposed to mean?"

"You have the heart of a lion, the courage of ten archangels, and the determination to succeed in whatever you put your mind to. I have faith that you can do what is needed."

"Ha," I said, chuckling. "That is not what you said to me before."

"No, I know that, and I admit I was wrong."

Memories of my time in Heaven flooded back to the front of my mind; one scene in particular from within my own castle. "I do believe I heard you tell Gabriel once that I had 'the charisma of a goat'."

His cheeks flushed with heat. "Well there are some who find goats charming…"

"You're not making this any better."

"I'm sorry." He ran a hand through his perfectly groomed blonde hair. "Look, let's not dwell on what has been, let's think about what is yet to happen."

"Which is?"

"Well, Lucifer wants to kill me, and the way things are going, he's going to succeed."

"And you want my help?"

He nodded.

"To do what exactly?"

"Make sure he doesn't kill me."

I laughed. I couldn't help myself. "And how do you expect me to do that?"

"Well, you've already started by collecting the daggers."

My stomach clenched with uncertainty. Everyone

seemed to be after the daggers but all for different reasons. "What do you want with the daggers?"

"Well they need to be returned to their rightful homes."

I narrowed my eyes at him. "Why don't I believe you?"

He gave me a brilliant smile and said, "It's only natural for you to be suspicious and paranoid. You have spent a long time on your own."

The way he said it made me even more suspicious of him. "No. You want the daggers for your own reasons."

"You're entitled to your opinions, I understand that now, and I was wrong to remove you from your home because you disagreed with me."

I raised my eyebrows. "And?"

"And what?"

"You've spent the last five minutes trying to convince me how I should help you and how you were so wrong in what you did to me, but not once have I heard the word 'sorry' come out of your mouth."

His jaw dropped. "I...I'm sorry."

"Kind of doesn't have much meaning to it now." I took a step back and thought over the conversation we'd just had. Then the penny dropped. "All you want is for me to do your dirty work so you can take all the credit and get control of Heaven again. That's it, isn't it? If all of Heaven thinks you've retrieved the daggers, they'll look at you as being mighty again when the reality is you need an angel from the bottom of the barrel to save your ass." I shook my head. "You disgust me. You're as despicable as Lucifer."

He closed the gap between us, his hands outstretched, and his face covered with desperation.

"I'll promote you. Give you your own clan. Anything you want."

"Of course you will. Because that won't scream you've had help."

"Doesn't our history mean anything?" he said, clasping his hands together as if he was praying. "Why won't you help me?"

Anger burned my soul. It bubbled inside me like a volcano waiting to erupt. "Why wouldn't you help me? I think you need to live two thousand years in all but solitary conditions, then come back to me and have this discussion."

"Angels are higher beings. The whole point of entering Heaven is that you've moved on from negative emotions. You've learned how to forgive and let go. You're better than this, Makeysha. You can't be an angel and hold a grudge. It's a total paradox."

I unfolded my wings and glared at him. "Well, here I am, in all my angelic glory, and my grudge is still firmly in place. It's an actual thing whether you like it or not."

"Do I have to pull rank on you again?" he said. A dark streak of power flitted through his golden eyes. "I will do whatever it takes. Don't push me."

I tipped my head back and laughed. "You can't do anything to me that would cause me more pain than the past two thousand years. You can't kill me because you need me. I would say that puts us at a stale mate."

A sickly-sweet smile spread over his pink lips. "You're right—I can't kill you. But I definitely can kill half of you."

Ronin. Nausea hit me with the force of a dozen minotaurs. "You lay one finger on him and I'll kill you myself."

"Fraternising with humans is strictly forbidden."

I smirked. "Indeed it is. Tell me, how is Joshua these days?"

The air around us suddenly became charged with danger. His face darkened, his hair started gaining streaks of black, and his eyes dulled as obscure shadows fought through his golden irises.

"Are you refusing to help me?"

I considered his question and all the possible answers carefully. After several strained, silent minutes, I replied, "No, but I'm also not saying I will help you. Neither am I saying I will help Lucifer either. I don't agree with either of you having the daggers."

"Well, I never thought history would repeat itself in this scenario again. Once more you refuse to take sides. I admire your tenacity."

I narrowed my eyes at him and ignored his statement. "I'm wondering what would make you so desperate as to call me here. What would make God feel so hopeless that he has to turn to Heaven's reject for help?"

"Look," he said, his tone sharp and demanding. "It took all of my power to summon you here. I wasn't kidding when I said we don't have long. My power is waning, and I need to send you back. What's your answer, Makeysha?"

I frowned as his words circled around and around in my mind. "What do you mean 'it took all of my power'?"

He fell silent and dropped his gaze to the smooth pavement under our feet.

As I waited for him to reply, pieces of the puzzle started to slot into place. "Oh my goodness," I said, sucking in a deep breath. "You're powerless…the angels…Heaven…no one has any faith in you anymore, do they? And all of your power comes from their faith.”

He lifted his eyes back to mine. All of the ire slipped away leaving nothing but despondency in its place. “I'm stuck in here,” he said, lifting his arms and motioning at the Gardens. “I don't even have enough power to get myself out of my own Gardens.” He gave a sad chuckle as he shook his head. “It's taken me fifty years to save up the power to call you here, Makeysha. Purely saved on what I get from humans.”

Thousands of humans followed God, but their faith in him gave him little power. Angelic faith is where he received the majority of his force. “This is quite the turn around of events. I would think about saying I'm sorry to see you like this but from my paradoxical grudge holding point of view, I would class this as karma.”

He sighed and raised his hand. “I tried. That's enough for me.”

He snapped his thumb and forefinger together, ejecting me at a rate of knots from the serene beauty of the Gardens of Eden.

***

I woke with a start, gasping for breath. My mind raced with my vivid dream. Had it just been a dream or had I really been there? As I debated this, a red rose petal floated down from the ceiling and landed on my lap. I smiled, wondering if that had sapped the last of his strength.

Replaying the conversation over and over to myself, I realised one thing about this whole twisted mess—faith gave power. Surely Ronin and I could survive these realms without completing the soulmate bond if we had enough faith, enough belief, in one another?

CHAPTER TWENTY-TWO

Ronin

Before Makeysha even said she was leaving for some time out, unease had started churning in my gut. Then when she announced she wanted time alone, it only became more intense. I didn't like the idea of her becoming more human and less likely to fend off attacks or potential threats.

I respected her wishes though and left her alone, hoping she would return soon. In the meantime, her words about not letting the third dagger out of my sight raced around and around my mind. What exactly did she mean by that? We were back with Wanda now which meant we, and the dagger, were safe.

"Right," Wanda said, clapping her hands together.

"Shall we make a start on this lavender juice?"

"Sure. Or should we concentrate on Caesar first?"

"Good idea. That could take more time." She stood up and grabbed a hold of the dagger. "I'll put this away safely with the others whilst I fetch the ingredients for the spell."

Panic swarmed me. How was I supposed to tell her nicely to leave it where it was? "Didn't Makeysha want to see the other two? So we could see which dagger belongs to who."

"Did she?"

I hesitated. Makeysha had asked twice. Wanda had acknowledged her the second time. What the hell was this? "Yes. Let's just leave it out for now. Perhaps whilst you're getting your candles and things you could bring the other two out of hiding?"

Wanda waved a hand through the air nonchalantly. "Oh, I'll leave them be until later when she comes back. Come to think of it, it might be safer if this is kept with them until then."

"It'll be fine," I said, giving her my best smile. "There's only us here. No one is going to break in and steal it."

"Well, stranger things have happened," she said, laughing.

I laughed with her, but I couldn't shake the feeling that she was faking hers. Wanda swallowed the last dregs of her coffee, tipping her head right back as she drained her plain white mug. That was when I noticed it—the twitching of her ring finger. It was like it had gone into spasm all on its own.

As it jerked, it seemed to gain a shadow of itself and for the briefest of seconds, there appeared to be two ring fingers. Then it would stop momentarily, letting me see there was in fact only one finger. It was as if the movement was so fast it was blurring itself, but the jolts weren't that quick.

Making a bold move, I reached forward and took hold of the dagger. Wanda snapped her attention to me in an instant. I tried to ignore her penetrating gaze as I turned the sacred item over in my hands, pretending to study it.

"Who would think that such a small thing could mean so much?" I said, lifting my head.

Her eyes were dark and stormy, nothing but hatred and anger oozing from their brown depths. When she realised I was looking at her, she blinked, the fury and animosity I'd just seen vanishing into warmth and smiles. I had to question myself as to whether I'd just seen it.

"Indeed," she replied. "It's often the trivial things that cause the most problems."

"So how do we know which dagger belongs to who?" I said, looking at the bottom of the handle for something obvious like a giant G for Gabriel.

"I don't know. I'm sure it'll be something simple." She stood staring at me for several seconds, to the point it became noticeably uncomfortable.

"Weren't you going to get your spell ingredients?"

Wanda shook her head, as if waking from a daydream, and plastered a smile onto her small face. "Of course. Yes. Shall I take that for safe keeping until Makeysha returns?"

She reached a hand out for the dagger but I pulled back. "No. It'll be fine out here with us. No point in traipsing it from one place to another for the sake of an hour or two."

Pulling her lips into a thin line, Wanda stalked out

of the room, her back ramrod straight and her shoulders visibly tense. Her behaviour around this dagger was starting to make me suspicious and combined with Makeysha's last words, I began to wonder if we had more problems on our hands than just Lucifer and his First Creations.

***

Half an hour and one locating spell later, Wanda had determined that Caesar was in fact in New Orleans as well.

"Everything is turning out to be nicely coincidental," I said.

"When the Universe wants something, it will happen."

I offered a smile but little else. I wanted to dig some more into Wanda's background but without it looking obvious. However, before I could even think of a way to ask the right questions, my phone rang. I pulled it from my pocket to see **MOM** flashing on the screen.

"Please excuse me a moment," I said, showing Wanda my phone screen. "I'll be right with you."

"No problem," she said, dabbing at the clean slit she'd made across her palm for the spell.

I stood up and answered. "Hi, Mom."

"Hello, darling. How are you doing? Have you had a nice chat with Wanda?"

I edged my way towards the kitchen, still holding the dagger. "I'm good. How are things back home? Wanda is lovely. Such a sweet lady."

"All good here, honey. How is Wanda? Is she still walking with that crooked stick of hers?"

214

My stomach somersaulted. Twice. "Err…yes, yes she is." I glanced over at Wanda to see her looking directly at me. I smiled at her and said, "Mom says hi."

She lifted a hand and waved back. "Say hi back."

"Wanda says hi," I said to Mom. "I have to go, Mom. We're kind of busy right now."

An excited squeal pierced my ear drum. "Have I got some good news for Leyani?"

I closed my eyes and sighed. "No, Mom. I told you that's not happening."

"Then why are you still with Wanda? What's going on?"

"Look, I can't talk right now, ok? I'll call you later, I promise."

I ended the call, cutting off her protests. I felt bad but now was not the time to be indulging my mom in a potential world ending scenario. There would be little she could do anyway—this was down to me and Makeysha.

"Everything ok?" Wanda asked.

"Yes," I said, wandering back over to the sofa. "Just Mom being Mom. You know what she's like."

Wanda laughed. "Bless her. She's a wonderful woman."

"Try living with her for a week, then tell me that." We both chuckled. Then I decided to test the waters. "Mom said she spent a lot of time here with you in the past. I think she misses you. How long has it been now? Four, five years?"

A lazy smile turned Wanda's lips upwards into a sadistic smirk. "Let's cut the crap, honey. I know you've worked me out."

My breath caught in my throat. *Shit.* My grip around the dagger tightened. I was not letting this thing go for love nor money.

"What was it that gave me away?" she asked, leaning forwards.

I debated telling her I had no idea what she was on about but figured we were well past that point by now. "Initially? Your finger."

Wanda raised an eyebrow. "Damn cloaking spells. They really are more difficult than people think. Especially when it comes to small parts of the body like a finger."

Wanda shook her left hand several times. When she stopped, her bent and twisted ring finger was as clear to see as a devil's horn. A cold chill ran down my spine. Our eyes locked. Then Wanda moved her focus to the dagger.

"I am taking that," she said.

"I beg to differ."

"Look, why don't we focus on the common goal here?"

"Which is what exactly?"

"Neither of us wants Lucifer to have the daggers so why don't we team up, exactly as we were, to achieve our aim?"

"That's all well and good, Wanda, – are you actually Wanda?" She nodded. "But I'm more a long-term planner so am currently thinking what will happen once we have all seven daggers away from Lucifer."

"Well that's easy," she said, with a shrug of her shoulders. "They'll come to me."

"I don't think so."

"Sweetheart, you won't get a choice."

"I'm afraid I disagree."

Wanda folded her arms over her chest and

smirked. "How exactly do you plan on besting a witch of my power?"

"With an angel," I said, giving her my own triumphant smirk.

"Ah, you mean the same one that seems to be turning human?"

Irritation rose inside me. This cross-breed mongrel was not going to get the best of me. "The same way I'm gaining more powers."

She tilted her head back and laughed. "Oh, darling. You are adorable. You can still bleed which means you can still die."

This chillingly calm conversation was starting to unnerve me. Wanda was very sure of herself. I was confident of myself as a hunter, but everything that had changed in the past couple of days had left me wondering exactly what I was capable of. I didn't know anymore and apparently, neither did Makeysha. This was not a winning advantage in a situation like this.

"Have you always been bad?"

She shrugged her shoulders. "No. I'm not a bad person."

I glanced at her ring finger.

"That's only been like that the past couple of years. Sometimes the greater good leads you down dark paths. It just so happens that my greater good has meant doing some unsavoury things."

"That doesn't justify any of this." I let out a sigh. "Ok," I said, deciding to go for the tactical route. "Let's focus on the joint aim for now—getting the daggers back from Lucifer. We'll deal with the other matter when the time comes."

She narrowed her eyes at me and studied me for several seconds. "Ok…but that dagger stays with me."

I shook my head. "No, it doesn't."

"Are we going to sit here all afternoon arguing about it or are we going to come to a reasonable agreement?"

"I don't see that there is a reasonable agreement." I sighed and cocked my head to one side, studying her. "What is your end game here anyway? Why do you want the daggers?"

She crossed her arms over her chest. "Have you ever felt like you don't fit? Like for some reason the Universe decided that you should live but it wasn't sure where you fitted best."

I pursed my lips. "I guess when it comes to being around normal humans, yes, I do feel like I don't belong around them. Around my own kind though, that's different."

"It's the same thing for us cross-breeds. We're an abomination, something that shouldn't exist yet for some reason we do. Lucifer is technically our creator through the fact he created our parents. We've all agonised over why he wouldn't want us to exist. Why he's hunted down and eliminated some of our fellow cross-breed siblings."

"And did you discover why?"

"Oh yes. You see, the pure-bloods are easy for him to control. If a witch steps out of line, he snaps his fingers and they're in uncontrollable agony. If he wants to punish a vampire, he forces them to stay in graveyards. When it comes to cross-breeds, that doesn't happen. He doesn't know how to control us, what our 'control switch' is so to speak."

I raised my eyebrows, the reality of what she was saying slowly dawning on me. "He doesn't know how to control you?"

Wanda shook her head, a broad smile spreading over her face. "All he does is send a hoard of demons after us to rip us apart. That tells us he's scared of our power. He doesn't know what we're capable of and that makes us more powerful than Lucifer. He views us as a threat yet still refuses to acknowledge our existence."

The penny dropped. "So you want to take the daggers from him to prove a point?"

She nodded. "And we want to lock him away in Tartarus until he agrees to take us seriously and stops sending demons after our kind."

"But witch cross-breeds are safe from him?"

Rage flooded her eyes in an instant. "It shouldn't just be witch cross-breeds that survive. We're making a stand for all the cross-breeds because we are the ones that happened to have survived. It doesn't matter if someone is a vampire-wizard mix, they're a part of our community and they should have a voice like the rest of us."

I had to give her kudos for being so passionate about this. "I understand, Wanda, I do, but these daggers aren't something to be caught up in the middle of some kind of political 'creature rights' revolution."

"We want his attention and the best way to get that is to take from him the most powerful thing he has. That happens to be the daggers."

"I see your logic, I really do, but the fate of the world literally rests with these daggers. You could simply lock him away in Tartarus and make your point."

"No," she said, shaking her head. "We need to make an impact. We need to hit him where it hurts as much as possible. Just locking him away isn't enough.

We need to make him see that we can do so much more."

I didn't know what to say to that. Before I got the chance to even think of anything, the living room door burst open. With the force of a Category 5 hurricane, Lucia exploded into the room, grasped my wrist with an iron like grip, and rushed me out of the house.

When the whirlwind around me stopped spinning and Lucia lessened her hold on me, I found myself in Odd Fellows Cemetery, staring at my beautiful soulmate. As I thought of something to say, Lucia approached her and held out her hand, offering two daggers to Makeysha.

I glanced down at my hand to see I still had my dagger. I raised my eyebrows as surprise took a hold of me.

"Hello, smooth dude," Makeysha said, grinning at me.

I chuckled. "I think after that little show, you're now the smooth one."

CHAPTER TWENTY-THREE

Makeysha

The realisation that something as simple as believing in myself was the key to all my power gave me a renewed sense of enthusiasm. I knew I could tackle this situation head on and come out on top.

I decided to give something a try. Lucia had been tamed by my magic which meant effectively that I controlled her. Certainly, the behaviour she'd expressed so far gave the impression that she served me, and anyone associated with me. I took a deep breath, closed my eyes, and reached out to her with my mind.

When she replied instantly, the grin on my face had never been so big. She had witnessed Wanda hiding one of the daggers and low and behold, both of them were together. In less than five minutes, she'd not only brought the two daggers but also my soulmate and the third dagger.

"Thank you, Lucia," I said. "Could you keep an eye out on the perimeter please and make sure we don't have any unwanted guests attempting to stop by?"

"Of course," she said, before gliding out of my crypt to start her border patrol.

"What have I missed?" Ronin said, walking to me and handing me the third dagger.

"Oh, nothing much. I had a chat with God and basically realised that I can do whatever I want."

He raised a sooty eyebrow and smiled. "You had a chat with God?"

"Yep. Right in the heart of the Gardens of Eden. Turns out he wants my help."

A soft chuckle sounded from him. "Forgive me, I'm not being rude, but what?"

"I pretty much responded in the same way. He admitted that Heaven has lost faith in him and as a result, he has no power."

Ronin's jaw dropped. "He has no power?"

"Well, he gets drips from the human's following him but it's nowhere near enough to power him. It's taken him fifty years to save up the power to get me up to Eden."

"Wow."

I nodded. "I know. That's when I realised that all we need is a little belief, a little bit of faith in ourselves and what we're capable of. We don't need this soulmate bond to define us and whether we live or die. *We* define us."

He took a hold of my hand and kissed the back of

it. "I admire your determination, I really do, but we're talking of literal life and death trials here. Those realms are going to push us to the brink of death and then some."

"I know," I said. "But I know we can get through this. I'm not going to allow some rumour to scare us into ruining our relationship."

"Relationship." He pulled his lips into a thin line and pondered over the word for a few seconds. "I never thought three days ago that I would be in a relationship. Definitely not one for life."

A vice of fear clenched my heart. "Is that a problem?"

"No, no, of course not," he said, scooting closer and taking hold of my other hand. "It just sounds strange to hear it."

"Is this where you tell me you're a commitment phobe?"

He laughed. "No, far from it. There's just such a lot changing right now, my feet haven't touched the ground since the moment I met you."

My heart skipped a beat at hearing his words. Warmth spread through me, igniting my soul with fire. "I know the feeling."

"If you think, I mean really think, that we can do this without being forced to…you know…then I trust you."

My eyes filled with water. "Really? You trust me that much?"

"More," he whispered, leaning in close. "I believe in you."

He brushed his lips over mine with such a soft sweeping embrace, he stole my breath away. As our minds reconnected, I revelled in the closeness, welcoming the strengthening mental link between us.

When he dropped my hands and wrapped his arms around my waist, desire flooded me in an instant. I loved the feeling of his big strong hands holding me tight and when he pressed his body against mine, I found myself secretly begging for us to be skin to skin.

His tongue stroked mine with a gentle but firm hunger. I couldn't hold back any longer. My craving for intimacy was becoming too much to bear. With our lips still locked together, I pushed him back onto the divine softness of my bed.

Breaking our kiss, he breathed, "What…what are you doing?"

I ran my hand over his chest, the hard muscles beneath his t-shirt making my want for him even greater. "I want to feel you…" I lifted the bottom of his shirt and settled my hand against his bare stomach "…skin to skin."

"Is that a good idea?"

"I don't care. I want it. I'm burning up here with this desperate need f—"

He pulled me back down to his lips, claiming me with such a carnal desire, my last hold of self-restraint was completely obliterated. His kiss turned frantic as I yanked at his t-shirt. He brought his hands up to the back of my corset, his hands struggling with the delicate hook and eye fastenings.

"Here," I said, waving a hand over myself.

"Whoa," he whispered.

I'd stripped my dress, leaving me bare and naked leaning over him.

"You know, half the fun is the undressing," he said, stroking his hands up and down my back.

"I can put it back on," I said, smiling.

He shook his head. "No, no, no. No need for that."

"Your turn," I said, waving a hand over his clothes.

His clothes disappeared, leaving before me the fine perfect form of a man. Ripped arms, toned pecs, chiselled abs, a delicious V pointing down to his groin, I couldn't help but give a groan of satisfaction.

"My oh my," I said. "The Universe loves me."

He roved his eyes over my body and bit his lip. "I think it loves me too."

I looked down at his crotch, eager to see what treat lay waiting for me. I was not disappointed. Fully erect already, just looking at him excited for me made my longing for him even greater. He was well endowed and the thought of the pleasure he could give me made my insides quiver in anticipation.

He pulled me down so I was laying on top of him. The second our bodies connected, bare skin to bare skin, a new wave of want rushed over me. I wanted more of him, I wanted him touching me everywhere possible all at the same time.

Kissing me again, he slid his hands down to my lower back and then cupped my ass. He groaned and squeezed me harder. I moved my kisses down to his neck, gently nipping at the soft flesh between his neck and shoulder. His breaths became short and shallow, spurring me on further.

I suddenly remembered that Lucia was walking the perimeter and would be coming back by any minute at which point she would get a full-on view of my bare ass.

"Lucia!" I yelled, grabbing the duvet to cover us over.

Ronin looked at me with raised eyebrows. "Bringing another woman into the bedroom when we've not even been together yet? This is interesting."

I slapped his shoulder playfully. "No. I don't share so get those ideas out of your head right now."

He grinned at me as he stroked his fingers along my thigh. "Aww, baby. So possessive already."

"I'm not possessive, I'm territorial. There's a difference."

He chuckled and kissed my shoulder.

Lucia appeared in the doorway. "Yes, Makeysha?"

"Lucia, do you think you could find Caesar? He's here in New Orleans, isn't he?"

"Of course, Makeysha." She clasped her hands together in front of her and then said, "May I please say something?"

I faltered for a second, surprised by her question. "Yes, of course."

"Whilst sealing your soulmate bond makes you immortal it also has repercussions."

I almost choked on the word. "Repercussions? Like what?"

"From what my parents told me and Kaspar, once you consummate the bond, it consumes you day and night until there is a product of it."

My jaw dropped. "What? What do you mean 'it consumes you day and night'? And what 'product'?"

"You will indulge in physical relations with one another until a product of that is created."

I sat, open mouthed, not knowing what to say.

"And by product," Ronin said, his voice very low and quiet. "You mean—"

"A child," Lucia replied.

I sprang away from Ronin like he'd just grown

thorns. "Whoa, now this is a whole other level of crazy. That's not possible."

"It is. I assure you, where a soulmate bond is formed, there are beings created as a result. My brother and I are living proof of that as are all the other First Creations."

My head spun like I'd just been hit with an eighteen-wheeler. "Wait, what? That's wrong. Only three instances of soulmates have been recorded."

Lucia offered a sad smile. "That you were allowed to know of, yes. God is not the honest being he tries to make Heaven think he is."

I pursed my lips. After my discussion with him earlier, I had to agree with her. "I thought the First Creations were what Lucifer made?"

Lucia shook her head. "All of the First Creations are the result of soulmates being forced apart by their war. All of the mothers were in the early stages of pregnancy when it happened, and they all sided with Lucifer."

"So why aren't all First Creations warlocks like you and Kaspar?"

"Lucifer did intervene but only with the permission of the mothers. He mixed dark magic and infiltrated the growing foetuses in the womb to make us what we are."

"He did kind of create you then?"

Lucia nodded. "In that way, yes. But we were already conceived. He just…tweaked our genetics if you like."

"If your parents reconnected, would there be more of you?"

"Potentially, yes. However, no one really knows what we would have been without Lucifer's intervention."

I didn't know what to do with this information overload. Everything I'd ever understood and known seemed to be crashing down around me, again.

"I'm sorry if I alarmed you," Lucia said. "But I felt I needed to warn you. Given the task ahead, you will not survive Lucifer's realms if you're consumed with thoughts of intimacy."

"But...but if we get pregnant, that means a Nephilim..." Ronin said, his voice now almost a whisper.

Lucia shook her head. "Nephilim are the result of 'sons of God and daughters of Men'. You are not that."

"So...so what would it be?" I asked, panic coursing through me like a tidal wave.

"I'm afraid I cannot answer that, Makeysha. You are an angel and your soulmate is a human graced with angelic powers. It would definitely be extremely powerful, that I do know."

I looked at Ronin, speechless. He shrugged his shoulders and gave me a cheeky grin. "I could live out the last days of Earth in bed with you."

Resisting the urge to laugh, I threw him a dirty look instead.

"Also," Lucia continued. "The closer Ronin is to death, the greater the desire to complete the soulmate bond will become."

Tears flooded my eyes instantly. "You mean my powers are overwhelming his body?"

Lucia nodded. "Yes, just as Wanda predicted. The urge to have intercourse will only become greater over the coming days."

"Until?"

"Until you give in or he dies. I shall go and find

Caesar now."

With that, she gave a slight bow and disappeared into the twilight leaving us revelling in her bombshell of information.

"Great," Ronin said. "So if we're not immortal going into Lucifer's realms then we're probably going to die. However, if we make sure we're immortal, we're not going to get to Lucifer's realms because we're going to be at it like rabbits whilst the world ends around us. Either way, people die. Fantastic."

"Quite a quandary, isn't it?" I said, furiously blinking away my tears. "Just when I thought things were going well."

"It's true what they say—if it's too good to be true then it often is."

"The First Creations are children of soulmates...look how powerful they are."

"But they were angel on angel pairings. This is something different."

"I know...that's besides the point anyway. I am not having a child."

Ronin gave me an unimpressed look. "I am not having a sexless relationship."

"There is a little human invention called a condom, you know."

"Makeysha, I have a feeling that a bit of ultra-thin latex isn't going to stop you getting pregnant. It seems the Universe has made things this way for a reason."

Growing more annoyed and frustrated by the second, I threw the covers off me and waved a hand over myself, redressing myself.

"Feeling different?" Ronin said, checking out my clothes.

I looked down to see a vibrant red jumpsuit

covering me. "Oh! Where did that come from?"

"I don't know," he replied. "But it looks good. Leave it on."

Smoothing the soft fabric down with my hands, I found myself quite enjoying the injection of colour into my otherwise dark life. "I think I like it."

"Do I get some clean clothes please? Seeing as you made mine vanish."

"I quite like your birthday suit in all honesty."

"Whilst that news delights me, I'd rather not have everyone staring at my junk."

I giggled and gave him some fresh clothes. He'd barely stepped out of the bed before Lucia was back, complete with none other than Caesar at her side.

"Well, this just gets even more interesting, doesn't it?" I said.

CHAPTER TWENTY-FOUR

Ronin

What a twist of events. I could barely get a grasp on one thing before everything changed and left me struggling to get a grip on the new reality laid out before me. One thing remained constant throughout all this—Makeysha. I had a distinct feeling that her theory of believing in ourselves was going to be our saving grace.

Right now though, I couldn't quite believe that just like that, Lucia had retrieved Caesar, the First Wizard. If I'd known it was going to be that easy, I'd have asked Makeysha to use her for Lasander. This did, however, bode well for our trip down to Hell.

The wizard standing in front of me was rather

unremarkable to say the least. He looked like a weedy teenage geek. Soft brown hair flopped over his forehead, skimming the tops of his thin framed glasses. Grey eyes stared back at me, no emotion flickering through them at all. His slight build did little for him, but he had good dress sense. He looked every inch the cool dude in his black and white striped cotton shirt, faded denim jeans, and smart brown leather shoes.

"Lucia tells me I am to help you," he said, his voice sounding like my brother's when he was thirteen.

"It would be most appreciated," Makeysha said.

"If I do, it is only because I see Lucia as someone I can trust."

Ouch. I frowned at him. "How are we supposed to trust you if that's how you view things?" I said.

He shrugged his shoulders. "That's your decision to make. I'm not the one asking for help."

Wow. This guy liked to play hard ball. I decided to go straight for the jugular and ask the one burning question behind all of this. "Why? Why are you helping Lucifer anyway? You do know he's going to destroy this world? That includes all of the animals that you profess to love and adore."

"Lucifer has made no threats to this world. I am unclear where that rumour has come from. As far as I am concerned, I am helping a greater power achieve his aim. By doing so, I am receiving something that I greatly want, too."

This was interesting. The First Creations were getting something in return for their labour. I had assumed up to this point it was purely because they were Lucifer's creatures that they were helping him.

"And what is that?"

"My parents, our parents…" he motioned

between him and Lucia "…back together."

"What?" Makeysha said. "Your parents back together? Is that what he's promised you?"

Caesar nodded. "Yes. When he ascends to Heaven, he will repair the rift between the angels, reuniting all of our parents once more."

"Why does he want to do that?" I asked.

"Because he knows how much pain we've been in," he replied. "How much our parents have suffered because they cannot be together. You haven't felt it yet, the completed connection between two souls, but when you do, you'll know how my parents felt and why I want to help them."

"What if we could help you?" Makeysha said. "Would you help us then?"

"Lucia has asked me to help you, so my help was never in question. I'm not sure exactly what you think you're going to be able to achieve. This hole between the angels needs a higher being to fix it."

"I disagree," Makeysha replied. "Lucifer is using you. He's emotionally blackmailing you to get what he wants."

"Does it really matter if the end result is what I want?"

Makeysha pursed her lips and sighed. The wizard had a point. From his perspective, he was getting what he wanted, regardless of the cost or manipulation at his expense. He didn't care. All he cared about was getting his parents back together.

"But you're all so powerful," Makeysha said, after a minute of silence. "You're First Creations. You could do this on your own."

Caesar gave an unnerving smile. It lacked warmth but was full of amusement. "We're not powerful because we're First Creations. We're powerful because we're the offspring of soulmates."

A lightbulb went off inside my head. All these years we'd assumed their power came from Lucifer, when in fact, it came from their very DNA, from their parents coupling. This was big news. And setting off alarm bells as to why Lucifer would want to reunite soulmates.

Makeysha gasped. "What are you saying? That if your parents had more children, they'd all be as equally powerful as you?"

Caesar nodded. "Yes. They wouldn't have the diverse gifts that Lucifer graced us all with, but they would have the same power. No one really knows in what form though. Would they be born angels, or would they be humans with super powers?" He shrugged his shoulders. "I'm curious if I do say so myself."

"What does he want?" Makeysha said. "What is he planning to gain by creating all these powerful beings?"

"He's essentially a mad scientist. He's curious. The magic he touched us with has affected us all in so many different ways, he wants to experiment some more."

"Experiment," I said. "Seriously? This world isn't a lab for some arch angel mad scientist."

"Why do you care?" Caesar said, narrowing his eyes at me.

"Because everything and everyone in this world deserves the right to live."

He tweaked the edges of his mouth up in a sly smile. "Why don't you repeat that to yourself the next time you squash a spider?"

I faltered, feeling like I'd just been hit with a baseball bat. Seconds ticked by until I found my voice. "What?"

"Your fear of spiders drives you to kill them, does it not? Have you considered that Lucifer perhaps fears humans?"

Makeysha looked at me, her eyebrows raised and an amused smile tugging at her pink lips. "You're scared of spiders?"

I scowled at her. "They have eight legs. That is not normal. The fact they can run with all eight of them at the same time is just…" I shuddered, then started scratching my arms "…they're all kinds of wrong."

She laughed. "I can't believe a badass supernatural hunter is scared of a teeny tiny spider." She clutched at her belly as she doubled over in laughter. "This is brilliant."

"Now is not the time to be discussing my phobias," I snapped. I turned back to Caesar. "Why would Lucifer be afraid of humans?"

"Think about it. He's spent years festering and boiling in his own bitterness and rage. He doesn't know love, compassion, and kindness anymore. Humans express that every minute of every day, despite what they do to each other. They're a threat to his emotional state of mind."

"What you mean is, he's jealous of them."

He shrugged his shoulders. "I guess so."

"What you're telling me is he basically wants to get rid of anything happy or loving."

Caesar nodded.

"So what makes you think he's going to help your parents rekindle their love?"

Realisation spread over his young face like

wildfire. He opened his mouth, but no words came out. After several minutes of waiting for his reply, he simply said, "I hadn't thought of it like that."

"Excellent," Makeysha said, clapping her hands together. "Are you still willing to help us now?"

Caesar, his features paling by the second, nodded.

"What can you control?" I asked. "With your wizard powers."

"Anything that isn't human."

"Would that extend to demons?"

He nodded. "I helped Lucifer create his realms. He used me to keep the demons at bay whilst he worked."

"This gets better and better," I said, smiling at Makeysha. "And sacred animals, like unicorns, would you be able to control them?"

"I don't see why not."

"Right," I said, clapping my hands together. "Let's get this show on the road then."

CHAPTER TWENTY-FIVE

Makeysha

Now the moment had arrived, nerves gripped me. Here we all were—a disgraced angel, a supernatural hunter, an evil warlock turned good, and a wizard, standing at the edge of a cliff ready to dive into the Hellmouth.

Ronin had a hold of my hand and gave me a firm squeeze of reassurance. "What was it you said to me? 'It's only a little jump'?"

I flipped him off with my middle finger. "A lot has happened since then. I'm not so angel powered anymore."

"Suddenly it's quite daunting, isn't it?" he said, wiggling his eyebrows up and down.

I gave him a playful shove in the shoulder. "Shut up. Let's just get this over with already." I bent down and grabbed a handful of loose stones from the dusty floor. When I stood back up and saw Ronin's questioning stare, I said, "We need to break the surface of the water. Otherwise it'll be like hitting concrete unless we dive properly."

"I get that," he said. "But those stones are going to hit the speed and get through the Hellmouth. Don't you think being showered in stones is a bit of a warning to them down there that someone is coming?"

I shrugged my shoulders. "The thought of hitting demons on the head with stones makes me want to find every last one and throw them all in."

He grinned at me and then looked to his right, where Lucia and Caesar were stood holding hands. "You guys ready?"

Lucia nodded.

Caesar gulped, then whispered, "Yes."

"Great," I said, taking a deep breath. "On the count of three. One. Two…" I threw the stones into the river "…Three."

We all stepped off the cliff at the same time. The sudden rush of falling through the air brought back vivid memories of when I'd fallen from Heaven. My instincts to release my wings and stop my tumbling descent became almost too much to bear. I dared to look down and saw the stones had hit the water already, ripples splaying out over the otherwise peaceful surface.

As the dark green water rushed closer and closer, I closed my eyes and squeezed Ronin's hand with everything I had. We hit the water. I couldn't help but gasp as the shock of its icy depths hit my body. Doing this at night definitely wasn't the cleverest idea.

Completely submerged in the cold river, my downward travel slowed almost instantly. When nothing happened, I began to wonder if we'd not reached the required depth. My lungs started burning, screaming for oxygen. I opened my eyes but could see nothing, not even the end of my nose. If it wasn't for the feel of Ronin's large hand still wrapped around mine, panic would have consumed me in an instant.

Then I felt it. A slight pull. Then a strong tug. All of a sudden, we were hurtling down through the bitterly cold waters at a frightening speed. I couldn't help it. I opened my mouth to scream but all that happened was I sucked in a lungful of water. My chest felt like it wanted to explode. My lungs were still desperate for oxygen, my heart raced at an insane speed. I wanted to take in a breath but all there was around me was water.

"Calm down, Makeysha. You're going to be fine."

Ronin's voice echoed around my mind. Instantly, my limbs stopped moving and my soul calmed to a quiet serenity. The worry of slowly turning human was beginning to affect me in more ways than I wanted to admit. How was I going to survive the deepest parts of Hell if I couldn't even handle being underwater for a minute?

A rod of fear struck my heart. *"Ronin, we didn't sort out our aura's being accepted into the Hellmouth! We're going to die."*

"No, we're not. Have some faith. Mind over matter."

"This isn't mind over matter, it's the laws of magic!"

"Makeysha, if you believe we'll be fine, then we'll be fine. Trust me."

Trust me. Trust me. How could will overcome the

basic rules of dark magic? Wanda had told us herself that she wasn't sure she could get us through the Hellmouth. Now, here we were, throwing all caution to the wind and leaping to our deaths, hoping it would work on nothing short of prayers.

We fell out of the water like sliding down a ride at a water park. I'd never been so grateful to hit a hard floor. I coughed and spluttered as I emptied my lungs of all the water I'd involuntarily swallowed. Opening my eyes, I looked around me as I took in breath after breath of sweet, fresh air. The bottom of the river was the ceiling, its murky waters shimmering above us. It seemed like we were in some sort of cave.

"You ok?" Ronin said, wrapping an arm around me.

I looked at him, never more thankful to have him by my side. "I'm sorry," I said. "I don't know what came over me."

"You don't need to apologise." He leaned forwards and pressed a kiss to my forehead. "I'm just glad I'm here for you."

I looked behind him to see Lucia and Caesar surveying their surroundings, water dripping from their clothes and hair. Caesar took his glasses off and shook them.

The cave we were in couldn't have been much bigger than a standard living room in a house. There was nothing in here but jagged rocks as walls and a sandy coloured dusty floor.

"Now what?" I said.

"We have to find the door," Lucia said.

"What door?"

"The door to the Hellmouth. This is like a reception room."

I stumbled to my feet and snorted. "Some welcoming room this is." I tripped over a pile of stones and laughed. "So much for hitting demons on the head."

"It's the thought that counts," Ronin replied.

Caesar and Lucia started feeling the rough walls with their hands, looking for this mysterious door. Minutes ticked by. Feeling Ronin's skin against mine as we waited for our aides to find the door started to consume my thoughts.

I started stroking my hand up and down his arm. When he gazed at me with those amber eyes of his, desire started to pool deep inside me. The longer we looked at each other, the greater our yearning became. Before I knew it, both of his arms were around me, pressing me against him. Then his mouth was on mine, claiming me, teasing me, promising me delectable pleasures I so deeply wanted.

"Found it!" Caesar yelled.

The wizard's voice broke through our connection like a knife through hot butter. When a rush of hot, stale air whirled around us, I realised this was it; the first test of our faith. We would either burn up and die, or we would survive and go on with our quest.

A narrow doorway had opened up in the walls, wide enough, just, for each of us one at a time.

"I suggest," Lucia said. "That one of us goes first, followed by one of you, then the other one of us, followed by the other one of you. To help disguise your auras."

I nodded. "Good idea."

"Ladies first," Caesar said.

"Age before beauty," Lucia quipped back.

I raised my eyebrows, wondering what was going

on. Up until the last couple of hours, she'd been nothing but a silent servant, only answering questions when spoken to. Now she was offering ideas and responding with witty remarks. Was whatever I did to her wearing off?

Caesar grinned at her and positioned himself at the open doorway. "Who's going first?"

"I will," Ronin said, boldly stepping forwards. He kissed the back of my hand and said, "Remember—we will be fine."

"Says the guy who thought it was all a load of nonsense."

"You believed in it so much you convinced me. Come on, beautiful. Don't let me down now."

My heart swelled when he called me beautiful. Cheesy I know, but that simple name/compliment made me feel all warm and cosy inside.

"I won't," I said.

Ronin stood behind Caesar. Lucia took her place behind Ronin and then held her hand out for me. I grasped hold of her small hand. The second I touched her warm skin, my world changed. Everything around me was ripped away, leaving me stood in the middle of a tornado of power. Panic swarmed me. I stared straight ahead, fixed on one point, desperate to see something of stability outside of the moving reality around me.

Just as I debated stepping into the whirlwind, everything stopped moving. A large grey room surrounded me, but I was alone. As I glanced around, I realised this was more than a room. This was like being inside a cathedral. Huge, vaulted ceilings loomed above me with thick towering stone pillars supporting the roof. A grey stone flag floor beneath my feet shone with layers of polish.

Then I realised there were no seats, no windows, and no doors. It was nothing but an empty shell of some kind of building.

"Makeysha."

A female voice, laced with authority, had me spinning around on my heels to see where it had come from. I did a full three-sixty, seeing nothing, but when I returned to my original position, three young women stared back at me.

I jumped back in surprise. "Oh!"

"Do not be alarmed, child," said the woman on the far left. Her white hair seemed to glow as she spoke.

These women were all identical, right down to their sapphire blue eye colour, except for their hair. One had white hair, another had black hair, and the third had grey hair. All of them were dressed in forest green tunics, cinched around the middle with a simple brown leather plaited belt. Their feet were bare.

"What is…where am I?" I said.

"We are The Fates," said the woman in the middle, with the grey hair. "We felt we needed to speak with you, Makeysha. Don't worry. No one knows you are here. Time has frozen for your friends whilst we meet."

"I am Aurora," said the white haired one. "These are my sisters, Freya, and Selene."

I offered a small smile but felt way out of my depth. Their power oozed into the air around them. It flowed from them like an aura for a human. I'd never been around such supremacy—even God didn't emanate power like this.

"You may have noticed how things have seemed

to be going rather perfectly for you," Freya said, her grey hair bouncing around her shoulders as she spoke. "This is not coincidental. It is our doing."

"We believe the Universe needs righting," said Selene. Her black hair glimmered as she talked, reminding me of a raven in flight and how its feathers gleam when the sun shone down on it. "And we believe you are the one to do it."

My mouth dropped open. "Wait, what?"

"This is a lot to take in. We appreciate that," said Aurora. "But we cannot continue to allow God to hide, Lucifer to destroy, and everything in between to die. We allowed for Lucifer's creatures. We even wrote them into the circle of life. They have helped establish a balance, surprisingly."

"But," continued Freya. "We cannot allow for either God or Lucifer to attain their aim of ascension. Not only are they not worthy, they do not possess the depth of character for such responsibility."

"Given your tenacity and belief in yourself," said Selene. "We all agreed that you would be the ideal candidate to aid us in our task."

"But…but if you have the power to bring me here, weave Lucifer's creatures into the fabric of nature, put things in place…why can't you fix all of this yourselves?" I asked, totally confused.

"There is only so much meddling we can do," Aurora said. "And whatever we do interfere with has to be put into place centuries before it happens. There is only so much we can do. Sometimes the finer details slip through the net, and that's where you come in."

"So you knew all of this was going to happen and you did nothing to stop it?"

"We couldn't. We don't just sit around here with

idle hands, Makeysha," Freya said. "We have constant work to do for the present and the future. To then take the past into account as well makes everything a lot more difficult. One tiny change two hundred years ago can wipe out an entire family or change the beliefs of a whole culture. It is not something to be taken lightly."

"By the time we realised what had happened in Heaven," said Selene. "The daggers were already free. We knew Lucifer's plans. We all agreed instead of affecting the past, we would affect the future. So we put things into motion to bring you and your soulmate into the equation."

"But," said Aurora. "There are glitches, such as your need to complete the bond before he dies. He is strong, but even his human shell has its limits. We have given you as much time as we possibly can."

Irritation sparked inside me. I couldn't help the flow of words that spilled from my mouth next. "Basically, what you're telling me is you've done half a job and you want me to pick up the pieces you couldn't be bothered to think about. In the meantime, you've endangered my life, my soulmates life, and the lives of millions of people because if we fail, Lucifer will kill them all."

"We have not done half a job," Freya said. Her blue eyes flashed with intense anger. "We have broken rules, Universal laws, to get this far. The least you could do is respect our position."

"I do understand that you have things going on I don't understand, but whilst you've tried to make things easy, you've also made them almost impossible at the same time. We need to be immortal to survive whatever is in Hell but if we do that, we won't even get to the first dagger because we'll be too busy humping each other's brains out. You really have created quite a conundrum."

The three sisters all exchanged a look. To me, it looked blank, but I'm sure something was being spoken between them.

"We cannot alter what it takes for soulmates to be completely bonded," Selene said. "There has to be a physical coupling for the two souls to fully reconnect." She held her hands out in front of her. In the blink of an eye, a uniquely decorated stone font appeared in between us. "This is where souls are created." She waved her hand over the empty space inside it. "When they are born, they are a physical entity."

Silence fell over us as she worked her hands back and forth over the font. A bright blue light started to glow from inside it, spilling out over the thick edge. Her sisters then joined her, all of them moving their hands over it. Then Freya reached in and pulled out a bright blue pulsing ball of energy. It was huge, at least the size of a car wheel.

Selene took hold of one side and Aurora the other. Gently, they started pulling. Just when I thought nothing was going to happen, a tear appeared at the top of the ball. As they continued straining against it, the tear grew into a rip, then into a total fracture of the once perfect ball.

When the last part was severed, a wave of energy burst through the air, knocking me off my feet. The sisters hadn't moved, except for their hair being slightly disturbed as if they were in a gentle breeze. I jumped back to my feet, watching in awe as two halves of a soul sat on the sister's hands.

"Touch it," said Selene, offering me her half.

I gingerly reached forwards, not sure if I would be

blasted with some sort of electrical shock or hit with energy I couldn't withstand. When my fingertips touched the soul, I was surprised to find it hard. Its edges were blurred, almost fuzzy, as it vibrated with energy.

"Now watch," said Aurora.

The two sisters approached one another, step by step, holding their halves with both hands. When they were toe to toe, they pushed the two halves against one another, but no matter how hard they tried, the two pieces would not glue themselves back together despite them fitting perfectly, as they had only moments ago.

"What's happening?" I asked.

"Whilst the two halves fit together physically, they no longer have a spiritual connection. They need a living existence to develop that," Freya said.

"And when there is a spiritual connection," Selene continued. "There needs to be a physical connection to complete it—more than just a mere touch or a deep kiss. The connection needs to be strong enough as if it's us piecing them back together."

"Whilst I appreciate you showing me this, it doesn't help me at all. The fact remains that once we complete the soulmate bond, we're going to be at it until I end up pregnant. From what I understand anyway. Am I wrong?"

"No, you're not," Aurora said. "Soulmates are a very special thing. Once we cast two halves out into the world, we don't interfere with them. We don't make it so that every soul finds their other half. If we did, there would be nothing unique about them because everyone would experience it. When two souls reconnect, that's something amazing, it's powerful, and with power comes desire. A product of that desire is the birth of something new."

"A child," I said.

"It's evolution," Freya said. "The human race cannot afford to stand still. Offspring of soulmates are merely a leap forwards in the evolutionary chain. Each child will be different and have its own powers. When they reproduce, be it with a regular human or a creature, something else will be born—something different. And so it goes on."

I couldn't believe what I was hearing. "Creatures…and humans can breed?"

"Yes," the sisters said, all in chorus.

"And not all soulmates are angels?"

"No," they all said.

"But so far," Selene said. "No human has found their soulmate, nor have they reproduced with anything but humans. Lucifer sees humans as beneath him and as a result, the creatures have only, naturally, reproduced with each other, despite his forbidding it. It's only natural to want your children to be the best they can be. Breeding with a species below you isn't forwarding your kind."

My frustration was growing. I still didn't understand, despite the fantastic show of watching a soul being created, what exactly I was doing here. "Why have you brought me here? I don't understand."

"We wanted to make you aware that you are on a higher path here. We have plans for you. Things will work out and you will be ok," Aurora said. "However, that doesn't mean you can blindly go into battle thinking we're going to save you if you die. It doesn't work like that."

"Don't think you're invincible," Freya said. "Not unless you complete the soulmate bond."

"That isn't going to happen," I said. "I'm literally about to walk into Hell."

Selene cleared her throat. "We could…alter what happened earlier. We could put you back to that moment in time so you can complete your bond. Nothing would be altered by doing that."

"Yes, it would," I said, wanting to scream in annoyance. "Because if we do that, we won't be in the Hellmouth, we'll be in bed. Time travel ideas make me very nervous."

"It's not time travel," Aurora said. "It's a correction of course. We need you to survive these tasks. As much as you want to believe in yourself, that alone is not going to save you. We can…ensure that once your bond is complete, you are able to leave the bedroom to carry on with your duties."

"And how are you going to do that?" I said, frowning.

Freya pointed to the half-soul in Aurora's hands. "By ensuring that your reconnection produces something immediately."

I stumbled back in shock. "You mean…pregnant. I'm going to be pregnant after my first time with my soulmate *and* going into the realms of Hell?"

"It's a lot to take in," Selene said. "We know that. But the power from your unborn child will help you in retrieving the daggers."

Nervous laughter erupted out of me. "This is insane. And how on earth can a foetus help me when it won't even be fertilised at that point?"

Aurora offered me a small smile. "When female angels are impregnated, they progress through the stages of pregnancy three times faster than that of a human female."

"Of course they do," I said, shaking my head. "And what if I say no?"

"We cannot force you," Freya said. "But we also cannot save you if you find yourself in a tricky predicament. We're offering a level of protection here for you. One that solves all the major problems you are currently facing."

"But it doesn't, does it? Because if I manage to survive and get the daggers, I have to deal with Wanda and her army of cross-breeds that want to prove a point to Lucifer. And you want me to do that whilst I'm knocked up?"

"I don't want to give away any spoilers," Selene said, giving me a sly smile. "But Lucia will deal with Wanda."

"So the option is yours," Aurora said. "You have the opportunity to go back a couple of hours, seal your bond, be with child, and continue onwards fearless and immortal. Or, you can carry on as you are, face almost certain death, but trust the notion that belief in yourself will be enough to carry you through three realms of Hell and fighting carnal urges to mate with and save the life of your soulmate."

I didn't know what to say, do, or think. I felt like I needed a panel of people around me to bounce all of this crazy off of, just to give me some sense of direction. Whilst their offer seemed like the best deal all round, I really didn't want to be getting pregnant the first time I slept with my soulmate. Meant to be or not, we still needed time to get to know each other. And the fact that this baby would be appearing in three months time really did not sit well with me.

"My dear," Freya said, approaching me slowly. "Let me show you something."

She held her hands out and motioned for me to give her mine. I hesitated. Was she going to manipulate my decision one way or the other?

"Do not be afraid," she said. "I am the middle ground of my sisters. Hence my grey hair. I see things from both sides."

I quickly glanced at Aurora and Selene. They were stood either side of the font, holding the two halves of the soul in their hands, watching me intently. I looked back at Freya and decided to hell with it. They weren't trying to hurt me.

Giving Freya my hands, I gasped when her searing hot skin touched mine. She pushed my hands together then clasped her hands over mine like a case. The heat from her touch intensified. My skin burned, heat propelled up my arms, through my shoulders, and then poured down through the rest of my body. Sweat broke out on my forehead. Yet, I felt no pain. Just intense heat.

Seconds later, my mind flooded with images. Images of death and destruction, Lucifer and his horrid demons flooding the earth like a plague, wiping out every living thing they set eyes upon. Everything was ablaze, the skies as far as the eye could see were orange with fire, tinges of grey swirling in the background from smoke. Buildings were destroyed, people scattered into pieces, animals tortured and crying their last woes of death.

Twisted metal from houses, cars, shops, were covered in blood. Limbs, heads, glass, children's toys covered in dirt—it was a scene of utter chaos and devastation. Then it flickered, rushing forwards in time. The warped scenery still remained, but in the middle of it stood Lucifer with his hands around God's neck, forcing him to take in the destruction of his beloved earth and humans.

Lucifer looked different. Every muscle on him throbbed with power. His eyes burned red. Everything about him shouted raw power. God saw the wreckage around him and cried out in anguish. Tears fell from his golden eyes, but they were tears of blood, leaving streaks of red pain down his pale face. Lucifer put a silver blade to God's throat, whispered something into his ear, and then with one swift, quick cut...

"No!" I screamed, wrenching my hands from Freya's. "Why are you showing me this? I don't want to see that."

I shook my head as if it would dispel the horrific things I'd just seen from my mind. It was then that I realised tears were streaming down my face.

"I am sorry if this shocked you," Freya said. "But this is what will come to be if Lucifer achieves his aim."

"But he won't. I have four of the daggers already. I don't have to go into Hell."

"Yes, you do. You know as well as we do that if he has three, he will stop at nothing to retrieve the remaining four. If, however, he loses all seven, and the support of the First Creations, then that will put him in quite a predicament."

"Why does he need the First Creations anyway? He has the means to collect the daggers himself."

"Because the First Creations are his link to his followers. Sure, he has his demons, but that's not the same—he created them. He needs the support of real living beings, generations of families, to back him and follow him."

I remembered my conversation with God. "No believers, no power," I said. "So will his power be waning already since I have four of the First Creations on side?"

Freya nodded. "Yes. He's worried, Makeysha. He's frightened."

"That makes him desperate," I said. "And a desperate archangel is a dangerous one."

"But one that you can handle. If—"

"I'm immortal. I get it." I sighed and shook my head. "Fine. I'll do it. Send me back."

Freya raised an eyebrow. "Really?"

"Yes. But do it now before I change my mind."

Selene lifted her half of the soul into the air and gave me a smile. Then, all three sisters clicked their fingers in unison, and my world changed again.

ANGEL OF THE CRYPT

CHAPTER TWENTY-SIX

Makeysha—Hours Earlier

"...I shall go and find Caesar now."

"Lucia!" I said, wanting to get her attention before she disappeared. "Once you find Caesar, can you keep him somewhere until I call you back? We would like some privacy."

Lucia gave a slight bow and disappeared into the twilight leaving us revelling in her bombshell of information.

"Great," Ronin said. "So if we're not immortal going into Lucifer's realms then we're probably going to die. However, if we make sure we're immortal, we're not going to get to Lucifer's realms because we're going to be at it like rabbits whilst the world ends

255

around us. Either way, people die. Fantastic."

"Quite a quandary, isn't it?" I said, furiously blinking away my tears. "Just when I thought things were going well."

"It's true what they say—if it's too good to be true then it often is."

"The First Creations are children of soulmates…look how powerful they are."

"But they were angel on angel pairings. This is something different."

"I know…that's beside the point anyway. I am not having a child."

Ronin gave me an unimpressed look. "I am not having a sexless relationship."

"There is a little human invention called a condom, you know."

"Makeysha, I have a feeling that a bit of ultra-thin latex isn't going to stop you getting pregnant. It seems the Universe has made things this way for a reason."

I gave him a beaming grin. "I think you're right. So let's embrace it fully."

He raised an eyebrow. "And by that you mean…?"

"Like you said, a condom isn't going to stop the Universe's will so let's just accept fate. Are you clean?"

A sheepish look crossed his face. "I've never had sex without a condom…this is a first for me."

"Ooo, this is nice. At least you're experiencing some sort of first with me."

He smirked and said, "And what first are you experiencing with me?"

I thought over his question for a moment. "I've never had sex with a human since I've been an angel."

"I'm not completely human."

"But you are half human."

"Fair point. I'll take it." He grabbed my waist and pulled me on top of him. "Now, where were we?"

He pressed his lips to mine, sealing our fate. He slid his hands up and down my body, covering me in goosebumps. I broke off our kiss and trailed kisses down his neck, loving the way he shivered underneath me. I took my kisses down to his chest, tracing my tongue over his deliciously hard pecs. Roaming my hands over his arms, I revelled in the rock-hard muscles I could squeeze to my heart's content.

His breathing started becoming shorter and shallower, and his erection was pressed firmly against my stomach, enticing me into heading further down to see how big of a treat waited for me. My entire body felt like it was on fire with tingles and excitement. I wanted him so badly, but I also wanted to savour the moment and enjoy this for as much and as long as I possibly could.

I licked and kissed my way down his abs, nipping at his taut skin every so often, grinning as he jolted from the surprise of it. When I finally reached his groin, I slipped a hand down the inside of his thigh, relishing in the way he shuddered as I skimmed past his balls.

Deciding to really tease him, I kissed my way slowly down the inside of each thigh, brushing my lips ever so lightly over the base of his penis as I moved from one leg to the other. His hands were in my hair, scrunching it up as he squirmed and wriggled in pleasure.

I reached up and gently scraped my fingernails down his torso right as I closed my mouth around the head of his dick. He convulsed, bucking his hips up as he groaned loudly. I flicked my tongue all around his engorged head, smiling to myself as I found one particular sensitive spot. I played with this area for several seconds, before letting him know I had no gag reflex.

Stroking my hand up and down his shaft as I made my way back to the top, I couldn't help but think about how he was going to feel inside me. He was a big boy and it had been so long since I'd had any sort of action, let alone something as amazing as reconnecting with my soulmate. I felt like a lion being set free into the wild.

His excitement started leaking out, spurring me on even more into a rhythm of deep throating him and playing with that delightful spot just under his head. It wasn't long before his balls were tight and his entire body tense and rigid. After a couple of minutes of delicious torture, he let out a hiss, pushed me back gently and took himself out of my mouth. Then he grabbed me, dragging me up the length of his body, and flipped me over, settling between my legs.

I giggled like a schoolgirl, loving the heat and the desire burning me up. The light from our connection was now blinding, filling the crypt and then spilling into the darkness outside. He nipped at my neck as he grazed a hand over my breast. I moaned as he touched my nipple, my most sensitive part. A potent throb shot straight between my legs, ramping my yearning up by a hundred degrees.

He moved down, licking and sucking my nipple. I writhed underneath him, panting and almost desperate for him to touch me down there and give me some sort of release. Something. Anything. When he switched his attention to my other breast, I couldn't help but cry out, partly from frustration, partly from pure bliss washing over me.

When he kissed his way south, I thought I was going to die from sensory overload. Then when he gently pressed his lips to my clit, I couldn't help but say his name as I struggled to stay still. I was lost in my own personal heaven, one that was just for me and him, and one I never wanted to be thrown from.

He slid his tongue into my folds, delving deep inside me. Then he slowly moved upwards before circling my clit over and over in a tantalising slow rhythm. As my release built deep in my core, he dipped back inside me to then repeat the whole thing over and over. Each time he stopped, I was only seconds away from my sweet, blissful freefall into oblivion.

After a couple of minutes of his relentless assault on my senses, I looked down at him, grinning at the sight of his handsome face between my thighs.

"You dare take that tongue off my clit once more and I'm going to ban you from blowjobs for a year."

He flashed me a cheeky grin, plunged his tongue back inside me, then crept his way back up to my clit. The slow, lazy pace he blessed me with pushed me towards my edge in such a delicate way, when I finally let go, it was a fall of decadence I'd never yet experienced. My ears were ringing, my head whirling, and my body fizzing like he'd filled me with electricity.

As I rode my high, delighting in the long wave he'd given me, he kissed his way back up to my face, then eased himself inside me, sending more ripples of bliss through me. We both moaned together, and I wriggled underneath him, trying to give him the best access to fill me up completely.

Reaching his end, he stilled for a moment, then

started moving. First he moved slowly, kissing my neck and stroking my hair. Then he started thrusting harder and faster, plunging himself in and out of me as he sought out his own release.

He was hitting all the right spots and it didn't take long before another promise of relief started climbing inside me.

"Don't stop," I whispered. "Harder."

His red puffed out cheeks told me he was holding his breath. When he heard my words, he let out his breath, groaning. He put his hands on my shoulders, shoving me down into the bed and he drove himself harder and harder into me. His relentless pounding quickly spun into a quick shower of ecstasy, giving me another orgasm.

I cried out his name and gripped his forearms as I rode out my wave of personal heaven. Seconds later, he moaned and stilled, pouring himself into me. I could feel him pulsing as he emptied his seed into my womb.

He lowered himself down and laid on top of me, trying to catch his breath. His forehead was covered in sweat and his entire body slick with damp. After a minute or so, he rolled off me, collapsing back onto the bed.

"Wow," I said. "That was…that was amazing."

"Tell me about it," Ronin replied. "Is sex with angels always like that?"

"No. Just sex with me."

He laughed and curled me against his side. "I think I need a long sleep after that."

"Time's up, buttercup," I said, pressing a kiss to his cheek. "Come on. We've got a world to save."

"Can't we just bask in this for a little longer?"

"Five minutes. Then we've got to go."

"I can do a lot in five minutes," he said, wiggling his eyebrows.

"I'm such a lucky girl."

He chuckled and kissed me. "You've broken a million hearts tonight by sealing our bond."

"Ditto, smooth dude."

We lay in comfortable silence for a few blessed minutes. Then it was time to get on with the task in hand.

"Lucia!" I yelled, throwing the covers off me. I waved a hand over myself, redressing myself.

"Feeling different?" Ronin said, checking out my clothes.

I looked down to see a vibrant red jumpsuit covering me. "Oh! Where did that come from?"

"I don't know," he replied. "But it looks good. Leave it on."

Smoothing the soft fabric down with my hands, I found myself quite enjoying the injection of colour into my otherwise dark life. "I think I like it. It seems you've made me a new woman."

"Do I get some clean clothes please? Seeing as you made mine vanish."

"I quite like your birthday suit in all honesty."

"Whilst that news delights me, I'd rather not have everyone staring at my junk."

I giggled and gave him some fresh clothes. He'd barely stepped out of the bed before Lucia was back, complete with none other than Caesar at her side.

"Well, this just gets even more interesting, doesn't it?" I said.

ANGEL OF THE CRYPT

CHAPTER TWENTY-SEVEN

Makeysha

... Lucia took her place behind Ronin and then held her hand out for me. I grasped hold of her small hand. The second I touched her warm skin, my head spun with a surreal feeling of déjà vu. I realised then that the 'course correction' The Fates had told me about was now complete. Like they said, everything up to this point had been the same, except for me and Ronin sealing our bond.

We passed through the doorway and into Hell. Blistering heat threatened to peel the skin from my bones, but my immortal status meant it could do nothing to me. Roaring energy whirled around us, almost blowing us off our feet.

"It's the Hellmouth not recognising your aura's," Lucia yelled. "It'll pass in a moment."

Like she said, in under a minute, the deafening noise stopped. Taking in what faced us, I realised the horrific images Freya had imprinted in my mind was what I was staring at right now. Lucifer was literally going to bring Hell on Earth if he succeeded.

Screams of agony shouted through the vast space, hands reached up through cracks in the fiery orange floor, heads looked at us, their mouths all shaped into 'O's of pain and suffering. Demons scurried about, their black bodies on all fours, moving like disgusting insects. They chattered like crickets, hissing and snarling at each other as they ripped into the souls around them.

"What the…" Ronin said, his features paling.

"Welcome to Hell," I said, trying to get a hold of my own shock.

"How do we get to the realms?" Ronin said to Lucia.

"We're in Lucifer's chambers. He will be here any moment to show us how to access them."

My mouth dropped open. "This is where he sleeps?"

"He doesn't sleep. But this is where he likes to spend his time, yes."

The ground beneath us started shaking and vibrating. Then, cracks started appearing all around us. Seconds later, the hard dirt floor fell away, dropping us through the earth to whatever lay below. I rode it out, quietly confident in my new immortal abilities. When we hit the bottom, we were in a huge shadowed cave. Easily the size of a football pitch, the darkness down here made it all the more eerie.

"Look," said Ronin, pointing at the far wall.

Set back in the jagged dark stone was a huge wooden door with a lion's head brass knocker on the front of it. A brass plaque read 'GLUTTONY' in italic scrawl. Glancing around, six other identical doors were in the stone walls, all with the names of the realms written on them.

"Well, this is easier than anticipated," I said, smiling to myself.

"Can you remember what gluttony was?" Ronin said.

"'In the circle of gluttony, souls are subjected to laying in vile slush created by a never-ending icy rain. The slush symbolises their personal degradation and overindulgence in food, clothes, and other worldly pleasures. They're blind and unable to see others around them, which represents their selfishness and coldness in life'. As quoted by Wanda."

"Very good," Lucia said. "What would you like us to do?"

"Guard the door," I said. "Make sure that nothing or no one comes in after us."

"Very well. We'll see you soon."

I nodded to her and approached the door, step by step. Despite the fact I knew I couldn't die it didn't mean I was going to find whatever was on the other side of this door easy. Ronin took hold of my hand and kissed the back of it.

"We're in this together."

I looked at him and smiled. "*Do we knock on the door or what?*"

"I don't think it's on there for decoration. I doubt there's many visitors down here."

I giggled to myself. We reached the door. Ronin

looked at me and motioned his head towards the knocker. I nodded. He picked up the handle running through the lion's mouth and banged it down against the wooden door.

Seconds ticked by. Then a slow rumbling came from the other side of the door. The rumbling turned into thundering, leaving me wondering if there was a stampede of rhinos heading our way. All of a sudden, the door was ripped off its hinges, sucked inwards by a massive draft. We shared a worried glance before we were swept off our feet and into the realm of gluttony.

Ice cold rain pelted my skin, leaving red marks where it hit me. I suddenly felt like I should be wearing battle armour, not some fancy jumpsuit. As I debated changing my clothes, we were thrown onto a smooth brown rock, several metres above the vile slush and piles of souls spread out as far as the eye could see.

As I inhaled a deep breath of air, I almost choked on the rotten, decaying smell overwhelming this place. It was a hellish stale mix of decomposing bodies, faeces, gone off food, and goodness knows what else. It made me want to hurl.

"Well, hello, Makeysha."

I whirled around to see Lucia, but as a man. "Kaspar," I said, completely thrown at how much like Lucia he looked. He had long silvery hair like his sister, but he'd drawn his back into a ponytail, reminding me of the handsome elf from Lord of the Rings.

"My sister has been speaking to me. Rest assured you will find no difficulties from me. But I do not have the dagger in my possession."

I frowned. "But I thought you were all in these realms to guard the daggers?"

"Oh yes. We are. But like I said, I am no threat to

you. However, that does not mean that I can hand the dagger over to you. You still need to retrieve it."

"Retrieve it? From where?"

Kaspar lifted a long bony hand and pointed his index finger over my shoulder. Far away on the horizon, hovering over a crooked tree, was the unicorn dagger, slowly twisting and turning in a pink bubble of magic. This whole realm was a depressing mix of browns and greys, making the bright jab of colour a welcoming sight. It was like finding a gem in a sewer.

"If you attempt to fly, your wings will be clipped," Kaspar said. "Not my rules. Just how the realms have been set up. No magic, except for that which holds the daggers."

"Flying isn't magic to me. It's natural."

Kaspar shrugged his slim shoulders. Dressed in a bright white suit, he looked insanely out of place in here. Yet, despite the mud, slush, and rain, he remained perfectly dry and spotlessly clean.

"If you wish to try it, then so be it, but don't say I didn't warn you."

"And you're staying clean and dry by pure chance, are you?"

"Lucifer guarded us against the elements before we came in here."

"Oh."

I quickly looked around me, hoping to spot an obvious way down. When I couldn't see one, I turned back to him and said, "How do I get dow—"

A firm shove on the shoulder had me tumbling over the rocky edge, falling into the oblivion of vile slush and torrential weather. Somewhere above me, I heard Ronin shout, "No!" but his cries were soon lost in the howling wind and driving rain.

I landed flat on my back, every last bit of air knocked from my body. I took the liberty of taking a couple of minutes to regain my breath. When I felt able to conquer the world again, I sat up and surveyed my surroundings. Where there wasn't sharp, roughly cut rocks, brown sludge marred the landscape. Hands and heads reached upwards out of the tarry looking substance, trying to claw their way forwards. As soon as it looked like they were getting anywhere, the ice-cold rain would concentrate on them, driving them back down beneath the depths of the thick mush.

Studying the quickest route to the dagger, I didn't pay any attention to where I'd fallen. My goal was to reach that dagger and get the hell out of here. So when a skeletal hand clamped down around my right leg, I screamed for all I was worth. It dug into my flesh, pressing down on me like a vice. I tried in vain to prise its fingers from me, but my attempts were proving futile. Just as I debated reaching into the slop to find its elbow joint and rip it off, a head began to rise out of the puddle of slush I was sat next to.

Washed out blue eyes stared into my very soul, chilling me to the bone. Dark curly hair clung to a feminine face of high cheek bones, a soft pointed noise, and pale pink lips. She lifted her chin out, showing me the beginning of her slender neck. The stubborn defiance in the tilt of her chin, the hatred in her eyes, pale porcelain skin…

I gasped, then screamed again. I jumped up, dragging her with me. Kicking at her face with everything I had in me, I managed to get her off me. I stumbled onto the nearest rock and fell back onto my butt, watching the zombie like skeleton scrabble its way along to the next slurry puddle.

My mind couldn't process what I'd just seen. It had been me, from a previous life. A life of...I sucked in a deep breath...gluttony. I'd been the spoilt daughter of a wealthy businessman. I had no compassion or empathy for anyone but myself. My overindulgence in the latest clothes, lavish food, and a stable of prized horses had been the only thing to rule my life.

Shaking, I stood up and gazed out over the terrain I still had to conquer. With a sweeping gaze, it could easily be missed, but as I paid attention to each soul reaching for air, I realised they were all me from my previous gluttonous lives.

ANGEL OF THE CRYPT

CHAPTER TWENTY-EIGHT

Ronin

When Kaspar pushed Makeysha off the rock face we were stood on, I lunged for him. Every instinct inside me screamed at me to punch his lights out.

"I wouldn't do that if I were you," Kaspar said. "You may be immortal, but you're not immune from pain."

"Why would you do that?" I said, all but growling. I had a hold of his stupid white suit by the collar, our noses almost touching. "I could end you, right now."

"But you won't," Kaspar said, gently pushing me away. "Because you need me. Your soulmate won't survive this realm if anything happens to me."

I shoved him away from me and walked off,

needing a few minutes to cool down. I walked to the cliff edge, scanning the horrid landscape below for my beloved. After a couple of minutes, I spotted her, screaming at something and scampering onto a rock.

"Makeysha!" I yelled, cupping my hands around my mouth. "Makeysha!"

She didn't look up. I shouted her name twice more, so loud my voice box cracked from the strain.

"She can't hear you," Kaspar said. "She'll realise in a moment that she's down there, all alone, surrounded by nothing but her own sins."

I spun around and narrowed my eyes at the arrogant warlock. "She's an angel. She doesn't have any sins."

"She did in her previous lives. And because she's an angel, she never atoned for those sins. This is her shining moment of glory." He outstretched his arms, motioning at the depressing realm we were stuck within. "She will be tempted by many things along her journey to the dagger. Her strength of character will determine if she's worthy."

I resisted the urge to grab him by the neck and throw him over the cliff. "And what if she fails?"

"Then we're in for a long wait. Or rather, you are."

I scowled at him. "So what are we supposed to do? You can't expect me to just stay up here and do nothing."

"That is exactly what you're going to do. Even if you went down there, she wouldn't see you. She's completely blinded by the actions of her past. Until she figures out how to move through that, it's just a waiting game for us."

"And what exactly is your purpose in this

anyway?"

"I'm your only way out of here," he replied, pointing across the wide-open space to a tiny spot across the valley. "So you'd best talk to me nicely."

I sighed and let out a shout of frustration. I looked down at Makeysha, seeing her stumbling across the jagged rocks, trying to stay out of the slush broke my heart. She needed help, my help, she needed me, but she had no clue I was there.

"Fine," I said, turning back around to face Kaspar. "Rock, paper, scissors?"

ANGEL OF THE CRYPT

CHAPTER TWENTY-NINE

Makeysha

I had enjoyed some fine lives, that I couldn't deny. In each and every one, I had indulged in the wealth I had been blessed with. Now though, it seemed all of that overindulgence was coming back to bite me in the ass.

The shock of what faced me had subsided to a degree. As far as the next mile or so looked, I could avoid the putrid slush by hopping from rock to rock. My shoes had become nothing but a hindrance, so I'd removed them and thrown them into the brown slurry bubbling away next to me. I can't describe how chilling it was to see several different forms of myself all reaching for a pair of red high heels, grabbing at them like they were starving hungry, fighting over them like their lives depended on it.

I made quick progress, albeit with a few cuts on the souls of my feet, and soon enough the dagger wasn't more than half a mile from me. But the rocks had ran out. I was at Land's End. End of the road. It was swim through the slush or fail.

Taking a deep breath, I quickly judged what I felt was the best place to jump into this disgusting mud. My hands, feet, legs, arms, and even my face, had long since gone numb from the never-ending driving rain. I kept repeating to myself over and over "It's just bad weather. It's just bad weather."

This was the point though where "It's just bad weather" wasn't going to cut it. The second I jumped into the slush, a new wave of freezing cold hit my body. Suddenly, what I understood to be cold, wasn't. This was. My breath choked in my throat. I literally couldn't expand my chest to even draw air into my body. I was paralysed. I willed my fingers to move but couldn't feel them moving. Then I started to panic.

As I became more and more consumed with not being able to feel any part of my body, my teeth started chattering, my heart raced to new speeds, and then I started sinking. I've seen people die in quick sand and quick mud, and it's one of the most unpleasant things I've ever witnessed. As I slowly sunk beneath the vile slush, inch by inch, I realised I was completely at its mercy and whatever this was, I was going to have to just ride it out.

Wanting a final glimpse of my handsome soulmate, I looked around, spotting the rock face I'd been pushed from. But no one was there. Had he really left me in here alone? I strained my neck, craning to see as far back onto the flat rock as I could, but there was nothing. Not even a hint of Kaspar in his bright white suit.

Despair flooded me. I opened my mind, calling for Ronin mentally through our link. Nothing came back. I couldn't even feel his heartbeat pulsing through my mind. Had Kaspar killed him? As endless possibilities swarmed through my mind, I found myself struggling against the slop even more, and thus bringing about my fate even quicker.

When my chin started to slip beneath the tarry mud, a sense of calm came over me from somewhere, urging me to be still and just let this happen. My mouth went under. Just as the level reached my nose, dozens of hands started grabbing at my body. A new lease of life took over me. I fought with everything I had, kicking and flailing my legs and arms to get whatever was touching me away from me.

Frantic and desperate, I focused on the dagger, imagining myself pulling along an imaginary rope that would bring me straight to it. My eyes started watering because I refused to blink and lose my target, my goal, the one thing that would keep my head above the horrid slush I was being forced to swim through.

I spotted a mangled shape a few feet ahead. Its twisted, pointed angles ignited hope inside me that I'd found a stray rock. With the mud sucking at my limbs, I dug deep and kept fighting to crawl my way forwards.

Three strokes away. A hand grabbed at my ankle, tugging at my jumpsuit. I took a wild aim with my free foot and connected with a face. I moved forwards.

Two strokes away. A head popped up in front of me, its haunting features inches from my face. Short blonde hair, pale green eyes, but the same high cheekbones and defiant tilting chin. This was me from one of my last lives and perhaps my most overindulgent.

I'd been a princess, a daughter of an infamous King of Greece—Phillip II of Macedon. When he'd told me who I was to marry, I'd cut off all my beautiful blonde hair in protest, enraging my father beyond belief. Then I'd spent a fortune on new horses, new clothes, and wild parties. It had not ended well, and I'd still been forced to marry the man I hated more than anything. I lifted my arm and pushed her out of the way, forcing her through the thick slush. She sank beneath the mud, leaving me alone.

One stroke away. I grunted with the effort of pushing myself forwards but I made it. When I grabbed hold of the rock, it turned over, revealing it was no rock but a twisted, mangled body of another version of me.

She curled herself around, like she was some sort of contortionist, and gave me a sadistic grin. This was an early life, one I really didn't want to remember. I'd been nothing but a cruel, emotionless bitch intent on nothing but furthering her own life, no matter the cost. To my utter surprise, she pulled from behind her a fluffy white blanket.

Just looking at the simple object made me feel warm. I wanted its softness caressing my skin and I wanted its heat enveloping my body. I would give anything to have that blanket right now, so I could feel my feet, my hands, maybe get some feeling back in my nose even.

"You know the cost," she said, all but hissing the words.

I frowned. It wasn't like I had any money down here. Then I remembered the worst thing I'd ever done in that life. I'd gone past a homeless man who was shivering cold, in the middle of winter, sat outside in the elements. He had a bread loaf in his hands and was devouring it to the point he was almost chomping on his fingers. I'd walked past, a big white fluffy coat wrapped around me. The man had grunted at me, making noises and motioning at my coat. In all my wickedness, I'd given him the coat in exchange for his bread loaf. It had been interesting to me at that point to see how desperate he was for warmth—was he desperate enough to give up his only food?

The answer had been yes. The next morning, however, he was found dead. The coat hadn't been enough to protect him from the deep freeze that night, but he had been so hungry, he'd eaten two of his own fingers. I'd taken my coat back, had it washed, and kept it as an interesting prize of a social experiment.

As I watched the glee filter through this woman's eyes, shame crashed through me like a tidal wave. What would Ronin think of me if he knew the lives I'd lived before now? Would he even want to be associated with me, let alone bonded to me? I knew that each life was something a soul had to live through in order to achieve enlightenment but that part of my history I wanted to forget.

I ignored the woman and pushed on past her. Even though I couldn't feel my legs or my arms, I could feel the fatigue fading my mind. Exhaustion and tiredness were starting to set in, and I had little left to dig for.

Checking how close I was to the dagger, I was disappointed to see it appeared no closer than when I last focused on it.

"You can do this," I said to myself. "You can do this. Mind over matter. Believe in yourself."

Stroke by stroke, I swam my way through the slush, painfully slowly, but each inch gained was a win. Eventually, after what felt like an eternity, I could see the edge of the slurry pit and the beginnings of more rocks. I cried in relief. It was the final push I needed to get me out of this damn mush.

I lifted my arm for the last time, finally grabbing hold of a large boulder. I'd never been so grateful to see a stupid rock. I didn't even care that its sharp edge cut my soft palm, spilling blood into the sludge around me. As I hauled myself up and out of the slush, hands upon hands seized hold of my lower legs, dragging me back down. I turned around to look behind me, shocked to see a crowd of me fixated on my body as their hands yanked at my clothes.

Then I understood. Like with my shoes, they wanted my jumpsuit. *No magic.* I remembered Kaspar's words. I sunk back down and stripped as quickly as I could, although it was nowhere near as fast as I would have liked. Finally, I pulled it over my feet and no sooner had the first peek of it appeared out of the surface of the slush had they all swooped on it like vultures on a carcass. I threw it at them and dragged myself up onto the rocks, away from all the evil past versions of me.

Laying flat out on my back, I panted for breath and fought against my eyelids closing. I was so tired, so tired I wanted to cry but even that seemed like too much effort. After several minutes, I rolled over onto my belly and crawled over the rocks, butt naked, like a baby. When I looked up to see how far I had to go, I sobbed. The crooked tree was a matter of feet away, the dagger hovering at the top of its gnarled branches.

I reached the bottom of the tree, then used its

sturdy trunk to help me to my feet. My legs quivered from exhaustion and I didn't know how much more I could give. As I pondered over the best way to climb it, a loud bang sounded around me, making me jump. I glanced up to see the pink bubble had popped, like a balloon being popped with a pin. The dagger fell to the floor, more or less at my feet.

Tears of joy mixed with relief fell down my face as I bent down and retrieved my prize. As I wrapped my hand around the handle, I expected something to happen, something that would transport me the hell out of here, but nothing did.

I scanned the landscape, looking for the rock face where Kaspar and Ronin had been, but it was still empty. "Where are they?"

"You know the cost."

That chilling, snake like voice sent chills rampaging over my body. I spotted her near the rocks, her head above the slush, staring at me like some wicked siren. I gulped. She couldn't be serious. I had to gnaw through two of my fingers to get out of here?

"You know the cost," she repeated.

Trembles took control of my body. I collapsed into a tired heap at the base of the tree, leaning back against it for support. I contemplated my options for what felt like an age. When still nothing happened, I figured I had no choice.

I lifted the dagger into my lap, then briefly wondered if I could use that instead of my teeth. Fingers were fingers, right? I placed my left hand on the flattest piece of rock I could find and spread my ring finger and little finger away from my middle and index finger. With a shaking right hand, I took the unicorn dagger and placed its serrated edge against my two precious digits.

Sucking in a deep breath, I lifted the dagger up and swiftly brought it down. My heart hammered against my ribs. My body shook from head to toe. I closed my eyes. I heard the blade hit the rock beneath my hand. Then the pain hit. The splicing, excruciating pain. I screamed and reached for something to wrap around my hand, then realised I had nothing.

Before I could think another thing, a burst of wind surrounded me, carried me up into its vortex, and lifted me over the stricken land I'd just laboured my way across. I gripped the dagger in my right hand, squeezing it like a stress relief ball as the agony from my left hand became almost unbearable.

Then, just as I thought I couldn't take anymore, I found myself outside the door marked GLUTTONY. I gazed around me, my mind foggy with pain and tiredness. When I saw I was in Ronin's arms, I let the darkness take me.

CHAPTER THIRTY

Ronin

Anxious didn't quite cover how I was currently feeling. Being forced to watch Makeysha struggle her way across that realm had been one of the worst things I'd ever endured. It broke my heart into a million pieces that I couldn't even speak to her to offer words of encouragement, let alone help her through what was no doubt one of the toughest moments of her life.

Now graced with my own angelic powers, as she lay passed out in my arms, I waved a hand over her beautiful body, washing her down. Then I dressed her in a pale-yellow figure-hugging dress before covering her in a blanket. I hugged her close to me like she was a precious baby.

"Is she ok?" Lucia said, bending down next to where I sat on the floor.

"She's so tired," I said. "And she's lost two fingers."

Lucia raised her eyebrows. "Let me see."

I gently reached beneath the fluffy layers of the blanket and brought her left hand to the surface. My jaw dropped. "What the…?" Her fingers were back. "I don't understand. I saw her chop them off with the dagger."

"What happens in the realm, stays in the realm," Lucia said. "She did what she needed to do in order to pass the test."

I buried her hand back beneath the blanket and pressed a kiss to her forehead. "But she's still so tired. Why isn't she awake?"

"Give her a minute," Lucia said. "She's been through a lot."

We waited, patiently, for my sleeping beauty to awaken. It felt like a lifetime passed me by before I saw her eyelids flutter. When she finally opened her eyes and looked up at me, I breathed a sigh of relief.

"Hey, smooth dude," she said, a pained smile tweaking her lips upwards.

I chuckled and bent down to kiss her. When our lips met, a bolt of electricity passed between us and she seemed to gain a whole new lease of life, like she'd had a shot of adrenaline. She leapt up, out of my embrace, and stood in front of me bustling with energy.

"Right, let's get on with the next one then," she said, putting her hands on her hips with some serious attitude. "Time's ticking." She glanced down at herself and noticed the dress. "Ooo. I like this colour. Good choice."

I stood up and took hold of her hands. "Just calm down a minute. We've got plenty of time. What's the rush?"

"I want to get the hell out of here."

"So do I but that doesn't mean you can't take a minute to compose yourself. You've been through a lot in there."

She shrugged her shoulders. "I'm fine." She held her left hand up and wiggled her fingers at me. "All back to normal."

I eyed her with suspicion. She seemed unusually chirp and positive considering what she'd just faced. "Ok. So what one is next?"

"Lust," she replied. "As quoted by Wanda, 'Those in the second circle are souls who were overcome by lust. Their punishment is to be blown violently back and forth by strong winds, preventing them from finding peace and rest. The strong winds represent their restlessness and desire for pleasures of the flesh.' Seems relatively easy after that." She jerked her head back towards the GLUTTONY door.

I pursed my lips and glanced around the room, looking for the door that said LUST. "Who is in this realm?"

"Bryn," Lucia replied. "I've already spoken with him. He won't be a problem."

"Where's your brother?" I asked, only now noticing that Kaspar wasn't here.

"He's on Earth. It's what the realms are programmed to do—eject us through the door and straight up to Earth. He'll be waiting for us along the river bed somewhere."

"What can we expect in the realm of lust?" I asked, not sure if I really wanted to know the answer.

Makeysha looked at me, then looked away. "Sex. Lots and lots of sex. People rubbing themselves with lots of expensive creams, covering themselves in silk, touching themselves. Basically, anything that makes the body feel good."

I raised an eyebrow. "That sounds…" I cleared my throat "…delightful."

"Actually, whilst I think about it, why aren't we currently trying to hump each other's brains out?"

She glanced at me, her cheeks blushing a new shade of red. *"I…we need to talk. When this is all done with."*

"Why can't we talk now?"

"Because we have an audience."

"They can't hear us."

"Perhaps not, but they know we can communicate telepathically. "

"So?"

"It's rude."

I pulled my lips into a thin line but left it. A niggling feeling deep inside told me she was hiding something from me, but I decided to leave it be, for now. After all, more pressing matters were at hand.

"Lucia," she said, throwing her the dagger. "Keep that safe whilst I go in for the next one."

"Let's go," I said, holding an arm out towards the door on the other side of the room. "Let's get this over with."

"Actually…I was thinking I should do this one alone."

I felt like I'd just been punched in the gut. And it hurt. "Oh. Ok. May I ask why?"

"I just think it'd be easier without having you as a distraction, that's all."

"I'm supposed to be your support, your help if you need it."

"I know but…" she shook her head "…I think I know what's going to be behind that door and that's not something I want you to see."

I frowned. "How could you possibly know what's going to be on the other side of that door?"

"Based on what I've just gone through, I have an educated guess."

"What do you mean?"

She ran her hands over her face and let out a long sigh. "There was a reason, a personal reason, why I had to chop my fingers off. That means that something else personal is going to be in the other realms."

"Ok," I said, reaching for her hands. "But what could be so bad behind that door that you don't want me there?"

She dropped her eye contact and stared at the floor. "I haven't been all sweet and innocent in my previous lives."

"No one is sweet and innocent. We all have a past."

"As a hooker?"

She looked up at me as she said that, her eyes watering with tears. I was stunned. Never in a million years would I have ever thought my darling soulmate would have lived a life like that.

"Like I said, we all have a past." My voice came out weak and quiet, not really commanding the belief that I wanted it to.

Makeysha gave me a sad smile. She let go of my hands and said, "Like I said, it's not something I want you to see."

"But it's still a part of you. It was a life from how

long ago? Thousands of years? It's not like it was yesterday."

"But it's still a part of me. You will look at me differently."

"No, I won't."

"You don't know that."

"Yes," I said, taking her hands in mine again. "I do. Look, you've told me what's going to be behind that door. You can't leave me wondering about you going into a realm with all that going on. You've got to take me."

"You mean in case I get tempted and end up cheating on you?"

I frowned at her. "What? No. It's like me telling you that I'm going behind a door that has thousands of me having sex behind it but you're not allowed to come. How would you feel?"

She pursed her lips as she thought over the question. "Ok. I see your point. But don't say I didn't warn you."

I grinned at her and pressed a kiss to the back of her hand. "Come on then, lover. Let's go see some porn."

CHAPTER THIRTY-ONE

Makeysha

I couldn't believe I was taking Ronin into this realm. As I lifted the handle on the lion's head door knocker, my heart beat so hard, I could feel my pulse in my ears. I don't think Ronin quite understood how much of a whore I'd been. I banged the handle against the wooden door, bracing myself for a storm to whisk us inside.

Instead, all that happened was the door creaked open slowly. Ronin pushed the door wider, striding through boldly. I meekly followed behind, swallowing the ball of fear lodged in my throat. I had no clue what to expect or on what scale.

Taking in my first sweeping glance, purple skies lit

a rocky chasm ahead of us. The door slammed shut behind us, making me jump. The air was humid and tinged with the smell of sex. Moans, groans, and shouts of pleasure echoed into the distance.

"Well, this is interesting," said Ronin.

We were on a narrow cliff pathway, a looming grey rockface to our left, and an intimidating fall into a black abyss on our right. Straight ahead of us lay a long winding path to the pointed edge of a cliff. Either side of the point stood two huge statues.

As we hurried towards the edge, I realised they weren't statues—they were the ends of a bridge, shaped into penises.

Ronin raised his eyebrows and scanned up the huge length of the phallic shaped stanchion. "I think it's safe to say I feel rather inadequate standing next to this."

I laughed. "Unless there's a giant woman wandering around here somewhere, I would say that's for show only."

"I know, but still. Damn."

Shaking my head, I carefully shuffled to the end of the cliff. There was no way down. Looking straight ahead, an identical cliff faced us, some fifty metres away over the yawning valley in between. It also had two giant penises as bridge ends.

"I don't understand," I said, shaking my head. "What are we supposed to do?"

"Jump?"

"I don't think so. I can't use my wings, remember?"

He scratched his head and frowned. "I don't know then."

We stood there in silence for several minutes,

trying to figure out what to do. Just as I started becoming really frustrated, the cliff edge started shaking. The rumbling of moving rocks thundered through the air. I grabbed hold of the huge phallus to steady myself.

As we watched, a stone staircase unfolded out of the cliff, descending into the darkness that lay below.

Ronin glanced over at me and then held his hand out. "Let go of the giant penis and take my hand."

I couldn't help but giggle. We gingerly stepped onto the first of the wide stone steps. As we did, two six-foot torches lit up either side of us. The torches were held by golden statues of people—naked people. On my side was a woman, nestling the handle of the torch between her breasts, her head thrown back and her arms reaching up the shaft of the torch. On Ronin's side was a man, the torch an extension of his erect penis. His stony eyes were staring straight at the woman statue, as if he was getting off on seeing her in such a provocative pose.

"How charming," I said, wanting each moment of this realm to end even quicker than the last.

"Isn't it?" Ronin replied.

We carried on down, taking in the bizarre torch holders for each step in silence. They all had different erotic poses, some quite disturbing, others not so much. When I came across a woman with her legs spread, a hand inside her, and her other hand gripping the torch handle, I cringed.

"Oh, come on," I said, shaking my head. "As if that's going to fit in there."

Ronin chuckled. "I say ten out of ten for effort. And ambition. Girl knows what she wants."

I glared at him.

"I'll shut up now."

"Good idea."

The darkness surrounding us seemed to have a life force of its own. If it weren't for the torches lighting our way, I wouldn't be able to see anything. Not even my hand in front of my face. The hairs on my arms stood up the entire way down and I couldn't shake the feeling of being watched. The more I tried to peer into the shadows enveloping us, the more it seemed to push back, promising me horrors yet to come.

We hit the last step, and as the torches lit up our final level of the staircase, the entire valley in front of us sprung to life. Thousands of torches flickered on like a switch had just been flipped, highlighting the landscape before us.

Except this wasn't rocks, or vile slush, or even anything scary, it was one insanely huge orgy. The stench of sweat and bodily fluids lingered all around us, hanging in the air so heavy, it felt almost physical. Men on men, women on women, men on women, women on men—anything went. The pleasure filled noises coming from all these souls almost deafened me. On this kind of scale, it was anything but erotic.

"What the...?" Ronin whispered.

"Wow," I said. "This is insane."

Ronin lifted a hand and pointed up towards the other cliff face. The dagger tumbled about inside a white magic bubble in between the two phallus bridge ends. A broad-shouldered man stood next to it, his muscular arms folded across his chest, and a dark, brooding look on his face.

"I guess that's Bryn," I said. "This seems easy enough."

"Getting through a sea of sex crazed people?"

Ronin laughed. "Yeah. We'll discuss this on the other side."

"Ready?"

He nodded, laid a kiss on the back of my hand, and said, "Do not let go of my hand. Understand?"

I smiled at him being all protective and sweet. Maybe it had been a good call to bring him in here after all.

We took a step forwards. The instant we did, we found ourselves swarmed by the throngs of lust driven souls. As I scanned over their heads, looking for the path of least resistance, a startling realisation hit me square in the stomach.

"Oh my goodness," I said, panic induced tears filling my eyes. "Look at all the men."

Every single man as far as the eye could see was an exact replica of Ronin. Everywhere I turned, there was my precious soulmate in the throes of passion with someone else. Jealousy twisted a knife deep into my soul.

"Hey," he said, squeezing my hand. "I'm right here."

I looked over at him just in time to see a slender female hand run through his hair. He brushed it away with his free hand, but where he removed one, two more appeared on his chest, sliding downwards.

"Get off him!" I yelled, slapping their hands away. I tugged his hand, urging him to follow me. "Come on. Let's move."

I bulldozed my way through several groups, focused on the dagger. My arm was fully stretched behind me, keeping hold of Ronin's hand. I looked behind me to check he was ok and noticed we'd barely moved twenty feet. This was going to be a long and testing realm.

"I'm ok," he shouted. "Just keep moving."

I pushed on, dragging him along. Focused solely on the dagger, I wasn't looking at anything in front of me, I was merely using my shoulders and upper body to barge my way through. But I didn't account for a couple being on the floor, humping each other's brains out. So when I tripped over, it was only natural that I would look at what I'd stumbled over. The man was laid on his back, the woman on top of him, riding him like her life depended on it. She was massaging her breasts as the man gripped her hips, helping her ride him harder.

The woman seemed familiar, but I couldn't place where she seemed familiar from. Long curly blonde hair trailed over her shoulders, her make-up perfect, and her nails long and sharp but carefully trimmed. When she opened her eyes and looked at me, I nearly fell over again. One blue eye, one green eye, there was no mistaking who this woman was.

She was the wife of a wealthy nobleman I'd seduced in a previous life. I hadn't been a hooker out of unfortunate circumstance, I'd been a hooker because I loved sex and I revelled in seducing men. The amount of married men I'd tempted into cheating should have set some kind of world record. It was a cheap thrill for me, back then, to know that I'd 'conquered' something, or someone, that should have been off limits.

I didn't know all of the wives whose lives I'd turned upside down, but I knew a fair few of them either because they'd confronted me, or I'd seen photos of them in the family home. Taking a deep breath, I dared to look around me. Within seconds, I realised my worst fears—all of those women having sex with Ronin, albeit his replica's, were women whose men I'd seduced.

"Well I guess that's karma at its finest," I said, to no one in particular.

"What is?" Ronin said, stepping to my side. He looked at the couple in front of us and raised his sooty eyebrows. "Nice."

I slapped his arm and said, "Would you mind not eyeing up the horny women?"

"I was talking about my abs," he said, pointing at his replica's body. "Didn't realise I looked that good."

"Nice try."

He grinned at me. "This doesn't seem too horrific in my opinion."

"That's because all you're seeing is yourself with thousands of women."

"Considering I was expecting to see you with thousands of men, I think I prefer this option."

I snorted. "I certainly don't."

"Why?"

"Because all of these women are women whose husbands have used my past…services."

His jaw dropped. "All of them?"

"I never met all of them, but I knew a fair few. I can't see that only a handful of them would be down here."

"This is…this is…*a lot.*"

Fear clenched around my heart. "Wishing you'd stayed the other side of the door now?"

"No," he said, kissing my hand. "That's a whole other life. Every experience you had is what has made you, you. If that means I have to deal with the fact that you had sex with like a thousand people, then so be it."

His joking tone of voice did little to ease my discomfort. "Stop it. It's not funny. I'm really ashamed of myself. Although I do have to point out that if a guy had slept with a thousand women, he'd be deemed a hero."

Ronin grinned. "Have you ever heard about the lock and the master key?"

"Err…no."

"If a key opens lots of locks, then it's a master key. But if a lock is opened by lots of keys, then it's a shitty lock."

I gasped and punched him in the shoulder. "That's disgusting."

He chuckled. "It's a well-known saying. I'm not implying it's applicable here, although that could easily be the case."

"Stop it!" I said, struggling not to laugh. "It's not funny."

"Then why are you laughing?"

"I don't know."

We both laughed, stepped over the Ronin and the woman having sex, and continued on. Whilst having Ronin with me eased my pain, the sight of seeing him with so many other women was starting to burn into my brain. Every time I blinked, all I could see was him and someone else. It was upsetting and soul crushing. After what I'd endured in the gluttony realm though, I understood that this was something I had to endure to understand what I'd done to all of those women in my past life.

Still, that didn't make it any easier of a pill to swallow.

"What is that?" Ronin said, stopping and staring. "I do *not* look like that when I'm jerking off!"

I giggled. He was staring at a lone version of himself, masturbating furiously, his mouth forming a perfect O and his eyes glazed over with a completely gormless look.

"Apparently you do," I said, struggling to contain my laughter.

"I do not."

"Drop 'em and show me then."

He spun around and looked at me, dumbfounded. "What?"

"There's only way to settle this," I said, shrugging my shoulders. "So drop 'em and show me." I motioned at his trousers.

"I don't think so."

"Well, until you can prove otherwise, that face is your masturbating face."

He scowled at me and took the lead, dragging us through the endless crowd of sexed up souls. As the other staircase came into view, the sex mad groups and couples lessened, leaving single people, and a handful of couples, indulging in rubbing lotions and creams on their bodies, or wrapping themselves up in fine fabric.

"This is not so bad at all," I said. "Aside from seeing you cheating on me a million times, this has been relatively easy."

"It's not me," he said. "I would never do that to you."

I motioned an arm around me and smirked at him. "My eyes are telling me otherwise."

"Let me show you otherwise," he said, wiggling his eyebrows.

"When we're done, wise guy. Got a world to save first."

As we reached the staircase, thunder rolled

through the skies above us. Seconds later, a streak of lightning hit the ground, not more than ten feet away from where we were. A gentle breeze started to blow through the valley.

"We need to move," I said. "Now."

We ran for the stone steps, but we'd barely taken five strides before the gentle breeze turned into a manic whirlwind. There seemed to be no direction to the wind, it blew from all directions, whipping around us and throwing us off track over and over again. We were two feet away at the most from the nearest torch statue.

Ronin let out a shout of pain as he battled against the wind trying to force him back. He yanked his arm to his side, dragging me through the fierce storm. My eyes streamed with tears, but I was at his side, safer here than being an arm's length behind him. I wrapped my free hand around his middle, hoping it wouldn't interfere with his forward momentum too much.

He moved a few inches forward, his fingers outstretched and millimetres from reaching the statue. He gave another yell, reminding me of a war cry, and hauled us to the statue, finally wrapping his arm around it. His chest heaved up and down as he fought to catch his breath.

"We can't go up these stairs in this," he yelled. "We'll get blown right off. It must stop at some point. We made it this far before it started."

I nodded, figuring it wasn't worth the effort of shouting.

"*Whilst we have a moment,* he said. *What did you want to talk about?*"

"*Now is really not the time.*"

"*We have time to kill whilst this wind passes. Humour*

298

me."

I sighed. *"Trust me, this is a conversation best saved for the right time."*

"There's never a right time for anything, Makeysha. You just have to seize the opportunity when it arises."

He had a point there. There would never be a 'right time' to have a baby, not with the lives we had. Despite the fact there was little I could do about it now, it made me feel some sort of peace that actually, perhaps I had made the best decision.

"Ok. I had a meeting with The Fates..." I explained our first 'timeline' and how we hadn't actually sealed the bond, what The Fates had said to me and shown me, and then the option I'd been given.

He glanced down at my stomach, nervousness filtering through his face. *"You chose their 'course correction' or whatever they called it?"*

I nodded. *"I figured it was the best option all around. I'm sorry I couldn't tell you at the time. They kind of didn't give me much time to make my mind up, let alone have a discussion with you about it. I just went with what I felt was the lesser of two evils."*

He wrapped his arms around me, letting go of the statue to do so. The violent gusts of wind battered against us, nearly knocking us off our feet. Inside his tight embrace though, I felt like nothing could touch me.

"You made the right decision. I just wish you'd told me before we sealed our bond."

"I kind of did, when I said not to bother with a condom."

"Makeysha, sweetheart, I'm male. We don't do well with hints. I knew it was a possibility but not a definite done deal."

I laughed. *"I didn't want to scare you...getting pregnant on our first time? That's a huge thing."*

"And something we should have faced together. I'm your other half, Makeysha, you don't need to hide anything from me."

"I'm sorry."

"It's ok. We're going to have bumps in the road, as well as a literal bump too." He squeezed me tighter and kissed the side of my head. *"You have no idea how happy I am right now."*

"One more thing…"

"Yes?"

"Apparently, angels progress through pregnancy three times faster than humans."

Silence prevailed for a few seconds, then he said, *"That's good. Patience isn't a strong point of mine."*

I smiled and snuggled inside his arms, waiting out the storm. What felt like an age passed by, but eventually, the winds died down to the extent that we could safely climb the stairs. We ran up them at warp speed, desperate to retrieve this dagger and get out of this damn realm.

"Hi there," said Bryn, as we reached the top of the stairs. His dark brown eyes gleamed with joy. "You progressed quicker than I expected."

"That wasn't too bad," I said, standing next to the dagger.

"Lust is seen as the least offensive sin, hence its relative easiness compared to the other realms." Bryn touched his index finger to the white bubble, bursting it in an instant. "There you go. Congratulations."

I grabbed the dagger as it fell like it was long lost treasure.

"How do we get out of here?" Ronin said.

Bryn motioned a large hand behind us. A bridge was manifesting between the two cliff points.

"Thank goodness," I said, putting a hand over my

chest. "I thought we were going to have to go back down there."

Bryn gave me a cheeky smile. "You can if you like."

As he turned to Ronin to shake his hand, another bolt of lightning lit up the sky, lighting up the area around us. For the first time, I saw Bryn's mark, the one that the hunter's use to identify him. It was a simple crescent moon in white, at the top of his forehead, right in the middle. It wasn't very big, probably the length of a fingernail at most, but it was definitely there.

He and Ronin shook hands before Bryn was catapulted through the sky at a rate of knots. We walked back to the door, hand in hand, dagger retrieved, and happily expecting parents.

CHAPTER THIRTY-TWO

Ronin

I was going to be a dad. In three months. Wow. This was a turn of events to say the least. I was slightly upset that she hadn't told me before we had sex what was going to happen. If she had, I would have done my best to make it even more special than it was. Still, the result was the same—we'd sealed our bond and we were expecting. A few candles and sweetly whispered words weren't going to alter that.

"Yay," Lucia said, clapping her hands together as we emerged through the doorway. "How was that?"

"Compared to the last one, a total breeze," Makeysha said.

"One more to go," Caesar said. "Then we have to

figure out how to get out of here."

"What?" I said. "You don't know how to get us out of here?"

"You're forgetting that our exits were all programmed into the realms. We have no exit strategy for getting out of here," Caesar replied, motioning to the room around us.

I felt like I was going to explode. "You brought us into the depths of Hell with no plans on how to get back out? Are you stupid?"

"No. It's just never crossed my mind until now." Caesar's faced creased with worry as I loomed over him, bristling with rage. "But I can control the demons, don't forget. I'm sure we'll be fine."

"I suggest you start thinking," I said. "Whilst I'm retrieving the last dagger."

"Greed," Makeysha said. "'Souls in this circle are divided into two groups—those who hoarded possessions and those who indulged in spending. They are punished by being forced to push great weights, namely boulders, with their chests, which symbolises their drive for fortune.'"

I flexed my arms and gave her a toothy grin. "You're definitely going to need me for this one."

"Steady on, Mr Muscles. This is going to be another one of my tests. I hoarded possessions and indulged in spending like wildfire."

"Let's see what's in there first. The last one wasn't quite what you thought it would be either."

"I like your optimism, smooth dude, but I don't see any other way of what this could be." She handed Lucia the dagger. "Maybe you can have a think on how we're going to get Mount Olympus tomorrow."

Lucia frowned. "Tomorrow?"

"Yes, it's a full moon tomorrow isn't it?"

"You mean today."

Makeysha gasped. "How long have we been in there?"

"Nearly a day. It's roughly two p.m. up on earth at the moment."

I looked at Makeysha. "No way were we gone that long."

"Time moves faster down here," Lucia said. "What your human brain attributes to being ten minutes is more like an hour."

"Might have been nice if you'd told us that before we started this," I said.

"Better late than never," Lucia replied, smiling.

"Come on then," Makeysha said. "Lots to do, not enough time to do it."

I held out my hand and glanced around, looking for the GREED door. When I found it directly behind me, I grinned. "It's almost like it's waiting for us."

"Imani can be a little tricky," Caesar said. "But I've spoken with her."

"Good to know."

Makeysha stepped to my side and took my hand. "Less chat and more action, smooth dude."

I gave her a cheeky wink and reached for the lion's head knocker. I'd barely knocked it against the wood before the door swung open. Peering inside, I saw nothing but a steep grass slope heading down to a flat meadow.

Makeysha opened the door wider, following me inside. The door closed gently behind us, leaving us no way to go but down. The incline was long and difficult. Several times we nearly ended up running or toppling over, head first. By the time we reached the bottom, the backs of my thighs and calf muscles were on fire.

To our left was a small hill, no more than the size of a house in height, but at least the length of a football field. As we hurried to reach the edge of it, the earth started shaking beneath our feet. The sound of crashing rocks rumbled through the blue skies, and the sour smell of sweat drifted through the air towards us.

We reached the end of the hill and found ourselves staring at an incline that could only be described as all but vertical.

"That must be at least seventy degrees," I said, absolutely shocked. "That's impossible."

"I think that's the point of it," Makeysha said.

The six boulders were easily the size of a car each, and the two dozen or so souls trapped in here appeared to be normal sized humans. Both men and women lined the bottom of the incline, all standing and waiting for their turn with one of the boulders.

We approached, slowly, weighing up the options here. Makeysha looked around her carefully, I presumed looking for the dagger.

"There," I said, pointing to the top of the incline, on the far left—closest to us.

A petite woman, much like Wanda, sat underneath a blue magic bubble. It hovered in mid-air, the dagger turning around inside it. As we approached the bottom of the incline, I could see she was of eastern descent. Sleek black hair was cut into a bob that hung level with her lower jaw. Her almond shaped eyes were narrowed in on us, watching us like a bird of prey eyes its next meal. She sat with one leg bent up, an arm resting on top of her knee. Every part of her oozed attitude.

"Oh no," Makeysha said.

I switched my attention to my soulmate, wondering what had her worried. When I saw it, dread filled me from head to toe. In front of us, at the beginning of the impossible incline, was a gargantuan pile of clothes and food. It was easily a foot taller than me and far too wide for me to get my arms around.

"What is this?"

"It's my overindulgence of spending and hoarding." Heat flushed her cheeks. "That's not even half of it."

I shrugged my shoulders. I knew this wasn't going to be just it, but I wanted to stay positive for Makeysha. "So we make a couple of trips up the hill. So what?"

"That's not even half of it for one life. Let alone the other two."

"So it's half a dozen trips up the hill. It's not a big deal."

Makeysha glanced down at the floor. I could see the shame flooding her eyes. "There's all the horses, and the dogs, and the cats, the birds…"

I pulled her into my arms and tilted her chin up, forcing her to look at me. "We'll get through it. You're not on your own, beautiful. Whatever this is, we'll face it together, because that's what soulmates do."

Tears pooled in her eyes as she gave me a sad smile. "It's not your job to absolve my sins."

"Maybe not. But it is my job to protect you and look after you and if that means carrying your punishment and doing your tests, then so be it."

She buried her head in my chest and sobbed. "I love you."

My heart bloomed with joy and pride. I'd never been so happy to hear three little words. Just hearing her say that made all of this worth it. I would walk to the ends of the earth for this amazing angel.

"I love you, too," I said, kissing the top of her head. "You know that's the first time we've said that?"

She nodded as she sniffed. "I mean it. I want to help you though. With this. I'm not going to let you do it on your own."

"Your pregnant, sweetheart, I'm not letting you take the strain of this."

"I'm pregnant, not disabled." She stepped back and glared at me, defiance shining in her golden eyes.

"I'm not putting you or our baby at risk."

"It's a few clothes. The Fates said that the baby's power would help me get through this."

"No."

"Ronin—"

"I said no. When I say no, I mean no. I'm not moving on this."

She sighed. "Fine. But if you need an extra pair of hands, promise you'll ask?"

I laughed. "Never."

Rubbing my hands together, I stalked towards the pile of clothes. Luxury dresses made of silk, velvet, fine cotton, all lavished with gems of some sort, stared back at me. Lots of bright red, gold, various blues and greens, all made me question why Makeysha had only ever worn black until a few hours ago. Still, now was not the time to ponder such silly things.

"Ronin, I'm so sorry," she whispered.

"Shush," I said, flexing my arms and eyeing up the first armful to scoop up. "What was it you said? 'Less chat and more action'?"

She grinned at me. "Fair point."

I bent down, hearing my father's voice and his monotonous 'bend your knees and not your back' saying. Somehow, I knew I would be thankful for that piece of advice by the end of this. I bundled a heap of Makeysha's past dresses into my arms, piled so high I couldn't even see over the top of it. Standing slowly, I grunted with the effort of lifting the surprisingly heavy clothes.

"Jeeze. How many clothes can one woman need?"

Step by step, I trudged up the incline, trying to ignore Makeysha's burning stare into my back. I could feel her watching me. I focused solely on putting one foot in front of the other. As the angle of the hill became steeper, and my foot falls become more and more angular, my muscles started complaining, burning with a deep ache I'd never felt before.

I pushed on, determined to reach the top. *Left foot. Right foot. You can do this. Left foot. Right foot. One more step.* I repeated the same words to myself, over and over in my head.

Sweat beaded on my forehead. My breaths were becoming shorter and shallower. As I started to wonder if I was anywhere near the top, I stumbled and fell forwards, face planting myself into the pile of dresses.

Scrabbling for a steady grip on the ground with my feet, I tried to stand up, but the incline was so steep, I couldn't find my footing after losing it. The only way for me to go from here was down, and down I slid, on my ass, surrounded by a load of women's clothes. Not my finest moment.

Makeysha stood at the bottom, one arm wrapped around her waist and the other lifted to her face, her hand covering her mouth. The creases at the corners of her eyes gave away the grin she was trying to hide. I narrowed my eyes at her but found myself chuckling.

"You were so close," she said, pointing to the top of the hill. "Another couple of steps and you'd have been there."

I turned around, gathering all the clothes back together, and noticed a stout middle-aged man pushing a boulder up the hill with his chest. As he neared the peak, giving hope that with a couple of more steps he'd reach the peak, he too tripped over his own feet and came tumbling back down to the bottom of the incline, the boulder careering down alongside him.

"I'll get it this time," I said, picking up the clothes again. "It's only a bit of grass."

Makeysha helped me pile the clothes into my arms, then gave me a kiss on the cheek. "I know you can do this."

Knowing she had faith in me spurred me on, making me even more determined to get this done and not let her down. My woman was depending on me and I would show her that she could rely on me even if it killed me.

I lumbered back up the hill, laden down with clothes, step by step. I took extra care with every foot fall I placed down, not taking my weight off one leg before I was convinced my other leg could take the strain.

Next to me, an old lady heaved a boulder up the hill, keeping pace with me. She had me questioning if she was superhuman or if I was just being too careful. Out of the corner of my eye, I could see her cheeks reddening, and her breaths were becoming louder and more laboured. As I placed my right foot down, my knee gave way, bringing me crashing to the floor. I roared with frustration, especially when I looked behind me to see how far I'd come.

The old lady next to me squealed. Her boulder hurtled down the hill at a frightening speed, thundering to the bottom for the next contender to attempt. She slid down on her ass, not that much ahead of me. Her grey hair was curled up into a bun, revealing the back of her neck. Her t-shirt had been caught under her ass, pulling the back of it down to expose the tops of her shoulders. Black writing spanned across the base of her neck.

It doesn't take strength to win. It takes the true heart of the team to win.

That made me start thinking. Perhaps letting Makeysha help me was the only way to complete this. Anger burned deep inside me. I was the man. I was supposed to take on the heavy side of the challenges we faced, handle all the physical side of things. That was the way I'd been brought up—old fashioned maybe, but I truly believed that was the way things like this should be handled. Regardless of the fact she was an angel and was probably stronger than me anyway.

As I reached the bottom of the hill, slowly sliding to a stop, I squashed down my male pride and forced myself to string together a sentence that hurt my very soul.

"Do you…" I cleared my throat "…do you want to err…maybe…give me a hand? Taking this up the hill, I mean."

Makeysha smirked. "Almost choked on those words, didn't you?"

The burn of my cheeks would have rivalled any degree of sunburn. "I should be able to do this on my own. I'm the man here. This is down to me."

"Calm down, Ronin. We live in an age of equality these days. Where have you been hiding all your life?"

I stood up and folded my arms over my chest. "Just because women now wear trousers, and body build, and run for president, it doesn't mean that I can't hold firm onto my beliefs. I've been brought up like the old days, where men were men, and women and were women. This is really hard for me."

She stepped forwards and placed her hands on my arms, flashing me a sympathetic smile. "Whilst I think that's really admirable, and very sweet, this—" she motioned a hand between us "—is supposed to be a partnership. We support each through thick and thin. Where one of us fails, the other steps in and picks up the pieces. It isn't a straight cut divide of you do this and I do that. And if in your old-fashioned beliefs, you have any ideas about me being pregnant and barefoot in the kitchen, you can get rid of them right now."

I grinned and slipped my arms around her waist. I pulled her close and said, "I quite like the idea."

"We'll discuss this later," she said, swatting my arm playfully. "Right now, let's get this done with. Seeing as you can't do it without me." She flashed me a grin.

Ouch. What a cut to the male pride. "You don't have to enjoy this so much, you know."

"Oh, I think I do. I tried to tell you to let me help you."

I laughed. "I see. So this is an opportunity for you to tell me 'I told you so'?"

She shrugged her shoulders. "Pretty much."

Shaking my head, I said, "Get the damn clothes."

Makeysha laughed and started gathering up the dresses. She picked one up and held it up in front of her. It was a beautiful midnight blue colour with a corset top and wide skirt at the bottom. Intricate gold lace stretched along its smooth surface, curled into swirling, pretty patterns.

"Do you think I can keep one?" she said, her voice all wistful and dreamy.

"I don't think so," I said, running my fingers through her long dark curls. Her hair was like silk to touch. "I'm sure we can buy you something similar when we're back on earth."

"Not quite the same though," she said, sighing. "I have lots of memories with this dress."

I raised my eyebrow. "What sort of memories?"

She turned and looked at me, then grinned. "Nothing that involves other men, don't worry. I used to wear this to family occasions. It's just a reminder of the closeness that I've been missing for so long."

I pulled her into my arms and planted a kiss on her soft lips. "Well now you have me, and my family. And we're creating our own family, too." I stepped back and laid my palm against her belly. "You're going to get all of that closeness back, and then some."

When I laid my hand against her body, a faint *thud-thud, thud-thud, thud-thud*, sounded in my head. I looked at Makeysha. The surprise in her golden eyes told me that she'd heard it too.

"What is that?" I whispered.

She settled her hand over mine and smiled such a warm smile, her eyes filled with water. "I think it's a heartbeat."

A lump rose in my throat and I choked back my own tears of joy. "That's amazing. How…how though? Isn't it a little early?"

She shook her head. "We're in Hell, time moves faster, the magic must have affected it in some way."

Fear gripped me. "Are you saying it's going to be

evil?"

"No," she said, giggling. "Just the magic down here must have affected my pregnancy, making it progress even faster than normal for an angel. Don't worry. We're not having Lucifer's spawn."

"I hope not. I'm telling you now, if it comes out with horns—"

"Then we'll love it anyway."

"Let's discuss that later," I said, grinning.

She draped her arms around my neck and kissed me with such sweet tenderness, I forgot we were stood in the depths of Hell. "Come on, smooth dude. Stop trying to seduce me and focus on the task in hand."

"Hey, you kissed me."

"Details," she said, laughing.

We turned to the clothes, piling them back up into a manageable heap. Then, we split it into two, which made life so much easier. We linked our arms together, lifted the clothes up, and set off up the incline. Our footfalls matched, helped no doubt by our synchronicity due to our bond. Both focused on the goal ahead, we stared at the top of the hill, determined to get there. Now my load had been halved and I could see where I was going, I knew we were going to do this.

A boulder crawled up the hill alongside us, pushed by a young man. As our progress matched, my heart leapt into my mouth as I began to wonder if the next step would be the step where we failed. The peak came closer and closer, and when the boulder next to us toppled back down the hill, hope flooded me in an instant.

"Come on, wise guy," Makeysha said, huffing and puffing. "We can do this."

One more step.

We were now the furthest anyone had ever reached. One final step and we'd be at the peak, having reached the first major milestone this realm had ever seen.

I let out a shout as I heaved us to that final step. Our feet stuck firm, not giving way, and I was able to throw the clothes onto the top of the hill.

"YES!" I yelled, gasping for breath. "We did it."

Makeysha shoved her clothes onto the peak and collapsed on the green grass beneath us, her hands holding onto the ledge that formed the beginning of the flat peak of the incline.

She turned her head towards me and blew her hair out of her face. "Key word there, smooth dude. WE."

I uncurled her fingers tightly gripping onto the ledge and took one of her hands into mine. "I admit it—you were right, and I was wrong."

She grinned and turned over onto her back. "Never have I ever been happier."

"Thought as much," I said, laughing and shaking my head.

She pushed herself down and tugged me along with her. "Time for the next load."

I looked at the bottom of the hill to see more clothes, complete with bowls of fresh fruit piled on top. "This is going to be a long ass day."

"Not that long. We're against the clock here, remember."

I pursed my lips and nodded. "We can do this."

Makeysha took my hand to her mouth and kissed it. "Yes, we can."

***

Sixteen piles of clothes later, fourteen horses, seventeen dogs, thirty cats, and goodness knows how many birds, I dared say we were done. Our own clothes were drenched in sweat, we were both weak and trembling from exhaustion, but the one amazing thing that had happened, just as Makeysha had said, was that our unborn child seemed to give us unknown strength.

With each trip up the hill we took, its heartbeat sounded stronger in our minds, and each time we thought we couldn't take another step, we somehow managed to find the stamina to carry on.

Now, as we sat hanging on to the ledge, looking at the bottom of the steep hill we'd climbed countless times, nothing sat waiting for us at the bottom.

"I think we're done," Makeysha said.

I took her hand and lifted it in the air, placing it over the top of the ledge. "One more push."

We turned over onto our stomachs and dragged ourselves up and over the peak, crumpling into drained, weary heaps as we finally found flat ground. As we laid there regaining our breath and allowing our jelly-like muscles to recuperate, a voice cut through the air.

"Are you coming to get this dagger or what?"

Grunting with the sheer effort of it, I lifted my head to see Imani, still sat as she had been the first time I saw her, but this time with the unicorn dagger in her hand draped over her knee. Her poker face and hard brown eyes gave off a sincere vibe of one unimpressed witch.

Makeysha rolled onto her side, facing Imani. "You've just seen what we've gone through. Have some patience."

A sinister smile tweaked at Imani's thin, pink lips.

"You should be careful who you speak to like that, Angel. I'm only on your side because of Caesar. Do not mistake me for a friend."

Makeysha forced herself into sitting up. "Don't start on me, Witch. That will be your last mistake."

"Whatever," Imani said, snorting. "Here. See you upstairs."

She threw the dagger at Makeysha with such force, it flew through the air as if it was a perfectly balanced throwing knife.

"No!" I yelled, launching myself over Makeysha to protect her.

The dagger whistled past my ear as I rolled over my soulmate to shield her from the angel killing blade. Immortal or not, I wasn't taking any chances that she could be hurt. A few seconds later, a heavy thud sounded somewhere behind us.

I looked up to see Imani still sat there, smiling maliciously. My blood began to boil.

"Calm down," Makeysha said, laying a hand on my forearm. "She's trying to goad you."

"It's working," I replied, shuffling off her, taking care to avoid her stomach. "Stupid bitch."

"Let's just get the dagger and go," she said, pressing a kiss to my lips. "I can't believe you threw yourself in front of me like that." Tears welled in her beautiful golden eyes. "I love you."

I stood up and took her under the arm, lifting her to her feet. "Guess it's just me and my old-fashioned ways," I replied, giving her a big goofy grin.

She laughed. "Get the dagger, smooth dude."

I strode over to the dagger, amazed that the small witch had managed to throw it so far with her tiny arms. I looked back down the hill, seeing the souls still trying to achieve what we just had. A slight twinge of sadness tugged at my insides as I realised they would be here forever, trying to attain an impossible goal.

Picking up the dagger, I walked back to my soulmate, took her hand and led us over to the angry witch who was our ticket out of here. We'd barely got within a foot of her when a whirlwind scooped us up high into the air.

We were tossed and turned inside the violent energy before being spat out in front of Lucia and Caesar once more. I looked up at Lucia and grinned, brandishing the unicorn dagger in the air.

"We did it!"

Lucia opened her mouth, but the voice that said, "Congratulations," was not Lucia's. It was a deep, gravelly male voice that oozed authority.

Makeysha gasped and scurried away from my side, her eyes filled with fear. From her reaction, I knew the answer to my wondering, but I had to turn around to see him for myself.

Lucifer.

CHAPTER THIRTY-THREE

Makeysha

Even though we were in Hell, in Lucifer's domain, I hadn't entertained the idea of seeing him again. The fact we had gotten down here, gone through all the realms, and retrieved all the daggers, had left me with an illusion that we would escape back out of Hell without seeing him.

Wrong.

Here he stood, feet away from me, in all his former glory that I remembered. A power house of muscles, towering height, a presence that demanded people bow down to him. His once bright golden eyes were now as dark as his raven black hair and they oozed nothing but hatred and negativity. He unfolded his wings, which had also turned the darkest shade of black.

"Hello, Makeysha," he said, tweaking his mouth up into a sarcastic smile. "Long time, no see. You've had quite the adventure these past few days, hmmm?"

I froze. He'd essentially been my MD all those years ago. With us both being angels, he technically was still my MD, just relocated. The fire burning deep in my belly was doused in fear the instant I saw him.

"I...I...I..."

"Leave her alone," Ronin said, stepping in front of me. "You got a problem with her, you got a problem with me."

Lucifer narrowed his eyes at Ronin, then tipped his head back and laughed. "Oh, dear human, you are amusing. I admire your bravery though. I may spare you a few hours of pain just for that."

Panic swamped me. I scrabbled to my feet and jumped up, grabbing hold of Ronin's forearm. "Don't antagonise him, Ronin. Seriously."

He slipped his arm around my waist and pressed a kiss to the side of my head. "Don't worry, sweetheart. I've got this."

"No, no, no, you don't," I said, shaking my head. "Please, just leave it."

"You should listen to your girlfriend, human," Lucifer said. "She's known me a very long time. She knows exactly what I'm capable of." He narrowed his eyes on me as he spoke his last words.

I swallowed the ball of fear choking my airway. Pissing Lucifer off wasn't something I was in a hurry to do again.

"You should be ashamed of yourselves," Lucifer said, staring at Lucia and Caesar. "I trusted you to carry out a simple task, something that no one but us should have known about. Instead, for whatever reason, you decide to collude with the enemy. Do you have anything to say for yourselves?"

Lucia offered him a small smile. "Your mistake was thinking you were the only one who could offer us what we all wanted. Turns out, you were wrong."

The air around Lucifer changed in an instant. His entire demeanour darkened to a degree I'd never seen. He seemed to visibly vibrate with rage as he stared Lucia down.

"And you thought that this disgraced angel would have the power to reunite your parents?" He bellowed with laughter. "I thought you were intelligent, Lucia. I never took you for a fool."

Lucia blinked. When she opened her eyes, the milky white eyes we'd seen for the past few days vanished, leaving behind a startling pair of sapphire blue eyes. I gasped.

Lucia grinned at Lucifer. "Who said anything about the angel helping me?"

Lucifer faltered, he even staggered backwards a step. "Then who?"

The warlock's grin grew even wider. "The Fates."

I choked on my sharp inhale of breath. Even Ronin sucked in a deep breath.

Lucifer's jaw dropped. "Impossible."

"Very far from impossible," Lucia replied.

The colour drained from Lucifer's face. The charge in the air his fury had brought dissipated, leaving nothing but a strained silence. His attitude shrunk, and if I didn't know better, I'd say he physically became smaller too.

Lucia suddenly sprung to life, moving her hands

in circular motions in front of her. A slight breeze stirred around us, then turned into a violent wind. A rounded portal opened in between Lucia's hands, the ripples in time and space wrinkling out through the air.

"Time for you to have some self-reflection," Lucia shouted, above the noise of the wind.

Lucifer attempted to disappear, but his magic failed him. His body flickered with colourful streaks of magic like a light bulb sputtering before it dies.

"What is happening to me?" he cried, hitting himself as his magic slowly faded him.

"You don't need magic where you're going," Lucia said, giving him a coy smile. "Don't worry. I'll bottle it all up and save it."

Lucia moved her portal, tilting the widening entrance towards Lucifer. She thrust it towards him. Lucifer screamed like a little girl as the moving mass engulfed him in one. Lucia brought her hands together, making the portal smaller. As her palms met, a 'pop' sounded around us, like bubble wrap being stomped on. Just like that, Lucifer was gone.

If I hadn't been holding onto Ronin, I think I would have fallen over in shock. "Where...where have you sent him?"

Lucia turned and gave me a warm and friendly smile. "Tartarus."

I smirked. "Wanda got her wish in the end."

"Oh, that wasn't for Wanda," Lucia said. "That was for the good of every living thing."

"Were you being serious when you said The Fates were helping you?"

"Oh yes," she said. "I met with them before we even met."

That had some questions churning around my

mind. "So you were on our side before we even had our fight?"

Lucia nodded, a sheepish grin sweeping over her face. "I'm afraid so."

"So I didn't…bewitch you or whatever?"

She shook her head. "Oh, no, you did bewitch me. It was more the fact I let it happen so easily. We felt it imperative that I needed to be subservient in order to gain your trust in me. If I'd looked like me, you wouldn't have believed my sincerity in helping you."

"But…but why are you helping us?"

"The Fates showed me a world where Lucifer gained his wish. It was not a world that I wanted to live in, nor have any part in creating. It was utter carnage, and whilst you may know me for being bad, I'm not really. I do have a heart and a soul."

"I saw it," I said, grinning like a Cheshire cat. "They showed me the same thing."

She nodded. "I told them they would need to take drastic action with you."

I laughed. "It was that that changed my mind."

"Sorry to interrupt the chat, ladies," Ronin said. "But aren't we on a time schedule here?"

Lucia nodded. "Well, no, not really."

"The full moon?" I said. "We need to get to Mount Olympus."

Lucia shook her head. She laid her hands out flat, palms facing up. The seven daggers we'd so painfully fought for over the past few days appeared on her petite hands. "These are going elsewhere. Whilst The Fates admired your plans for them, and it was a very good one, they have a better home for them."

"Have you met The Fates since all of this started?"

Lucia nodded. "Yes. They helped me convince the others."

"I'm guessing," Ronin said. "That the daggers are going with them?"

"Yes," Lucia replied.

As she said this, a crack of lightning struck the middle of the cave we were in, opening up a chasm. The rift widened and as it did, Aurora stepped through, followed by her two sisters.

"Hello, Makeysha. Congratulations," she said.

Lucia stepped forwards and bowed down, offering the daggers up to the sisters. Freya had a brown hessian sack in her hands. She opened it and one by one, placed each dagger inside it.

"We do believe, Makeysha," said Selene. "That Heaven needs a helping hand getting itself back on its feet. There are some archangels that need rescuing and some soulmates that need reuniting."

"How do I...how do I even do that?" I said.

"Open the Heavens so what is below can come above, and vice versa," Aurora said. "God sealed himself and the angels inside when he threw you and all of the others from Heaven. It was a small rip in that seal which allowed his angels to come down to earth in the first place. When he discovered it, he created a triple layer, stopping any further visits from angels to earth."

"Wow," Ronin said, letting out a long breath. "It really is by chance that we exist."

Freya glanced at him and smiled. "Everything happens for a reason. Don't forget that."

"I can't go to Heaven," I said. "I tried so many times to go back up there but whenever I flew too high, my wings would burn up and I'd come crashing right back down."

"Lucia?" Selene said, turning to the warlock who'd apparently been a secret aide all this time.

Lucia rubbed her hands together then faced her palms at my head. Slowly, she moved them downwards, until she was on her knees, at my feet. Then she worked her way back up at the same leisurely pace.

"There," she said. "All cleansed. All done."

"Now I can fly to Heaven?" I asked.

She nodded. "Free as a bird. God put a restriction on you when he cast you out."

"What will happen to him?" I said.

Lucia smiled. "I think he needs some more reflection time yet. He and Lucifer have some big egos to get over before we consider helping them out of their respective prisons."

"I don't understand. God is in The Gardens of Eden."

"Yes," Aurora said. "We took the opportunity to seal him in there after his revealing conversation with you. He had already shut himself away anyway."

I couldn't help but laugh. "Oh, I bet he is livid."

The three sisters all smiled, confirming my suspicions that God was not a happy being right now.

"Heaven needs a strong leader," Freya said, looking at me. Her blue eyes burned right through my soul. "One who understands the true tests of purging their sins, facing their worst fears, and teamwork."

My jaw dropped. "Wait, what?"

"The time has come for a new age," Selene said. "And we believe you are the one to lead us into that, Makeysha. You, Ronin, and your baby. An age where soulmates are no longer a hidden secret, a power to be controlled by egotistical maniacs, and everyone has the opportunity to be something special."

"What about Lucifer's creatures?" Ronin said.

"They shall continue as part of the circle of life. As shall your kind, Ronin," Aurora said. "But not all of them are evil. It is up to you hunters to distinguish the good from the bad."

"As if we didn't have enough to do already," he said dryly.

"I'm not an archangel," I said, anxiety slowly squeezing my heart. "I can't possibly be any sort of leader."

"Hierarchy doesn't mean anything," Freya said. "Your experiences and your strength of character far outweigh any political advantage the archangels have. This is the way the Universe has willed things to be. Embrace it."

"I can't just go strolling in there after all this time and suddenly say I'm their new leader," I said, my voice getting squeakier and higher.

"You won't need to. Once you release the archangels, everyone will look to you with a new faith," Selene explained. "It will be fine. Everything will work out."

I looked at Ronin, the reality of this still not really sinking in. "Can you pinch me and wake me up please?"

He took my hand and kissed the back of it. "I'm afraid it's all real, sweetheart."

Caesar walked up to me, his young face devoid of any emotion. "If you do this, reunite our parents, you'll have restored faith in every angel that ever was. I want you to do this because I don't want to have to hate you. You've grown on me."

I laughed, fighting back the tears. "I won't let you down."

"We must be going," Aurora said, turning her and her sisters back towards the lightning chasm.

"But we will always be watching," Freya said.

"And planning," said Selene.

The Fates disappeared back into their realm, another crack of lightning sealing their doorway shut. It seemed oddly quiet and surreal now that they'd left, along with the daggers.

"Well, I guess there's one less thing to do now," I said, sighing in what I would dare call contentment.

"Actually," Ronin said. "I was kind of thinking, now we have some spare time, that we could do something else."

I grinned at him and ran my hands down his chest. "Oh really?"

He chuckled. "Whilst I definitely want to take you up on that, I was thinking, especially as it seems we're going to be in Heaven for goodness knows how long, that maybe we could go see my family?"

I took a moment to soak in his words. His family. I hadn't even thought far enough ahead to consider the prospect of meeting his parents and fellow hunter community. It was daunting to say the least.

"I…err…I don't know. I mean, isn't it going to be a little weird, rocking up with me in tow, announcing we're soulmates and pregnant and all?"

"Are you kidding?" he said, grinning like anything. "My mom is desperate for grandkids. She'll be ecstatic."

"I'm sure she expected a human grandchild, not some hybrid super powerful baby that is capable of who knows what."

He slid his arms around my shoulders and drew me into his arms. "Are you nervous?"

"No," I said, shaking my head. "Me? Nervous? Never."

"I promise I'll protect you. Ok?"

I grinned and kissed him. "That could be something I can live with. The thought of you protecting me makes me feel all funny inside."

"I can do other things to make you feel all funny inside," he said, wiggling his eyebrows.

Lucia tutted. "Get a room already."

My cheeks burned with heat as I turned my attention to her. "Sorry."

She threw me a cheeky wink and lifted her arms up towards the ceiling. Waves of bright red energy blasted from her hands, penetrating the rocky cave above us. Within seconds, she'd created a hole that went straight up, through the depths of Hell, and right up to the blue skies of earth.

"Up you go," she said, motioning for us to move underneath it. "It'll take you back to the cemetery."

"Thanks, Lucia. For all your help. We really appreciate it."

She smiled, and if I didn't know better, I'd swear blind I saw some water welling over her blue eyes. "I'll see you soon."

We stepped underneath the hole and found ourselves being propelled past all the layers it had pierced through at such a speed, everything became a blur. When everything stopped moving, I dared to move my head, only to be relieved when I realised we were back in front of my old crypt.

I sighed and wrapped my arms around Ronin. "We're home."

CHAPTER THIRTY-FOUR

Ronin

Whilst my intention was to dive beneath the soft covers of Makeysha's bed and shower her in my undivided attention, unfortunately all that happened was both of us crashing out into a deep sleep the second our heads hit the pillows.

I woke up to blinding sunlight piercing through my darkened eyelids. As I forced my eyes open and revelled in waking up to a beautiful day, I sighed in contentment. I turned my head to see Makeysha still fast asleep, her long dark eyelashes resting against her smooth pale skin.

After a decent night's sleep in the world's most comfortable bed, I felt able to tackle anything;

including my family. I knew Makeysha was nervous about meeting them, despite what she said. In all fairness, I understood where she was coming from. She'd been on her own for two thousand years, then all of a sudden within the space of a few days, she'd gained a soulmate, been thrust into the middle of an apocalyptic event, gotten pregnant, and now faced meeting even more new people who would love and cherish her just as much as I did. I could see how claustrophobic it must be making her feel.

I debated whether we would drive back to my parents or whether Makeysha would want to teleport, so we had a quick way out if needed. Driving would give us an opportunity to relax and at least attempt to be normal whilst enjoying some gorgeous scenery.

The rhythmic thud-thud, thud-thud, thud-thud of our baby's heartbeat was growing stronger every second. In some ways it was an ominous reminder of how our lives would be turned upside down very soon, but in other ways, it was a privilege to have a direct link to our child's life force and was a comforting reassurance that it was growing well.

Makeysha stirred in her sleep and let out a gentle moan. Desire tugged at me instantly as my mind filled with memories from our first time together. The feel of her silky soft skin, her sweet kisses, the way she twizzled her tongue around me when she took me in her mouth…

I shook my head, trying to dispel the thoughts away. Now was not the time to be getting horny. I let my mind wander to thoughts of Heaven and what exactly it would be like up there. After meeting Apnastin, I couldn't help but feel dread when I thought of what must be the current state of affairs in Heaven.

"Morning, Handsome," Makeysha said, breaking through my thoughts.

I turned to her and smiled. "Good morning, Beautiful."

"How are you feeling?"

"Like I saved the world."

She grinned at me. "You mean 'we'."

I reached out and slipped an arm around her waist, loving how warm and silky she felt. "Of course I mean 'we'." I took a deep breath and then said, "I thought we should go see my family today, get it out of the way so we can go and save Heaven."

She immediately tensed up. She dropped her eye contact and said, "Oh, I err…I figured saving Heaven would be higher up on the agenda…"

"Well we don't know how long we're going to be up there. And it would be nice for my parents to meet you before we throw a grandchild into the mix."

Several seconds ticked by, then she said, "Ok. But we can't stay too long. We've still got angels to save."

I gave her a gentle kiss and brushed her dark curls from her cheek. "If it helps, we can teleport there. That way when you've had enough, we can just leave instantly. Plus, I was thinking the dramatic entrance might help me persuade my mom that all of this is true and I'm not lying."

Makeysha laughed. "Ok, smooth dude. You've got yourself a deal."

Several minutes later, after a fresh change of clothes and some croissants and orange juice, I felt ready to tackle the world.

"Ready?" I said, holding my hand out to my soulmate.

She grasped my hand and nodded. "Ready as I'll

ever be."

We'd decided teleporting was the best way. I wanted the drama factor to shock my mom more than anything. How else would she believe that her son has found his soulmate, who happens to be a legendary angel, and has a child on the way with said legendary angel?

I closed my eyes and filled my mind with thoughts of home. Makeysha took the driving seat with the magic side of things. Whilst I could feel her power bubbling through my veins, magic was more her domain than mine. I didn't feel comfortable even turning a light on with the click of my fingers for fear of setting something on fire. It was just safer for the world if I left that part of me alone for now.

The ground started shaking. I squeezed Makeysha's hand for comfort. This was still bizarre for me despite everything we'd been through.

"We'll be fine," she said, her sweet voice echoing around my mind.

No sooner had she said that than my world became still again. I didn't even get time to open my eyes before dishes clattered to the floor and my mom screamed, "Ronin?"

I opened my eyes to see we'd landed right in the middle of my kitchen, whilst Mom was cooking breakfast. Bacon and eggs lay splattered against the wooden flooring, the frying pan a little way away, turned upside down. My mom stood in front of us, her hands over her mouth and her big brown eyes wide open in shock.

"Honey?" Dad said, rushing into the kitchen. He stopped and stumbled back when he saw us. "Oh my! Ronin?"

"Hey, Mom. Hey, Dad." I lifted mine and Makeysha's clasped hands and gave them my best smile. "This is Makeysha."

Mom's knees wobbled and she fell forwards onto the kitchen table, clutching at it for support. "She's a…she's the…*the* angel…" Her voice trailed off into a whisper.

I nodded. "Shall we go sit down?"

Dad, clutching onto the kitchen doorway, nodded, the colour rapidly draining from his face. "I think that would be a good idea."

I took the lead into the cosy living room. Seeing the aged red sofas, the coal-burned wooden floor in front of the open fire, and the spread of family pictures on the wall made me realise how much I missed home. It had only been a few days, but the familiar smell of recently washed clothes in Mom's special citrus laundry powder, cooking breakfast, and the fresh outdoors blowing in through the open windows made me so grateful for my upbringing. And at the same time, it made me sad for Makeysha. She had missed out on her home comforts for much longer than a few days and yet here I was, appreciating the small things after a mere few days.

Makeysha's lips were pulled into a thin line and her golden eyes were full of uncertainty.

"We're going to be just fine," I said to her.

"I know. I trust you."

I lifted her hand to my mouth and kissed the back of it. Dad took his seat in his favourite armchair. Its well-worn red fabric was close to being threadbare, but he refused to throw it out.

"That's what makes it so comfortable," he'd say. "It takes years to mould furniture to you."

Mom perched herself on the arm, holding onto Dad's shoulder for all she was worth. Her hands were white from where she gripped Dad so hard.

"It's been an interesting few days," I said, looking at my life givers with a renewed sense of love.

Dad, with his cart-horse build, bald head, and stern features, looked surprised. I felt like I'd managed to achieve at least something by wiping the angry look off his face he usually had.

"It turns out," I continued. "That the angel from all our stories is true. And this is her. She happens to be my soulmate, she's pregnant with my child, and we also kind of saved the world."

Mom raised an eyebrow. Dad narrowed his eyes, his eyes glassing over with his normal hard stare. Seconds ticked by. I hadn't really known how else to deliver the news other than to just come right out with it and lay it all bare on the table.

All of a sudden, Mom burst out laughing. She clutched a hand to her chest and doubled over in laughter, nearly falling off the chair in the process. Dad took hold of her forearm, keeping her from tumbling to the floor.

"That's not funny, son," Dad said.

"It wasn't meant to be funny," I said. "I'm being serious. Did you miss the part where we teleported into your kitchen?"

Mom's laughter died down, gradually coming to a stop, at last. "You're...you're actually serious?" she said.

"Do you see me laughing?"

Makeysha squeezed my hand and then cleared her throat. "I understand this must be a bit of a shock for you, but I can assure you, what Ronin just said is one hundred percent true." She outstretched her hand towards my mom. "I can let you hear the baby's heartbeat if you like."

Mom's eyes fluttered. Then she fainted, falling off the chair and landing in a crumpled heap on the floor.

Dad looked at me and lifted his eyebrows. "Well done, son. You've managed to shock your mother more than your brother."

***

Twenty minutes later, Mom came around on her own. Makeysha offered to bring her back around sooner but I told her Mom had had enough shocks already, let alone being magically brought back to consciousness. Besides, the time might help her soak in all this crazy.

Laid out on the sofa, Mom looked up and saw Makeysha and I stood over her, concerned. "You're really here?" she said.

I chuckled. "Yes, Mom."

She sighed and slowly sat up. "I'm so sorry. That was just a bit too much to take in." She pressed her hands to her mouth and smiled, the corners of her eyes creasing up. Tears filmed over her eyes. "Are you really pregnant? With my boy's baby?"

Makeysha gave her a dazzling smile and nodded. "It's complicated, how it's all happened, but yes. And we are soulmates."

Mom dropped her hands and reached for Makeysha. "And the whole saving the world thing?"

"Yes. Lucifer up to his usual tricks. But he's safely locked away in Tartarus for now."

Mom gripped Makeysha's hands and dropped her

gaze to Makeysha's stomach. "And you can really let me hear the heartbeat?"

"Sure," Makeysha replied, grinning wildly. "Here." She put my mom's hand on her stomach and then pressed two fingers to her temple. She closed her eyes and said, "And there. You should be able to hear it."

Mom gasped and then burst into tears whilst grinning like a kid a candy shop. "Oh my goodness. This is amazing. Mary Whittaker is going to wipe that smug grin off her face now."

Dad rolled his eyes.

Makeysha looked at me with a questioning glance.

"Don't ask," I said.

"What about Leyani?" Dad said. "She's going to be extremely upset."

"Leyani?" Makeysha asked.

"Long story. I'll tell you later."

"A hunter?"

"Yes. It was a marriage that our parents wanted, and Leyani, but I never did. I've never spoken more than a few words with her."

Makeysha smiled at me. I presumed what I said scored me some brownie points.

"I can't go against the will of the Universe, Dad," I said, shrugging my shoulders. "Things happen for a reason. For whatever reason, Makeysha is my soulmate and this is my life. I'm not going to apologise for that."

"What am I supposed to tell Brian Shipton?" Dad said, frowning at me. "We presumed your absence and lack of communication was because you were finalising things with Wanda. Now you turn up and tell us this?"

"Bert," Mom said, her tone harsh. "Their life path has nothing to do with anyone else. The Shipton's will just have to deal with it."

"They've refused offers from other families, even the Greenacres, because they wanted this union. Now I've got to tell them that their daughter isn't good enough. Do you have any idea what kind of a position that puts me in?"

Makeysha's eyes darkened and the buzz of her energy in my mind told me she was feeling something very strong about my dad's appalling reaction.

"I'll go and smooth things over with them," I said, hoping my offer would help diffuse the situation. "It'll look better if I do it anyway. It's more respectful."

Dad stood up and folded his arms over his chest. "Too damn right you will. I don't care if your soulmate has turned up, all angelic wings and all, you're making me break my word, Ronin. If there's one thing I've ever been in my life, it's a man of my word."

"I think you're being extremely cruel and unfair, Bert," Mom said.

"Where's Brandon?" I asked.

"He's out on a werewolf hunt in Washington."

I nodded. "Ok. Well, we can't stay long. We've still got things to tie up and sort out."

"Just make sure you go and see the Shipton's before you disappear to wherever it is you're going," Dad said.

"I'll go now," I said, narrowing my eyes at my father. "Ok?"

He scowled at me before storming outside, no doubt to go and play with his guns and knives, which is what he normally did whenever he was in a bad mood.

"Don't pay any attention to him, honey," Mom said. "You know he doesn't like change. He had this whole idea in his head of how things were going to be once we were coupled with the Shipton's. He's just a bit shocked, that's all. Give him a couple of hours and he'll be fine."

I sighed. "But still, he's being really rude and very unwelcoming to Makeysha. Hardly a great first impression for her is it?"

"It's ok," Makeysha said. "I know males can be like children at the best of times. I can imagine this is all a bit of a shock for him and he doesn't really know how to react."

"Oh really?" I said, raising my eyebrows. "We act like children, do we?"

Makeysha grinned at me. "Yes, you do."

"I'm going to do the manly thing and go over to the Shipton's. Then we'll get on our way. Ok?" I gave her a cheeky grin.

"Let her down gently, Ronin," Makeysha said. "Poor girl will be devastated."

"I'll do my best."

I gave her a parting kiss then headed out to the Shipton's cabin. I was determined to smooth things over with them so I could patch things up with my dad more than anything.

CHAPTER THIRTY-FIVE

Makeysha

Whilst Ronin went to break some hunter girl's heart, I helped Irene, his mom, clean up the mess in the kitchen that we'd inadvertently caused.

"I'm so sorry about Bert," she said, scooping up the bacon and eggs. "He's really quite a sensitive man at heart. He doesn't take too kindly to massive changes."

"Honestly, it's fine," I said. "I understand. All of this still seems surreal to me to be honest."

"Can I just say I'm so honoured to meet you. You're a real legend in our world. I can't believe you're stood here in my kitchen, pregnant with my son's child. This is…" she shook her head "…beyond my wildest dreams."

"Thank you," I said, grabbing the mop from near the back door. "But I'm really not such a legend. You do know I'm pretty much the lowest form of angel and then some?"

"You're still an angel. The only link to those who created us. Do you know which angels were responsible for giving us our powers?"

I shook my head. "I'm sorry, I don't. I can try to find out for you, if you're really interested?"

She nodded enthusiastically. "We've always known our powers are thanks to the angels, but we're all so different, it must be down to what angel blessed who. Right?"

"Possibly. Or it could be how your ancestor's DNA responded to the angelic powers."

"So we could all have been blessed by the same angel?"

"Maybe."

"Funny how things work, isn't it?"

She started humming to herself as she picked up the last of the bacon and headed to the trash can. I scrubbed the floor with the mop, thinking how homely and comfortable I felt here. It felt like a home from home.

"How long have you and Bert been married?" I asked.

"Over thirty years," she replied, smiling wildly. "Rupert was my—" she slapped a hand over her mouth "—Bert was my childhood sweetheart. My one and only."

"Rupert?" I said, giggling.

"That's his official name, but he hates it. He can't have 'Pert' as a nickname, so we call him 'Bert' instead. Makes him seem more manly."

I laughed. "I don't think I can look at him in the same way again knowing his real name."

"Don't tell him I told you. He won't speak to me for weeks."

We laughed together as we finished cleaning up. Then we sat and chatted over a cup of coffee whilst we waited for Ronin to come back. As we drained the last dregs, he breezed back in through the door, complete with Bert lazing a hand over his son's shoulders and a broad grin on his face.

"Congratulations to you both," Bert said. "I'm so sorry about before."

"It's ok," I said, giving him a smile.

"No, it's not. I behaved totally inappropriately and all for nothing. My worries and concerns should not reflect on your moment of joy."

"Honestly, it's fine," I said. "Thank you for apologising." I looked at Ronin. "How did it go?"

"I left out the part of my soulmate being, well, you, and filled him in on everything else, except of course the apocalyptic scenario. He was totally fine, completely understood that I needed to be with whoever the Universe had matched me with, especially as I was lucky enough to find them."

"And Leyani?" Irene said.

"She cried but said she was happy for me. She also hinted at being interested in Brandon when he's ready to settle down."

Irene squealed and clapped her hands together. "See, Bert? It's all working out nicely."

He slapped Ronin on the back. "Never doubted you'd smooth things over, son."

Ronin looked at me and said, "Is it time to go?" Then added in my mind, *"Please. Get me out of here. Small doses and all that."*

I smirked. "Yes, we ought to be going really."

"Where are you going?" Irene said. "Can we help?"

"No, Mom," Ronin replied. "You can't go where we're going."

She pouted. "When will you be back?"

"I don't know. Could be a few days, could be a few weeks."

"Well don't be gone too long. I want to see this one blooming in her pregnancy," she said, gripping my arm in excitement.

"Of course," Ronin said, widening his eyes at me in such a way that clearly said 'time to go'.

Ronin kissed his mom on each cheek, shook hands with his dad and then stood by the door. Irene embraced me in a tight hug, then pecked both of my cheeks. Bert merely raised his hand and nodded his head.

I took hold of my soulmate's hand and with a final wave goodbye to his parents, I teleported us back to my crypt.

"Thought we were going up?" Ronin said, looking up at the clear blue sky.

"We are. But I didn't think you'd want your entire community seeing us flying into the Heavens."

"No, not really," he said, chuckling.

"Then let's go," I said.

I uncurled my wings, revelling in feeling them fully stretch. Ronin hadn't developed wings when we'd complete the bond, but he had the same powers. I don't think he quite trusted in them yet though as he seemed to like leaving the magic side of things to me.

Taking in one last sweeping glance of my cosy

crypt, I pushed upwards with my feet and flapped my wings to get us in flight. Ronin curled his arms around my waist and nestled his head on my breasts. I couldn't help but smile.

We reached the clouds, bursting through them at a rate of knots. I carried on going, beating my wings harder and faster in a desperate bid to get into Heaven as quickly as possible. As we reached the outer edge of the earth's atmosphere, we surged into a sea of thick fluffy clouds.

I grinned. This was the layer—the one God had sealed me out of. I pushed through, finally exploding into bright rays of sunshine. I slowed my ascent and looked around for somewhere to land. When I took in the sight before me, I gasped in shock, tears flooding my eyes.

The once Great Hall lay filthy and abandoned, its doors wide open, the glass table still shattered into millions of pieces. The layer of dust covering the floor must have been a good inch or more thick. Panic swarming me, I rushed through the thermal waves, divebombing through them to the castles. I hadn't yet seen one single angel.

"What's wrong?" Ronin said.

"There should be more angels roaming freely and going about their daily tasks, but there's no one. It's like Heaven is shut down."

"I do believe your friend said Heaven is in chaos."

"He's not my friend. And we need to decide what to do with him."

Ronin snorted. "I think you know my answer."

"Murder isn't the answer to everything, smooth dude."

"It is where I come from."

I laughed. "Well not where I come from."

The black roof turrets of Gabriel's castle peeked at me through a thin layer of cloud. Dirt and grime lined its once pristine exterior, making it look like a derelict building. As I flew down, I saw the white walls were a murky grey, the windows misted up and impossible to see through. If a building could look sad, this former home of mine was the epitome of sad, lonely, and neglected.

Outside, on the cloudy expanse where we used to gather to sun gaze, stood a small group of angels. A few stragglers sat upon the stairs leading up to the huge double doors that were wide open, revealing more forlorn looking angels.

As I came into land, a sea of blonde heads turned upwards, watching me in shock and awe. Their golden eyes glistened with hope. I landed on the top of the stairs and folded my wings away. Ronin uncurled himself from my body and looked around him, the amazement on his handsome face matching that of my former comrades.

"Makeysha?"

I turned to the pitiful female voice and saw it came from an older angel by the name of Jeshya. Even though aging in Heaven was impossible, Jeshya looked like she'd aged by a thousand years. Her once senior beauty was now shrouded in confusion and sorrow, her eyes no longer gleamed bright with life but were shadowed with distress.

"Hi, Jeshya."

"What…what are you doing here?" She laid her eyes on Ronin and gasped. "And you brought a human?" She narrowed her eyes at him, scrutinising his aura. "But he has angelic powers. What's going on?"

"It's a long story," I said. "This is Ronin. He's my soulmate and is a hunter from earth. He has my angelic powers now we've sealed our bond."

Jeshya's hand flew to her mouth. "Oh my goodness. A soulmate? Really?" Her eyes glistened with tears. "This is amazing. The best news we've had for I don't know how long."

"I'm here to help, Jeshya," I said, reaching for her hand. "Tell me where Apnastin is."

Her pale features immediately darkened. "Nasty, nasty being. Do you know what he's done?"

I nodded. "That's why I'm here. I'm here to free the archangels and put everything right."

"So God can return?"

"I'm afraid," I said, squeezing her hand in comfort. "That God needs some time for self-reflection. He won't be coming back for a while."

A strangled sob left her throat.

"I can't explain everything right now, Jeshya, but you need to trust me, ok? Higher powers are at play here and this is their will."

She nodded and sniffed loudly. "He's down by the Pegasus fields. The archangels are bound and gagged in the middle of the fields. That's why we couldn't help get them back. They're out of our bounds."

"Don't worry," I said. "I'll sort it." I turned to Ronin, who was staring inside the castle, his mouth wide open as he soaked in all the architecture. "You can marvel at it later, smooth dude. Grab a hold of me, we're off again."

He turned to me and grinned. "Grab a hold of you? Do you even need to ask?"

I laughed at him as he wrapped his arms back around my waist and clung on to me whilst I took to the skies once more. The Pegasus fields were at the highest point of Heaven. The unicorns also grazed here and were protected by the Pegasus. Only the archangels and God's confidantes could go there. On the rare occasion a regular angel needed to go up there, they were blessed with specific powers to aid them in their quest.

Many years ago, one of the Pegasus had escaped and gone on a rampage around Heaven, trashing everything he came into contact with. He ended up flying right into Gabriel's castle, where I was cleaning the marble floor in the entrance hall. I somehow managed to calm him enough to get a rope around his neck. Gabriel had instructed me to take him back immediately, blessing me with the powers to do it. Of course, afterwards, I'd sneakily tried my luck in going back up to the fields and found that my powers were still intact. I had no doubt that they still would be valid now.

Soaring up through the thermals, disturbing them all once more, I headed up and up until I felt my wings couldn't carry me any further. Then, just as I thought I was going to fail and crash back down to Heaven, the lush green pastures of the Pegasus fields came into view.

A fresh burst of energy propelled me towards my goal. Seconds later, I was landing on soft grass, immediately scanning the rolling horizon for Apnastin. Ronin let go and gazed around him.

"Wow," he said, breathless. "This is absolutely stunning."

"I know. It's so peaceful up here. Well, until one of the Pegasus decides to try and kill you."

He raised an eyebrow. "You are joking, right?"

I grinned. "They are quite hostile. They're wild and they know that when angels come up here, it's usually because one of the unicorns is going to die."

"Made yourselves some friends then," he said, chuckling.

In the far distance, against the backdrop of some beautiful hills, I saw what appeared to be a small cluster of…something. I just couldn't quite make out what exactly it was.

"There," I said, pointing to it. "I think that's our archangels."

Ronin squinted, trying to make out the odd shape stuck in the middle of the otherwise flat landscape. "What is that?"

"The archangels. Jeshya said they were bound and gagged in the middle of the fields."

"Can we fly or have we got to walk?"

I threw him a cheeky smile. "Depends how adventurous you're feeling."

He frowned. "Why?"

"Well, we could fly, but the Pegasus don't take kindly to angels being up here, let alone flying. We can risk it, but there's no telling—"

"We'll walk."

I laughed at him and held my hand out. "Come on then, smooth dude. Time for a walk."

He grasped my hand and started marching towards the bundle of archangels. "Your friend up here somewhere?"

"He's not my friend," I replied, rolling my eyes. "But yes, he'll be hanging around somewhere."

"Where? It's not like there's millions of places to hide."

I hadn't taken my eyes off the vast expanse in

front of us, searching for Apnastin, but I could see no sign of him. "I'm sure he'll make himself known when the time suits him."

"Have you got any ideas on how to take him down?"

I faltered for a moment. "Actually, no. I've taken the daggers for granted the past few days, always having one to hand. It hadn't even occurred to me I'd need a weapon for this."

"He's a fruit loop, Makeysha. He's gone in the head and you're telling me we've come up here with nothing?"

"We've got our powers. And we're immortal don't forget."

"That doesn't mean I want to suffer pain unnecessarily."

I giggled at him. "We'll be fine. I have faith in the Universe, even if it does work in mysterious ways."

He looked at me out of the corner of his eye but said nothing as we continued heading towards our target.

As we neared the odd shape, it was clear to see that it was in fact a bundle of archangels tied together. Legs and arms were all tied together, and each archangel was bound to the one next to them. Silver tape sealed their mouths shut.

Seven pairs of burning golden eyes settled on us as we cautiously approached. Gabriel was the closest to me. His usual bright appearance was shadowed with exhaustion and he looked like he'd lost a lot of weight. As I scanned quickly over all of my former superiors, they all harboured the same haunted, dark eyed look, as if death was looming over them.

I bent down to Gabriel and rested my hand on his

forearm. "Bet you didn't expect to see me."

His eyes softened slightly before he lifted his eyes upwards, widening them as much as he could. He started making noise and moving his head towards the sky. I looked up to see Apnastin plummeting down towards us, an antique angel blade in his hands and pointed directly at me.

"What the hell is that?" Ronin said, his eyes bulging at Apnastin's silver sword.

"It's an old blade that the archangels used to carry."

I waited until Apnastin was too close to change his trajectory, then jumped out of the way, leaving him no choice but to land where I had been stood. The thunderous look on his face made my heart skip a beat. Perhaps relying on my immortality had been a really stupid move. His golden eyes were almost black with rage and hatred.

"Traitor!" he yelled, lifting his sword. "You are not welcome here."

"Calm down," I said, holding a hand out. "We can talk things through."

He laughed. "I don't think so. I said all I had to say when I visited you in the cathedral. You turned me away!"

I opened my mouth to respond but was stopped in my tracks when I noticed a Pegasus galloping towards us from across the field. His head was low, his ears pinned back, and his teeth bared. His wings were still tucked up which meant he was intent on charging us, like a bull. Except he'd hit with the force of a thousand bulls.

Apnastin turned to see what had my attention. He flapped his wings, getting ready to fly, but he didn't take off. He fluttered them harder and faster but still nothing happened—he wasn't gaining any air.

Then I saw it—the haze of purple flitting around his dirty white wings.

"Is that…?" Ronin said.

"Pixies," I said, nodding and grinning.

Apnastin shouted in frustration, and probably a little bit of pain. He swung his sword from side to side, swiping at the tiny creatures buzzing around him like a swarm of bees. The ground started to vibrate as the Pegasus hurtled towards us. Apnastin dropped his sword, clutching at one of his hands as he howled in agony.

"Get the sword!" I shouted at Ronin. He dashed forwards and swept the relic up in one smooth move. "Cut them free!"

I ran away from the cluster of bodies, hoping to draw the Pegasus' eye and steer him towards me, but he was locked onto the small crowd of angels in front of me. Panic flooded me. I didn't know what to do for the best. I rushed to stand in front of the archangels as Ronin cut through their magical rope ties.

The Pegasus flicked an ear forwards and seemed to hesitate in his stride but still he kept coming. A whooshing noise from overhead stole my attention upwards. Three more Pegasus were circling overheard like sharks waiting for the opportune moment to strike.

I looked behind me to see Ronin had freed Michael and Uriel. Apnastin was now hysterical, looking like an insane man from a mental asylum as he swatted at the almost invisible pixies and shouted at them furiously. He stumbled around as he twisted from side to side in his vain attempts to fend them off.

Another Pegasus careered towards us from the

other side, its expression just as menacing as the first.

"Makeysha!"

I turned my head to see Michael beckoning me with his hand, an urgent look painted across his face. I ran to him, the enraged snorts from the Pegasus now rumbling through the air. Daring to see where the Pegasus was, I was shocked to see he was less than a hundred yards away. I tripped over and hit the ground. My teeth smashed together, making me bite my tongue. The metallic tinge of blood filled my mouth but all I could think of was that Pegasus, bearing down on me like a demon.

Time seemed to slow down. Ronin yelled my name. Apnastin roared in pain, no doubt now driven crazy by all the pixie toxins. The Pegasus let out a squeal, mere feet away from him, but I was in the way, my legs right in its path. I closed my eyes and waited for the excruciating agony to hit me.

But it never came.

Instead, a breeze of air blew over me. A deafening thud echoed around us. Apnastin fell silent. I dared to open my eyes to see the Pegasus had jumped over me and taken flight, kicking Apnastin in the head. The rogue angel lay in a crumpled heap, unconscious, and his body swelling from the toxins pouring into his nervous system.

The Pegasus from overhead divebombed at him, all taking their turn to whack him in the head or kick his torso. Within minutes, Apnastin had been reduced to nothing but a limp ragdoll useful as nothing but a punch bag for the Pegasus.

Ronin's hands were suddenly around me, lifting me to my feet. "Are you ok?" he said, breathless. His eyes were wild with fear as he looked me up and down, checking me over.

"I'm good. Have you freed them?" I glanced behind him to see the freed archangels helping their fellow beings.

"Is the baby ok?" He touched a hand to my belly, concern filling his eyes.

"Yes," I said, smiling and pressing my hand to his. "We're both fine. Let's just get out of here."

He nodded and wrapped his arms around my waist. I unfolded my wings and spared Apnastin one final glance. With the combination of the pixie toxins and the brutality of the Pegasus attack, I doubted he would ever open his eyes again.

I lifted us into the sky and plunged down to the Heavens below, thankful this was all over at last.

Epilogue

Ronin—Two Months Later

Life had never given me such a wild ride. If someone had told me six months ago that I would find my soulmate, save the world, have a child on the way, and have visited Heaven, I'd have laughed at them and referred them to my family psychiatrist.

Now though, I couldn't be more grateful for the way things have turned out. After that fateful day in Heaven, we spent a couple of weeks up there, helping the angels return everything to its former heavenly glory. The archangels held Makeysha up on a pedestal and begged her to stay and reign in God's absence.

Flattered, but not really feeling the love of Heaven like she once had, she politely declined, and instead suggested that she be a silent 'CEO'. She created a council of the archangels, leaving them in charge of the daily running of Heaven. Makeysha graciously said she would visit once a month for a day to meet and iron out any problems. If something urgent cropped up in the meantime, they could call for her, but with the baby's birth due within a couple of weeks, I hoped they wouldn't.

We had settled in an old plantation, just outside of New Orleans. Its sprawling gardens, private lake, and spacious house provided us with enough privacy from prying eyes and any potential supernatural creatures, but also kept us close enough to the city that we both adored.

The archangels couldn't give us any sort of clue as to what our baby would be in terms of its potential power. The whole children of soulmates and First Creations thing had been news to them. We had reunited all of the broken soulmates, making some very happy First Creations in the process.

Lucia had taken over the running of Wanda's Voodoo Museum. Wanda now worked as Lucia's faithful servant, minus her powers. We all agreed she deserved some self-reflection time, despite her intentions being for the good of her people.

Cross-breeding between species had erupted almost overnight. What potential new creatures the hunter community would face would remain to be seen, but I would do my best to help when I could. For now, my focus is on my beautiful soulmate and her swollen belly.

I had no doubt that the future would bring us many challenges, but I knew whatever life threw at us, we would face it together, and win.

A NOTE FROM THE AUTHOR

I hope you enjoyed Makeysha and Ronin's story. If you did, I would be eternally grateful if you could leave a review to let others know how much you enjoyed it. Even one sentence is fine. Thank you so much!

If you want to follow me and keep up to date with all my latest goings on, visit www.cjauthor.com and sign up for my newsletter, join my Facebook group:

www.facebook.com/groups/lollipoplounge

or look me up in the places below:

www.facebook.com/CJLaurenceAuthor

www.twitter.com/cjlauthor

www.instagram.com/cjlauthor

https://www.bookbub.com/authors/c-j-laurence

I love hearing from my readers and will always reply to you!

ALSO BY THIS AUTHOR

Want & Need
Cowboys & Horses
Retribution
Unleashing Demons
Unleashing Vampires
The Red Riding Hoods – The Grim Sisters Book 1
Game Changer

Printed in Great Britain
by Amazon

85015434R00212